MANHUNTER'S MOON

ALSO BY WAYNE D DUNDEE

MANHUNTER'S MOON

A LONE MCGANTRY WESTERN

WAYNE D DUNDEE

WOLFPACK
PUBLISHING
— EST 2013 —

Manhunter's Moon
Paperback Edition
Copyright © 2024 Wayne D. Dundee

Wolfpack Publishing
1707 E. Diana Street
Tampa, FL 33609

wolfpackpublishing.com

Paperback ISBN 978-1-63977-625-2
eBook ISBN 978-1-63977-624-5
LCCN: 2024946024

MANHUNTER'S MOON

CHAPTER ONE

HALF A SECOND SHORT OF PULLING THE TRIGGER ON A warning shot, Lone McGantry's finger was stayed by a pulse of silver-white lightning that revealed the rain-beaded, pain-racked face of Charley Bourbon. The curse that ground out between Lone's teeth got swallowed by a growl of thunder rolling across the black, boiling night sky.

But Charley's curse, coming a moment later, could be heard plainly. "Jesus Christ, McGantry! Wavin' a hogleg under the nose of an old friend who's come callin' is a helluva rude thing, don't you think?"

"Not as rude as plunkin' a .44 slug through that soggy sombrero plastered atop your head would've been. Which, skulkin' around like a horse thief in the middle of the night," Lone told him, "you damn near earned yourself."

"Labelin' me—a US Marshal—a horse thief?" Charley protested. "Now you've gone beyond rude to bein' downright insultin'!"

"I said skulkin' around *like* a horse thief," Lone

reminded him. "And if you're so thin-skinned comes to folks formin' a wrong notion about you, then maybe you oughta avoid rootin' about inside a fella's horse barn after dark."

"You call this lopsided contraption a barn?"

"Now who's bein' insultin'? It's a work in progress," Lone growled defensively. "In any case, don't make me look bad in front of my horses. I got them convinced it's a *fine* barn."

The object under discussion was, in fact, not a barn. Rather it was a large lean-to shelter built in the near corner of a peeled pole corral, all part of the modest headquarters for Lone's equally modest Busted Spur horse ranch. The lean-to's back wall and the slope of its corrugated roof were set to the northwest where the worst of inclement weather tended to come out of. Due to the scarcity of lumber in these southern reaches of Nebraska's treeless Sandhills, the back and side walls were made from thick cuts of sod anchored for added stability by deep-set posts placed at regular intervals. The front was open, facing Lone's house, also made of sod, located about fifteen yards outside the corral.

The lean-to was undeniably not much to look at. This was due largely to the crude components it was made from. But part of it, Lone would be the first to admit, was also due to the fact that his background of years spent as an Indian scout, tracker, and drifter did not include developing carpentry skills of any note. Yet regardless of some odd angles and misaligned joints, the structure served its intended purpose of providing his corralled horses a welcome measure of shelter against bad weather. Like tonight's rain.

Adding to his defense of the outcome, Lone now

went on to say, "And no matter what you call it, barn or otherwise, I'll point out you seem to find it suitable enough to have plopped yourself on the inside—where it's warm and dry, just the way it's supposed to be—instead of out here in the rain. How do you account for that?"

"Aye. It's warm and dry, I'll grant you that," Charley allowed. "But that don't mean I was plopped here with any intent of settlin' in. No longer, that is, than it took for me to try and spot that big gray stud of yours so's I'd know if I had the right place or not. I forgot what a blamed good watchdog he makes and how, once he spotted me snoopin' around, he'd be bound to cut loose and carry on loud enough to wake the dead."

"Leastways loud enough to roust me, even over the rain and thunder. That's why I built the corral and lean-to so close to the house," Lone said.

Charley nodded. "Smart plan."

Lone held off for another one-two punch of lightning and thunder to play across the sky. Then he said, "I'll tell you what ain't so smart, and that's me standin' out here in the rain talkin' to you holdin' in there where it's dry. And something else that don't seem so smart—why the need for you to come pokin' through these horses to determine if this was my place when you could've simply knocked on the door and asked? It ain't that late, there's light glowin' plain in the window."

"In case it wasn't you who answered my knock," Charley explained in a gravelly voice, "I got reasons for not wantin' to be seen by nobody else."

Lone gave it a beat, considering what might be behind such a statement. Then he said, "You're safe from not seein' or bein' seen by nobody but me. Come on, let's go inside where we can both be dry and you can tell me what this is about."

A handful of minutes later they were inside Lone's soddy. It was a single room layout, spare and tidily arranged, more than adequate to meet the former scout's simple needs. There was a kitchen area at one end with cupboards, a rough-cut square table and two straight-backed chairs, and a big iron stove that did double duty for both cooking and to provide heat. A middle space boasted a roomy buffalo hide chair for just relaxing or maybe sitting and reading of an evening. Occupying the far end was a spacious rope bed, a storage trunk at its foot, and a tall chest of drawers.

Shedding the rain slicker he'd hastily thrown on before heading out to see what Ironsides, his stallion "watchdog," was fussing about, Lone hung the dripping garment on a peg just inside the front door. He was a big man, just shy of six-three in height, thick through the chest and shoulders. For all that, he moved smooth and light on his feet. A plain, squarish face, built around a prominent nose and alert cobalt eyes bracketed by deep crow's feet, showed the wear of having been exposed for much of his near forty years to the battering of sun and wind. His thick shock of brown hair, however, exhibited not the least hint of gray.

After hanging up his own wrap, Lone next reached to assist Charley in getting off his even more thoroughly drenched long coat. This resulted in Charley instantly shying away from his touch and hissing, "Take it easy, friend. Easy."

Lone then remembered the pained expression on Charley's face when the sudden flash of lightning had first revealed his identity. In the conversation that followed, Lone had forgotten that unguarded look. He also hadn't paid much attention to the slow, awkward manner in which Charley had exited the corral by squeezing out between the railings and then his equally slow, carefully measured gait when walking to the house. The latter Lone had laid to just being cautious not to slip on the rain-slick grass. But the whole of it, he now realized, totaled up to his old friend trying to mask some kind of physical misery he was packing around.

Before Lone could ask, Charley went ahead and addressed it, saying, "One night ago, right about this same hour, I ran into some misfortune that left me a mite stove up. Sorry to bring it to your doorstep, but you're the closest person that came to mind I felt I could trust. I'd be obliged if you went ahead and helped me out of this coat, like you started, but I'll ask you to go at it easy-like. I got some damage to my back I ain't rightly been able to get a look at, but it hurts something fierce."

Lone first turned to a coal oil lamp that was burning on a nearby stand beside the buffalo hide chair and adjusted its wick brighter. Then, re-positioning Charley slightly so that his broad back was better illuminated by this increased light, he again reached to help remove the sodden coat, this time lifting it off slowly and care-fully. Charley braced his feet and held himself rigid yet, even still, another faint hiss of discomfort escaped him as the weight of the heavily soaked garment slipped away. When Lone saw what was underneath, he had to grit his teeth to keep from sounding a reaction of his own.

The shirt under the coat hung in blood-stained shreds. As a man of color, Charley's natural skin tone was dark as strong-brewed coffee. Much of this showed through unmarred, as nature intended. In several places, however, it appeared charred and blistered by burns. To an even greater extent, it was torn and slashed by deep cuts, some showing pieces of debris embedded in them. One large gash over his left shoulder blade had what appeared to be a chunk of jagged wood jutting out from it.

"Jesus God," Lone said. "What the hell happened to you?"

"Railroad freight car explosion on the UP line due south of here. You mean you ain't heard nothing about it?"

"Afraid my setup here is kinda lackin' for regular newspaper delivery," Lone replied dryly.

"Well, it happened," Charley harrumphed. "I was in the next car, the caboose, up near the front end. Too damn close. Luckily I was facing away, so the blast tore up mostly only my backside." Charley spoke in terse, tight sentences. "I was ridin' in the caboose along with another marshal, escortin' a fugitive prisoner back to the territorial pen outside of Laramie, Wyoming. There was a brakeman in the car with us, too. Those other three was sittin' farther back. The explosion ripped off the front of the caboose and de-railed it. I got flung away and sent rolling down a long slope, several yards clear of the tracks.

"Fiery, flyin' pieces of the freight car side boards and whatever it was carryin' filled the air and started landin' all around me. Thankfully none of 'em landed directly on me, leastways not none of the bigger ones. But soon they was layin' in burnin' heaps on all sides and settin' the grass and brush on fire too. At the bottom of the slope was a narrow ditch filled with a half foot or so of muddy water. I managed to crawl into it and scooped mud and water all over myself to keep from takin' flame like everything else."

"Okay, I get the picture. That's enough for right now," said Lone, interrupting him. "You can break it down in more detail while I'm workin' on that back of yours. But we need to get started pronto on cleanin' and treatin' all these cuts and burns before the chance for infection increases more than it already has."

"That don't sound like nothing to look forward to," Charley muttered. "But I reckon it can't hurt much worse than the misery it's givin' me the way it is."

"Step over to the kitchen table and straddle one of those chairs," Lone directed him, taking the lamp on ahead and placing it atop the table. As Charley settled carefully onto one of the straight-backed chairs, Lone rummaged in a cupboard and from it withdrew a bottle of whiskey that he thumped down before the patient. "There. Start fightin' your misery with some of that while I get a pot of water boiling and lay out the other things I'll need."

Charley wasted no time reaching for the bottle, declaring as he did, "I don't know what credentials you have for practicin' medicine, but I can tell right away that my first impression is you got the makin's of a fine doctor."

For the next forty minutes, that assessment was put to the test as a somber-faced Lone focused intently on ministering to his friend's savaged back. During this, the two men continued to talk intermittently, and Charley gradually layered on more details about how he'd ended up in such sorry shape.

When asked if he had any idea what had caused the

freight car to explode so violently, he responded in a prompt snarl, "You damn betcha I do. The prisoner bein' transported by me and my partner—a new kid, nice young fella by the name of Hank Wordell—was Rip Hardessy. I expect you've heard of him?"

"Theodore 'Rip' Hardessy," Lone recited tonelessly. "Got his name from the hook he sports in place of a hand at the end of his left arm, and the charmin' habit he developed for usin' said hook to rip the gizzard out of any hombre unfortunate enough to have to face him in a close-in fight."

"The very same," Charley confirmed.

"But I thought he got put away a long while back."

"He did. I'm the one who nabbed him. He got sentenced to twenty-five years hard, in the Laramie pen. Bloody bastard should've hung right then, but he got sentenced by one of those newer lily-livered judges who don't believe in goin' the way of the rope near as quick as the old drop-'em-and-be-done boys used to." Charley heaved a remorseful sigh. "So, anyway, Rip went behind the walls for a few months but then managed to bust out, with some outside help from his old gang. Wasted no time takin' up with 'em again and goin' right back to robbin' and killin' same as before. Lasted a year or so before he got nabbed once more, this time by the marshal of a little town off to the east called Gothenburg. Bunch of Switzers settled there, used to be a Pony Express relay station.

"So the place has a bank. For a small town, it tends to hold a tidy sum of money. Enough to attract Rip and his boys. They hit it, clean it out, make their getaway. But later that night, sufferin' what must've been a powerful case of horniness, that bold bastard Rip doubles back to pay a visit to a local whore before movin' on to the tall and uncut. Just by accident, the marshal spots him headin' for his mattress dance. Gives the lawman enough time to round up some deputies and then put the grab on their man."

"I'll be damned," said Lone.

"Those local boys did a good job of latchin' onto Rip and holdin' him. But they was on pins and needles the whole time, expectin' his gang was lurkin' close itchin' to try and spring him on account of their boss's well known practice of bein' the one to hold the money ridin' away from a job. He didn't have it on him when the law nabbed him, though, so he must have stashed it somewhere before he went to have his poke. Either way, it was a safe bet the rest of his crew wanted him back— not just for him, but for the money they was lackin' their cut of." Charley gave a throaty chuckle. "So those Gothenburg fellas was mighty relieved when me and Hank showed up to take Rip off their hands. And where we was assigned to take him, while the legal minds are tallyin' up all the new charges to bring against him in a new trial—for which he's expected to certain hang this time—was back to the Laramie pen until the new trial details are finalized and a date set."

"Makin' the train you and your partner was haulin' Hardessy in on," said Lone, "what the gang ended going after—by means of the explosion—in order to save Rip from ever havin' to once more see the inside of those walls."

"Not a whisker of doubt in my mind. Like I said, there was plenty of warnin' they was itchin' to try something. Which was why," Charley explained, "I got called in to side Wordell for gettin' the job done. Also why we switched up our plans three different times for how we was gonna go about makin' the trip—meanin' to confuse the gang and make it hard for 'em to get set for how and where to make a play against us. By the time me and Wordell settled on invitin' ourselves and our prisoner aboard that no-account freight run, wasn't but three or four other men in the whole state who knew what we finally decided."

"Yet if it was Hardessy's gang who blew that freight car—like you suspect—then word somehow got leaked or passed on."

"Yeah, that's the only sad and damnedably infuriatin' explanation for it," Charley growled. "Once they knew it was that freight run we was usin'—however they found out—the skunks waited until we reached a long, lonely stretch between North Platte and Ogallala before they struck. I picture the devils had a charge set on the tracks and then triggered it to blow just as that freight car ahead of our caboose was passin' over. The idea bein' to uncouple the caboose and at the same time jar the hell out of us who was inside so's we'd be easy pickin's for 'em to swoop in and snatch away their man."

"Would've took awful tight timing, but I guess it's workable as an idea," Lone allowed. "The thing about it, though—the way you described that hellacious blast— it sounds like they must have gone way overboard on the size of the charge they used for what they was meanin' to do. Wonder they didn't blow hell out of Hardessy in the process."

Charley grunted. "You ain't tellin' me nothing about the strength of that blast. I got picked up and sent for a ride by it, remember? And as far as Hardessy, you make a good observation concernin' him. One he himself was also quick to make. You see, even though I was able to drag myself into that muddy ditch, I was in kind of a daze for quite a spell after bein' flung down that slope. Sort of driftin' in and out, at times near blackin' out completely. Thinkin' back, it's a wonder I didn't drop my face into that muddy water and not lift it out in time to keep from drownin' myself.

"But it never came to that. And durin' the periods I had my senses about me, through the fire and smoke and the ringin' in my ears, I could make out some of the activity takin' place up on the tracks. I could hear men hollerin' and cussin'. Gunfire. The last told me that Wordell must have come out of the blast in good enough condition to make a fight of it. At least for a while. And plenty of the hollerin' was comin' from Hardessy—cussin' the chowder-brained idiots who near blew him to bits. That told me the lowdown skunk had survived too. It was the last bitter thing I remember thinkin' for a long damn spell..."

CHAPTER TWO

AFTER CUTTING AWAY WHAT WAS LEFT OF CHARLEY'S shirt, Lone had begun treating the wounds one by one, working from most to least serious. The worst was the shoulder gash with the jagged chunk of wood still in it. Once the wood was pulled out, the torn flesh bled so badly it required both cauterizing and stitching to get stopped. From there it was a methodical progression of salve application to the burns, more removal and cleaning of cuts with foreign particles in them, more stitches where required, and yards of bandage wrapping. Through it all, Charley endured stoically, continuing to fill in added details behind his receipt of so much damage. Lone prodded him with a few questions here and there, but for the most part Charley told it at his own pace and in his own manner.

Charley Bourbon was also a big man. Equal in height to Lone, maybe even a fraction of an inch taller, half a dozen years older; less muscular in the chest and shoulders, though of greater girth through the middle. He had bold, strong-jawed facial features, with penetrating dark eyes. Circling his mouth was a neatly trimmed goatee sprinkled with flecks of gray, as was the tight cap of hair covering his head. Stripped to the waist, thick forearms resting across the top of the chair's backrest (except for frequent lifts of the whiskey bottle in order to gulp down long swallows), his pose and brooding expression might have been that of a gladiator or Nubian warrior from ancient times, contemplating an upcoming battle. In truth, Charley *was* contemplating a battle of sorts. A desired one, and likely to require confrontation on multiple fronts.

"Way I see it," he told Lone, "there's two men I gotta go after. First, the fugitive Hardessy who I damn well ain't gonna let spoil my record of never lettin' a prisoner escape alive. And second, the double-crossin' polecat who tipped off Hardessy's gang what train we was transportin' him on so's they could rig that explosion and spring their ambush."

"I can track along with all that okay. Wouldn't expect nothing less out of you, and reckon I'd feel the same," allowed Lone. "But where our trails fork is me not understandin' this business of you hidin' the fact you're still alive and kickin'. If you'd've done otherwise come daybreak this mornin', after you came around mostly out of that fog you'd been in, you could have made yourself known to the track clearers who were startin' to show up by then and they would have hauled you out of that ditch pronto-like. Instead of bein' here gettin' patched up by me and my half-assed skills, after draggin' your wounds across rugged, open country all day to get this far, you could've long since been under the care of a proper doctor in either North Platte or Ogallala. What's more, it would've also given you the chance to have the law in one of those places filled in thoroughly on what took place so they could already have posses out on the trail of Hardessy's bunch."

Charley made a face. "You can bet Hardessy's crew wouldn't have left no easy trail to follow, especially not for no hastily throwed-together town posse. And when this rain hit just before evening, that would have finished erasin' their sign good and proper. So me hurryin' to the law in one of those towns wouldn't have gained hardly nothing, not in the short term. Might as well accept that, after last night, it's just plain gonna take some time—for anybody, includin' me—to get a line on Hardessy again. And as for a doctor's care, the job you're doin' is suitin' me just fine and I oughta have the right to say if I'm satisfied. Ain't that so?"

"Not necessarily. If you start runnin' a high fever from one of those burns or that bad gash," Lone warned him, "I'll chunk you on the head to put you back in a daze and haul your stubborn ass to a doctor myself."

"*That* would count as a definite slip in the bedside manner I just got done givin' you high marks for."

Lone took the much depleted whiskey bottle, threw down a big slug of his own, handed it back. "Damn it, Charley, quit beatin' around the bush and tell me what you're up to with this stunt about playin' dead."

Charley waited a long beat, then said, "Did you ever notice how, if you listen real tight, you can sometimes learn almost as much by what *ain't* said as by what is?"

Lone cocked a brow in a show of annoyance. "If that's the case, then I oughta be a lot smarter than I am about what you're tryin' to pull. Because you ain't sayin' shit, yet I still got nothing figured out."

"When I was finally comin' out of my fog back

around daybreak," Charley told him, "there was still a lot of smoke hangin' in the air above my ditch. Comin' from the heaps of smolderin' debris and the burned grass and bushes scattered all across the slope between where I lay and the tracks up higher. I knew right away that's why none of the men I could hear workin' up there had seen me or come to my aid. My first thought was, just like you said, to holler and let 'em know I was down there. But then, while I was still kinda gatherin' myself, gettin' ready to call out, I heard one of the men say something about 'the dead nigger marshal.' That gave me pause. Not because it offended me or nothing like that. Hell, I been hearin' the word nigger tossed around—though not to my face, not since I got my growth anyway—too many years for it to rankle me every time it falls outta some fool's mouth. It's been used for a long time, gonna be used by some a lot longer I expect.

"But the thing that struck me about what I heard the worker say in this case was the 'dead' part. And there's what I mean about also hearin' what *wasn't* said. Do you see? Nothing was mentioned about anybody else from the caboose bein' dead—not the brakeman, and especially not my partner Wordell. Don't get me wrong, I ain't sayin' I wanted him to be dead or nothing like that. But, doggone it, it just seemed reasonable to expect he would be. You understand what I'm drivin' at?"

Lone scowled. "Yeah, I think maybe I'm startin' to. With you blown clean out of the car and only your partner left to hold off the gang when they came swarmin'—and you did hear gunshots soundin' like he tried to make a fight of it—then it seems most likely he'd be left shot to pieces."

"Uh-huh. The fact he wasn't makes a body wonder. Leastways it does this body. Then, if you got a suspicious damn mind like mine—made that way by too many years dealin' with sneaky connivers of every stripe —you are quick-like reminded of something else you've already been wonderin' about...like how the Hardessy gang got tripped to the freight run me and Wordell decided at the last minute to take."

"You're suspectin' him? Your own partner?"

"Ain't like it's what I want, damn it," Charley growled. "But until I for sure know otherwise, my habit is to suspect every critter in sight. Comes to this particular matter, though, unless I'm wrong in my belief about what *wasn't* said and it turns out young Hank *is* plugged full of holes...well, he ranks pretty high on the list of who I mean to take an extra close look at."

"And you're figurin' if him and everybody else thinks your fried carcass is buried under one of those smolderin' piles of debris, Hank might be a little less careful about hidin' the dirt on his hands."

"That's the general idea. Like I said, there'll be a small army out tryin' to run down the escaped Hardessy. I'll join 'em in due time but, like I also said, it's gonna take a while to flush him again. Meanwhile, I got a more personal reason for wantin' to first flush out a certain back-stabbin' weasel."

"But what about the shootin' you heard?" said Lone. "If Wordell was their inside man, why would he turn around and blaze away at the gang when they sprang the ambush he supplied information for?"

"I took the gunfire I heard as Hank puttin' up a fight because that's what I had reason to believe at the time. But pullin' a trigger don't necessarily mean a body's aimin' to hit something," Charley countered. "I never actually saw who was poppin' off those rounds. Or at what. Coulda been the gang members throwin' lead to keep everybody in line. For that matter, it coulda still been Hank, only just puttin' on a show for the sake of the brakeman—or maybe even for me, since they likely hadn't yet writ me off for dead."

Lone once more cocked an eyebrow. "Gropin' around to come up with a range of possibilities like that, maybe you *have* been hangin' around shifty-minded characters too much. For all the different angles you're takin' into consideration, though, it seems to me you still got a chink in your figurin'."

"How so?"

"If you're supposed to be dead, how you reckon to go snoopin' about and keepin' an eagle eye on Wordell in order to gain some proof he's your man?"

Charley grinned slyly. "Well, for starters, I had in mind that a certain old friend of mine—while I'm grabbin' at least a day or two of healin' for this poor beat-up body of mine—might have cause to ride into town for supplies or some such. And, while he was there, he'd just naturally keep his ears perked for any news about things in general. In the process, he might even be inclined to ask a question or three on my behalf. You know, makin' what those fancy-talkin' lawyer types call 'discreet inquiries?'"

CHAPTER THREE

IT STOPPED RAINING SOMETIME DURING THE NIGHT. LONE rose with the sun, dressed quietly, made his way with equal stealth into the kitchen area, passing where Charley Bourbon was curled fast asleep in the big buffalo hide chair. Charley had declined the offer of Lone's bed, not wanting to take the risk of possible leakage from his numerous back wounds fouling the nest. Besides, he insisted, the chair was plenty roomy enough and comfortable enough to accommodate even his large frame just fine. Since Lone knew this to be true from his own experience at sometimes dozing off while sprawled there on quiet evenings and then snoring away for as long as two or three hours before finally getting up and shuffling to bed, he didn't argue the point. Evidence that it hadn't been an inhospitable allowance came in the form of the contented expression now on Charley's face as he continued to sleep deeply and peacefully, occasionally issuing volleys of his own snoring that rivaled last night's thunder.

At the cook stove, Lone got a small fire going in one

of the side chambers and set a pot of coffee to start cooking over it. Then, from the warming box, he took a plate of day-old biscuits that he placed on the table along with a clean cup. He left these out in case Charley woke up before Lone returned from a piece of business he needed to take care of outside.

Once again slipping quietly past his slumbering guest, Lone paused only long enough to snag his hat and gun belt from pegs beside the front door before stepping on through and exiting the soddy.

The morning air was crisp, still carrying a dampness from last night's rain. The rolling, grassy hills that extended off in all directions for as far as the eye could see glistened with sparks of silvery wetness when caught just right in the slanting rays of early sunlight. A glance at the clear sky overhead told Lone that the dampness in the air and the wetness clinging to the grass would disappear quickly, however, as the sun climbed higher and hotter.

While he stood buckling on and adjusting the gun belt around his waist, several of the horses in the corral came shuffling forward, eyeing him expectantly in hopes he might again shovel over a few scoops of grain like he'd done the previous evening to stoke their bellies with some added warmth to counter the chill of the then approaching storm. "Oh no, I ain't gonna spoil you no more than it looks like I already have," Lone told them with a grin. "Mother Nature provided you a trough full of fresh, clean water and in a minute, I'll be turnin' you out so's you can graze to your heart's content on her sweet spring grass. That'll do you just fine, with no more coddlin'. But who I *will* be givin' some extra attention to is one of your cousins who wasn't lucky enough to spend the night in near as much comfort as you critters."

The "cousin" Lone was referring to was the mount Charley had arrived on but then left tied in some gully back a ways while he came the rest of the way on foot to check the horses in the corral for verification he had the right place. Once past that and ushered inside, the demands of getting his injured back taken care of and relating the story of what had caused it crowded out any thought of the left behind horse. Until, that was, it was time to turn in for the night. Charley's belated mention of the abandoned animal at that point made it impractical, given the dark and the storm and all, to go out and try to bring it in right then. Charley was in no shape to go himself, and his vague indication of where it was he'd left the critter might have sent Lone stumbling around for who knew how long out in the rain and blinding lightning pops before he came upon it. The only sensible thing was to wait for morning. Yes, the horse would be cold, wet, and generally uncomfortable, but conditions weren't so harsh as to pose any actual threat to its survival. As a matter of fact, a handful of Lone's own horses—those who were too widely scattered for him to get rounded up and herded into the corral for shelter when he saw the storm coming—had to endure a taste of the same.

Nevertheless, Lone's affinity for horses in general— perhaps more so, when it came right down to it, than for people in general—made it a priority upon waking this morning not to leave Charley's mount unattended any longer than necessary. Taking only additional time to swing open the corral gate, as he'd promised the critters on the inside so they could get back out to seek good graze, he commenced his search. Ironsides, his tall, deep-chested, faithful gray stallion, trailed close behind. It was as if the big gray sensed Lone had something weighing on his mind and felt he ought to remain near in case needed. Only when he was sure everything was okay would he go in search of some graze for himself. Even then he would never wander beyond earshot of a summoning whistle that would bring him at a gallop.

They found what they were looking for in a shallow, weed-choked gully a couple hundred yards southwest of the corral. It was a bedraggled, forlorn looking steel dust gelding tied to the base stalks of a bramble bush. It was somewhat stubby-legged, making it limited if called upon for speed, but was otherwise built with a broad back and rump that marked it as being sturdy enough to carry Charley's bulk. Or, as was the base truth of the matter since the animal didn't really *belong* to Charley, anyone of similar bulk.

The wrap-up of Charley's tale about all that had brought him to Lone's place the prior evening included relating how he'd come by the steeldust. At first, upon slipping away undetected from the train wreck scene, he'd started north across open country on foot. He knew that the train had reached a point roughly halfway between North Platte and Ogallala when the freight car blast happened. He additionally knew—from interim talk he'd heard in the months since he and Lone had first met and ended up throwing in together to take down the vicious Eccles gang in the Devil's Tower region of northern Wyoming—that Lone had returned to his small horse ranching operation near a tiny settlement called Sarben. Said settlement, Charley was further aware, happened also to be located about halfway between the two larger towns, though some dozen miles north of the UP track and across the north branch of the Platte River. This, then, became his goal. Reach the vicinity of Sarben and from there determine where Lone's ranch was. Having to do so, the way it looked at the start, plodding stubbornly afoot with a ravaged back.

He hadn't trekked far before he came to the river. Finding it running broad but shallow at the spot he encountered it (living up to the Platte's legendary description of being "a mile wide and a foot deep" as pegged by early mountain men who followed it to their hunting and trapping grounds in the Rockies) it posed no great obstacle, except for avoiding pockets of quicksand. First, though, before starting across, Charley waded out just far enough to sit down and lean back on his elbows in order to allow the cool, fresh water to flow soothingly over the wounds and burns on his back that were otherwise unreachable to do any other ministering to. This brought considerable relief and was overall revitalizing to his battered condition, causing him to soak there for several minutes. It was when he pushed back to his feet that he spotted the saddled horse standing and watching him from the bank about twenty yards upstream. Only after getting past a wave of concern over being spotted in turn by whoever the horse belonged to, did Charley come to realize that whoever that was didn't seem to be anywhere around.

What he next concluded was that the horse, like him, must be a refugee from the train wreck—most likely the mount of one of the Hardessy gang spooked into terrified flight by the violent explosion. No matter its origin, the steeldust now represented a means for

Charley to proceed under far less trying conditions than on foot. With soothing words and soft clucking sounds he'd been able to approach the animal and, when his hand clamped possessively around its reins, he felt another surge of relief even greater than that provided by the dip in the river.

Being mounted naturally made the rest of what Charley had in mind much easier to accomplish. Yet navigating through an unfamiliar area while taking care to remain unseen and all the while enduring the pain of his many wounds, still made for a long, grueling day. There was nothing in the saddlebags of his confiscated horse to provide any clue as to the identify of its true owner. Nor was there anything else of much use, except for a bent and battered old sombrero stuffed in one of the pockets which, when tugged back into serviceable shape, helped keep the hot sun off Charley's bare head (and later, in the stormy dark, became the target for damn near catching a warning bullet from Lone). Also rolled up in the bedroll was the long coat, though unfortunately not a water-shedding garment, that nonetheless provided a layer of protection against the same storm when it broke.

"You been of service deservin' better treatment than you got in return, that's for sure," Lone told the steeldust now as he untied it and gave some comforting pats to the side of its strong neck. "But you come along with me, and we'll square things up a bit. How's that sound?"

Keeping hold of the reins, Lone turned and began leading the way out of the gully and back toward the corral. The gelding followed along obligingly. Ironsides, apparently sensing things were now well enough in hand, gave a sort of farewell snort then wheeled away to go tend some business of his own.

Plodding through the still wet grass with his retrieval satisfactorily in tow, Lone's thoughts began to roll ahead toward what else the day held in store for him. After stripping the saddle and other gear off the steeldust then giving it a dry straw rubdown, he'd leave it in one of the lean-to's stalls with some grain and hay until he found out what Charley had in mind for it. If simply turned loose, the animal might mingle in with the rest of Lone's herd or it might take a notion to wander off in search of its former owner and thereby draw unwanted attention. Lone and Charley would have to hash out a decision about that over breakfast. Next, depending on how Charley's wounds appeared to be healing, it seemed likely that Lone would be heading into town to, among other things, make some "discreet inquiries" on behalf of the laying-low marshal. Any question about pitching in however he could to aid an old friend never crossed Lone's mind.

"Hello, the house! Anybody t'home?"

This shout-out caused Lone to halt in his tracks. The nose of the steeldust trailing behind bumped lightly against his shoulder before it too came to a stop.

Lone frowned and perked his ears sharper. Visitors to his remote ranch were uncommon. Mostly only wranglers off a couple of the bigger spreads to the north, coming from or headed to a letting-the-wolf-howl night in town, stopping on their way by to water their horses and maybe their morning-after parched throats from the cold, clear contents of Lone's deep well. But this was mighty early for any such as those. And the harsh-sounding voice—coming from up near the soddy though its source currently not in sight due to the speaker being at an off angle to the faint slope Lone was still ascending out of the gully—had a different ring from any the former scout recognized.

Lone started forward again. But, before he did, he shifted the steeldust's reins to his left hand and, with his right, reached down to slip the keeper thong off his holstered Colt.

CHAPTER FOUR

"Hello, the soddy! Ain't nobody up and about yet?"

This second shout-out sounded just as Lone topped the slope at an angle that gave him a view of the man behind the shout. The hombre was sitting his horse a dozen or so yards back from the southeast corner of the house. Another man was reined up alongside him. A quick appraisal by Lone judged them not to be a couple of ranch hands on break from their chores, but rather a pair cast from the shiftless hard-case mold. Both were generally rumpled in appearance, unshaven, flinty-eyed, and heavily armed. The owly countenance of each might only be due to having been caught out in the open by last night's storm—or it could be the habitual look of their kind always being half-assed on the prod. In any case, it wasn't something Lone favored seeing. Especially not here on his spread.

"Can I help you fellas with something?" he called ahead as he continued moving toward them.

Two faces snapped around to aim matching scowls

in his direction. He met these with a stony look of his own.

Drawing closer, Lone saw that the one who'd been making the noise was a whip lean number with a wedge-shaped face, a hawk's beak for a nose, and squinted eyes set too close on either side of the bony bridge. He had a thin-lipped slash of a mouth perfect for twisting into a sneer. He packed a walnut-handled Colt .45 holstered high on his right hip and a second handgun, same make and model only this one sporting ivory grips, tucked in his waistband off center to the left. A Henry repeating rifle was nestled in his saddle boot.

His so far silent partner was a considerably larger cuss. Tall in his saddle, wide shouldered, too much gut. He had a moon face with a big, blunt nose, beady eyes under a heavy ledge of forehead and bristly brows, a wide mouth with a sagging lower lip. He had a Henry in his saddle boot too, and was also heeled with a Colt .45, though worn on his left hip for the cross draw—which meant, seeing how he'd have to reach across that big gut to grab it, he sure as hell was no quick trigger threat.

But that didn't much lessen the overall aura of threat —or maybe menace was a better word—that seemed to hover over the pair. Lone was feeling glad he'd slipped the keeper thong off his Colt, not to mention taking time to strap on his gun belt in the first place. He only wished he had also included bringing his Winchester Yellowboy along. And while he was wishing, he went ahead and did some hoping as well; namely, hoping that Hawk Nose's shouts to the cabin had rousted Charley and he was now on the inside making his own covert assessment of the visitors.

Before either of the men spoke in response to Lone's

query, the big one, Moon Face, shifted his gaze to the steeldust and it resulted in a reaction that caused him to reach out and give an urgent tug on Hawk Nose's sleeve. Hawk Nose shrugged off the tug and kept his own expression impassive.

By then Lone had advanced onto the flat area in front of his soddy and once more came to a halt, holding off several paces from the mounted men.

Hawk Nose formed a crooked grin. "Well now. Looks like I was wrong. You not only are up and about mighty early, but it appears you have been plumb busy already."

"Way it is on a ranch," Lone replied.

Moon Face grunted. "You call this patch of nuthin' in the middle of nowhere a 'ranch'?"

"What it is to me," Lone grated. "Now I'll ask again, what brings you fellas here to the middle of nowhere and what is it I might could do for you?"

"Well, for starters, what I hope you'll be willing to do is forgive my partner here"—this coming from Hawk Nose as he cast a disapproving sidelong glance over at Moon Face—"for his rude comment. All I can say is that, through nobody's fault but our own, we got caught ill prepared by last night's storm and are fresh from a cold, wet camp that has left both of us some out of sorts."

"True enough that a storm rollin' up on a body in all this wide open can make for some misery," Lone allowed.

"Boy, don't we know it," said Hawk Nose. "But what we *didn't* know, in the dark and rain, was how close we was to this spread of yours. Making it even just to that horse shelter would've been a big improvement over what we had to settle for instead. The sight of your chimney smoke shortly after sunup, though, held the hope of a better start to a new day. If you was to say you had some hot coffee you'd be willing to share with a couple sorry storm riders, that would add to it all the more."

Lone's habitual caution when it came to strangers— heightened by his particular suspicion regarding this pair—caused him to shade his response by saying, "Reckon some coffee could be arranged. But I'm afraid I'll have to fetch it out here to you boys. Can't invite you inside on account of I got a sick wife and child in there, and don't want to disturb 'em."

Hawk Nose eyed him shrewdly. "Sick wife and kid, eh? That's a shame."

Lone shrugged. "You know how it is. Always something." It wasn't hard to see that Hawk Nose was harboring some suspicion of his own. What was more, though he had no way of knowing the story behind these two, Lone had a growing sense it was something lowdown and, before they were done here, them showing up was going to boil into trouble. He wished to hell he had some idea whether or not Charley was awake and aware of what was going on. But, since he didn't, Lone had no choice but to figure on having only himself to count on for handling whatever might boil up.

It didn't take long for things to edge closer toward finding out for sure.

"I see you got yourself a horse all saddled up and ready there," drawled Hawk Nose, still with the shrewd glint in his eyes. "That mean you're headed somewhere —maybe to fetch a doctor for your poor ailing family?"

"Whatever it means," Lone told him in a flat tone, "I'd say falls under the headin' of my business."

"Now who's bein' rude?" spoke up Moon Face. "Man asked you a civil question, mister. No call to give back such a snotty answer."

"Where I come from," Lone said, "man standin' on his own property has the right to say pretty much as he pleases. What I'm about to say where you're concerned, Fatty, is that you've near wore out your welcome. So, unless you're ready to keep that hole under your nose shut until I fetch some hot coffee to pour in it, we can call quits to this whole business and you fellas can both be on your way."

"Now just a minute—" Hawk Nose tried to say.

But Moon Face wouldn't let him get any more out. "Too hell with that! What are we pussyfootin' around for, Simon? That's my goddamn horse, and the fact this lyin' bastard has got his grubby paws on it can only mean he must know something about that nigger marshal."

In response to this, the front door of the soddy was suddenly jerked open and there stood Charley Bourbon. He was shirtless, his thick torso crisscrossed with strips of linen wrapped around to hold in place the numerous bandages applied to the wounds on his back. Along with a fierce glare from his narrowed eyes he was aiming the black bore of Lone's Yellowboy, held loosely at waist level. "You wanna know about the nigger marshal?" he bit out through clenched teeth. "How about askin' him to his face?"

A whole new layer of tension crackled in the air.

Reluctantly, guardedly, the eyes of both mounted men lifted off Lone and shifted to the sight of Charley filling the open doorway. Hawk Nose fought hard to hold his expression flat, unchanged. But Moon Face couldn't keep from gawking, his sagging lower lip dragging his mouth open wide.

Lone also cut his gaze to Charley, feeling instantly relieved by him stepping forth. But then, regarding his old friend closer, he saw signs that quickly put him less at ease. The lawman's eyes, narrowed into that well-practiced glare, were red-rimmed, maybe even a bit feverish. And his bold stance, feet planted wide with the Yellowboy gripped casually yet menacingly in an equally well-practiced manner, didn't appear all that steady. To the extent it was, Lone realized sinkingly, was at least partly due to how the thick bulge of his left shoulder was braced against the door frame. Shit. It was good to have Charley show up to side him—but at the same time it was clear he was doing so in a weak, tenuously stable condition, not fully recovered from all the punishment he'd endured.

Whether Hawk Nose picked up on this too, or he was merely moved to put on a display of bravado, he acknowledged Charley by saying, "Well, well. What've we got here? I see a big pile of bandages with a noisy Black man poking out of 'em. But what I don't see is any sign of a badge."

"Sometimes," Charley drawled, "a body oughta be just as careful about what he don't see as what he does."

"What the hell's that supposed to mean?" Hawk Nose sneered.

Charley wagged his head. "Never mind. What I see before me is plain as can be. Simon Redsleeve and Boyd Cramer...two pus drippin's off the diseased ass of Rip Hardessy. Nothing more, nothing less."

That tore away the bravado and all the rest of hawk-nosed Simon Redsleeve's composure. His eyes blazed and his mouth twisted savagely. "Why, you uppity Black bastard. I take that kind of talk from no man—especially not no stinking nigger!"

"The words've already been spoke," Charley snarled back, leaning away from the doorframe and standing straighter, more rigid. "You got a problem with 'em and mean doin' anything to try and...try an'..." His words abruptly trailed off in a slur, eyes growing momentarily very wide before going into a series of rapid blinks. He lurched drunkenly then seemed to teeter in an attempt to remain upright at all.

In his battered, weakened state, Charley was being struck by a sudden wave of dizziness, struggling not to black out completely. This was immediately clear to Lone—and, unfortunately, also to the two horsemen looking on.

Not hesitating to seize this unexpected opening, Redsleeve instantly clawed for the gun on his hip while bawling to his partner, "Take the rancher—time to cut down both these sonsabitches!"

And in the furious seconds that followed, that's exactly what the pair of tough nuts tried their damnedest to do. Just as quickly, however, they found it a task not easily accomplished.

Lone had been poised and ready all along and, though he in no way fancied himself a gunslick of any note, he was nonetheless a fair ways from sluggish when it came to clearing leather. It worked in his favor, too, that it was moon-faced Boyd Cramer who got sicced on him. In keeping with Lone's initial assessment of the man, his oversized gut and his gun worn for the cross draw made his grab for the weapon too damned cumbersome. His meaty paw had barely closed on the hoglrg before Lone's Colt was in his fist, angled upward, spitting flame and lead.

With Cramer having obligingly twisted in his saddle to face Lone, his wide frame made an easy target. Lone's slug smashed into his chest, just off center to the left. The big man shuddered and rocked back from the impact, but stayed in the saddle. Until, that was, the shudder running through his body reached his gun hand and caused the finger slipped inside the trigger guard to jerk and inadvertently fire off a round. The bullet thus released went sizzling at an angle down across the ribs of Cramer's horse. The animal screeched in alarm and pain, rearing on its hind legs and dumping its flailing rider heavily to the ground.

Through all of this, Lone was gripped by concern for the fate of desperately vulnerable Charley. Bad as he'd wanted to help his friend against the threat stated in no uncertain terms by Redsleeve, the former scout had had no choice but to deal first with Cramer in order to keep from getting his own hide ventilated. But now, having succeeded at that, he whipped his gaze anxiously to determine what was taking place between the other two men. Even as he and Cramer were burning powder, he'd heard the crashing reports of additional gunfire.

With Cramer's horse continuing to rear up and thrash about, jumping forward to block Lone's line of sight and kicking up swirls of dust to mix with the rolling powder smoke, it took Lone frantic seconds before he was able to make out how things stood. He could see that Redsleeve was still in his saddle, though being pitched to and fro now as his horse had also begun acting up in response to the shooting and the antics of Cramer's horse. None of it was keeping Redsleeve from blazing away, though, thrusting out a wildly swaying gun arm and cussing a blue streak as he pumped lead at the soddy's doorway. In the doorway, Charley was dropped to one knee, slump shouldered and head hung low, as bullets tore away pieces of the frame above and beside him.

Lone lunged forward, breaking into long, ground-eating strides. "Over here, you piece of shit!" he hollered at Redsleeve, swinging his Colt in chopping motions to drive Cramer's damn horse out of his way. The frenzied beast sprang to one side, shrieking. And then, except for the dust and smoke hanging in the air, there was nothing but open space between Lone and Redsleeve. The latter, rein-jerking his own horse once more under control, snapped his face around at Lone's shout. His lips were peeled back, teeth bared in a snarl. After only a fraction of a second's hesitation, his gun arm also started to swing around—pulling his aim away from Charley and bringing it to bear on Lone.

Lone dug in his heels, skidding to a halt and dropping into a half crouch. He braced himself, gun arm rising and steadying again at an upward angle.

Over in the doorway, Charley was suddenly, shockingly jolted out of his seeming collapse. His head lifted, his shoulders quit their slump, his gaze made a clear-eyed sweep of all on display before him. Re-tightening his grip on the Yellowboy still at his side, he immediately swung the barrel up and thrust its muzzle forward.

Three firearms discharged in a nearly simultaneous roar.

Redsleeve's bullet punched scalp-close through the crown of Lone's Stetson, singing tufts of hair and knocking the hat away into a wild spin.

But failing to score a meaningful hit on his intended target was the least of Redsleeve's bad luck. The lead thrown his way in return did *not* fail to score. Charley's slug hammered square to the center of the hawk-nosed varmint's chest, Lone's drilled into the side of his neck just above the shoulder. Redsleeve was lifted out of his saddle by the double impact and deposited five feet away, dead before he hit the dirt.

CHAPTER FIVE

BOYD CRAMER LASTED ONLY A LITTLE WHILE BEFORE exhaling a final raspy gurgle that marked the end for him. Lone did what he could, but the bullet had gone in too deep and too close to the heart. Stanching the bleeding on the outside did nothing to address what was torn up internally.

Before he died, Cramer did some talking. He confirmed that, just as Charley pieced it together afterward, the plan by Hardessy's gang to stage a rescue of their leader had hinged on dynamiting the freight car in front of the caboose holding the marshals and their prisoner, then extracting Hardessy out of the chaos. Nobody could explain why the explosion was so massive—the gang member who rigged it, a man named Posey, swore vehemently there was no way his charge was anywhere near big enough to cause such a result. The only possibility he could think of was that part of the contents of the freight car must have been some kind of additional explosive that was also set off by the dynamite.

At any rate, once they'd ridden clear of the destruction with a badly shaken Hardessy now in their midst—along with the body of a gang member who'd been shot and killed by Marshal Wordell, and also the injured dynamiter who got caught too close to the blast—Hardessy called a halt and began questioning everybody about Marshal Charley Bourbon. He himself had seen Charley hurled out the front of the caboose by the explosion, but he demanded to know if anybody could give an account of him after that. The answer came back no, at no subsequent point, not during the shooting or within the scattered wreckage and thick clouds of smoke from the heaps of burning debris, did anybody spot further sign of the Black marshal. This made Hardessy highly agitated. It was like he became obsessed with not wanting the notoriously dogged Bourbon left still alive to hound him any more in the future.

In order to make sure, he sent Cramer and Redsleeve, who was the gang's best tracker, back to the scene. Their instructions were to confirm that a dead body already existed or hunt down whatever remained of the lawman, who in Hardessy's mind *had* to have at least suffered serious injury, and finish the job. The sheer devastation at the site made the task challenging enough, but then the arrival of railroad personnel and a track repair crew—forcing Cramer and Redsleeve to dodge being spotted by any of them—made it damn near impossible. When they were on the brink of giving up without finding any shred of Bourbon, Redsleeve finally cut sign where he had crawled away through the muddy ditch. This meant bad news as far as their quarry remaining alive, but there was good news in that he was for some reason on the move *away* from where the derailment had taken place and where the cluster of prying eyes was now gathering. That gave Hardessy's men the chance to still hunt him down and finish him before he reached whatever alternative destination he was bound for.

Trouble was, tracking Bourbon's erratic route over open terrain that was by turns grassy and yucca-choked then rocky and cut by gullies and washouts, was slow and tedious and proved a strain on Redsleeve's ability. When they at last felt they'd nearly closed the gap on him, the late evening storm had intervened and left them no choice but to hold off until morning...neither Lone or Charley needed to be told what happened then.

Though an attempt at more questioning was made, Cramer divulged nothing further. Not the location where he and Redsleeve were set to rejoin Hardessy and the others, not how information on the train selected to transport Hardessy had been gained. Nothing worthwhile.

Once Cramer had breathed his last, Lone promptly wrapped his body and that of Redsleeve in canvas tarps and temporarily placed them in a shaded spot beside the grain bin. That done, he turned his full attention to getting Charley back inside the soddy so he could have a fresh look at his injuries and address the matter of his near black-out.

Regarding that, Charley wasted no time expressing lamentations and apologies. "Damn, Lone, I surely regret that display. Bargin' out like I done, all full of bluster and tough talk—only to buckle at the crucial point and most near cause us both to buy the farm!"

"What the hell're you talkin' about?" Lone countered. "If you hadn't shown up when you did to split the attention of those two jaspers, I'd've been in a fine pickle on the short end of two-to-one odds. They were seconds away from openin' up on me when you flung that door open."

"Yeah. Flung the door but then melted in on myself like a glob of lard on a hot griddle," Charley muttered sourly.

"What matters," Lone said, getting the lawman once again sat astraddle one of the kitchen chairs, "is that we're the ones left upright while their carcasses are stacked outside drawin' flies. I'd call that an outcome in our favor. And you not endin' up with any bullet holes after the way Redsleeve was blazin' away at you, I'd call that damn near a miracle."

Charley frowned. "Reckon I'd've expected a miracle to leave me feelin' better than the way I presently do. But don't get me wrong, I ain't complainin'. If you want to label it a miracle how Redsleeve's horse went to hoppin' around and kept him from bein' able to steady his aim, I won't argue."

"Maybe he was just a piss poor shot. Main thing is, you came out of it with no lead rattlin' around inside you to go with this chawed up back you're already sportin' on the outside." Lone reached to briefly press the back of his hand against Charley's forehead. Drawing it back, he said, "I'm surprised you ain't burnin' up. That's good. But the way your eyes looked just before you went all woozy before, I had a notion you'd likely took on a fever."

Charley's frown deepened. "That damn wooziness. I don't know what brought it on, but it sure fetched me a wallop. Maybe it was the sight of my own Colt .45—the one I lost, along with my hat, when that explosion flung me out of the caboose—stuffed in the waist of Redsleeve's britches." It was a fact that during Lone's treatment of his savaged back the previous night, Charley had lamented less about his physical pain than the loss of one of the two guns he was notorious for packing in a custom two-holster gun belt. "I'm happy to reclaim that shooter now," he continued, "but, to clean off the taint of that lowdown cur havin' handled it, I'll definitely be scaldin' it and givin' it a good gun oil bath before re-holsterin' it for my own use."

Lone grinned. "Yeah, you'd better do that. How about the stubby-legged gelding that saved you from bein' stuck shank's mare? Talk about irony, you heard Cramer claim that critter was his, before it ran off spooked by the train explosion. You gonna give it a bath and scrub it down too, before you'll ride it again? Or you just gonna shove it aside and mooch a horse off me instead?"

"Nossir," Charley said sternly. "That horse came along like a blessing when I sorely needed one. Reckon I'll go ahead and keep him in that spirit."

Lone made no response.

His expression remaining stern, Charley said, "Gettin' back to that shootout. I came out of my chair when I heard you and those peckerwoods jawin' outside. Felt plenty stiff and sore. Yet steady enough. Or so I thought...until all of a sudden that damn wooziness hit, and then I wasn't."

"How is it now? Any dizziness or a light-headed feelin'?"

"Not no more. Might be a little wobbly-kneed was I to stand up too sudden."

"You still got a heap of healin' to do. Your body's

been through a powerful lot in a short amount of time."
Lone had begun gently prodding and peeling back the
edges of some of the bandages on Charley's back. "Don't
look like you floppin' around dodgin' bullets in that
doorway tore these wrappin's loose or re-opened your
wounds any, though. I think it's best to just leave things
be for the time bein'. When I go to town, I can bring
back fresh bandagin' material and maybe some added
salve or other treatments to help."

"You're the doctor," Charley allowed. "But if I can
make a suggestion...is that coffee I smell cookin' on the
stove? I think a cup of that'd be sure to help my healin'
along, especially was you to splash in some more of that
redeye you was dishin' out last night."

"Coffee it is. I'll pour us both some. There's biscuits
there on the table, too. Wouldn't hurt to get some food
in your stomach."

"Sounds good. Coffee, biscuits, and don't forget the
redeye. Strictly for medicinal purposes mind you.
Remember, I got a heap of healin' to do."

Once Lone had cups of coffee poured for each of
them and a bottle of "medicinal" whiskey placed in
front of Charley, he also took a seat at the table. Their
talk quickly picked up where it had left off last night
regarding the loose ends trailing from Rip Hardessy's
escape. The encounter with Redsleeve and Cramer had
provided little in the way of worthwhile new information. That didn't mean, however, it didn't present some
new things needing consideration.

"If Cramer was accurate in what he said about my
partner shootin' and killin' one of the gang members,"
said Charley, "then that kinda goes against my notion of
Hank maybe bein' the inside man for 'em, don't it?

Unless, that is, they tried some kind of last minute double cross on their deal with him and he didn't give in without a fight."

Lone gave him a look. "Jesus. When you latch on to a suspicion you don't let go of it easy, do you?"

"I told you. Until I know for certain, I see everybody who ain't already planted in the ground as a possible suspect...and even then, there could be times I might still wonder a bit."

"Speakin' of bein' planted in the ground—or least-ways served up as buzzard bait—it seems Rip Hardessy is hell bent on arrangin' that for you," Lone pointed out. "You been that much of a burr under his saddle for him to want so bad your wick gets pinched out once and for good? Peelin' two men off a getaway run and sendin' 'em back to make sure strikes me as a mighty bold move."

"Maybe bold, maybe just desperate. Either way," said Charley somewhat smugly, "I hope them skunks failin' to return to the varmint hole gives ol' Rip a pump-kin-sized knot of worry in his gut. Let him fret about what happened to 'em and how much they might've spilled in the process."

"Sounds like Hardessy's dislike for you ain't exactly a one-way trail."

"You got that right," Charley affirmed in a somber tone. "Him and his bunch are a bad lot, Lone. Deservin' of havin' the earth scraped clean of 'em a long time ago. I've chased 'em plenty and done my damnedest to get the job done—reckon that's why Rip is so anxious to have me got rid of—yet the sorry sonsabitches are still runnin' loose."

"But not so many now as there was a little while ago," Lone reminded him. "They're less the two outside, plus, if Cramer told it straight, one more killed durin' the train attack and the dynamiter hisself maybe laid up. How many usually run in Hardessy' pack?"

"Half a dozen to eight. Thereabouts."

"So that means we've whittled 'em down considerable. Half or more."

Charley drank some of his coffee. "Reckon so. I guess that's encouragin'. But it still leaves the head of the snake, Hardessy. And, since Cramer didn't mention him otherwise, his second in command too. That'd be Whitey Culp. With their combined reputations, it won't take long to attract more scum for fillin' their ranks back in." The lawman took a bite of biscuit and chewed it furiously. "That is, unless we can come up with a way to lure out some of the ones who're left before they're all the way done lickin' their wounds."

Lone eyed him. "You've got something besides wooziness swirlin' around inside that cracked noggin of yours. What is it?"

CHAPTER SIX

"YOU KNOW, JUST THE OTHER DAY I WAS THINKING HOW long a spell it's been since you've come to town. Made me wonder how you were doing, what you've been up to." Keith Overstreet paused, his eyebrows pinching together in a display of remorse. "And now here you are, and I see what it is you *have* been up to, and you know what? I gotta say—I could've stood you staying away a while longer."

From his saddle, Lone gazed impassively down at the town marshal of North Platte. The latter stood looking back from his stance on the boardwalk out front of the city jail building. He was tall and lanky of build, not far past the thirty-year mark, still with traces of boyish handsomeness. A feature of his countenance happened to be a mildly jutted jaw that at the moment was thrust forward in a particularly pronounced way. In response to this and the greeting that came with it, Lone drawled, "Jeez, Keith, that's a helluva rude welcome to an old friend. Not to mention a mighty ungrateful way for a lawman to show appreciation at havin' his peace keepin' load lightened for him."

Overstreet glanced past Lone to once again regard the two horses in tow behind him, each with a canvas-wrapped body slung belly down over their saddles. Bringing his eyes back to Lone, he then said, "I take it by that remark you're saying these packages you're so ostentatiously delivering are a pair of wanted hombres —or *formerly* wanted, I guess I should say. That it?"

"Uh-huh. They ain't exactly strikin' their best poses right at the moment, but if Deputy Jeff takes a close look I think he'll recognize 'em okay. They'll prove to be what's left of Simon Redsleeve and Boyd Cramer...a couple upstandin' citizens known for their good deeds as part of the Rip Hardessy gang."

The mention of Hardessy's name sent an excited ripple through the knot of townsfolk gathered close around in the lengthening shadows of late afternoon. Having reached a dozen or so in number, they'd begun forming in Lone's wake as he rode into town and proceeded leisurely down the street toward the marshal's office and jail. Deputy Jeff Tully had also shown up to fall in and walk alongside Lone and Iron-sides. Lone's calmly stated, "Everything's okay, Jeff, I'll explain it all when we get to the marshal" had mollified him enough to merely stick close and make sure nothing got out of hand. Considering the make-up of those taking an interest at that point—bored old-timers with nothing better to do, a few housewives distracted from last-minute shopping, some store clerks with the day's business at a lull—nothing like that had been apt to happen. Now, however, with awareness ramped up by the words "Rip Hardessy gang members" flapping on tongues, that could change in a hurry. A more boisterous element could become attracted.

Sensing this, Marshal Overstreet moved forward off the boardwalk and quickly began dispersing what crowd there was. "All right everybody, let's break this up. Clear out and go on about your own business. There's nothing more to hear or see here. Not now, not until we've had a chance to check out things farther." He motioned impatiently to his deputy. "Jeff, gather up those damn horses. Take them and their passengers over to the undertaker and get 'em out of sight. Not that I doubt Lone's accuracy, but confirm it truly is Redsleeve and Cramer. Then get back to me."

"Will do, Marshal."

With Jeff leading away the corpse-laden horses and the crowd breaking up as ordered, Overstreet turned his attention back to Lone. Jerking a thumb over his shoulder, he said, "Inside with me, amigo. We got some talking to do."

Lone was hardly a stranger to the North Platte marshal's office. He'd been there many times in the past. Never as a detainee, though often—like now—still in conjunction with some trouble or other of the type that seemed to find him wherever he went. It found him perhaps more frequently in this Nebraska railroad town because of the fact that here was the place he'd regularly gravitated back to during his drifting years following the end of his days as a scout for the Army out of nearby Fort McPherson. What kept bringing him back, in addition to the town's proximity to the fort where he'd grown up and been stationed out of, was the presence of an elderly widow named Adeline Sharples.

Though barren in reality, Mrs. Sharples ran a popular boarding house and grew to commonly be called "Ma" by most everyone. But to Lone, more than the rest, it was a particularly suitable title because it was she and her late husband, a crusty old sergeant also stationed at McPherson, who primarily saw to Lone's upbringing at the fort after his true parents were killed in an Indian massacre.

Much had changed over the intervening years... things like Ma having relocated to the small settlement of Sarben off to the north, Lone more or less settling down to try and revive the Busted Spur operation he'd originally started a number of years back with a now deceased one-legged ex mountain man named O'Malley, and Keith Overstreet growing from a green deputy to full marshal...but the one thing that seemed unchanged, at least on an intermittent basis, was Lone coming around packing some new kind of trouble.

Exhibiting a well-established familiarity with that fact, Marshal Overstreet wasted no time addressing it on this occasion. He'd barely closed the office door behind him and Lone when he wheeled with an exasperated look on his face and declared, "Jesus Christ, Lone! Do you have any idea what a hot button the name of Rip Hennessy is right now?"

Lone walked over and hitched up one of the straight-backed chairs situated before the marshal's desk. "Right now?" he echoed. "I'd expect Hardessy's name to be a hot button most any time."

"True enough," allowed Overstreet. "But take into added account how he escaped custody from a pair of federal marshals less than forty-eight ago and how, to help him accomplish that, his gang blew hell out of two railroad cars and tore up a section of UP track only about thirty miles from here...does that give you a better idea why interest in him is right now at a heightened level?"

Lone issued a low whistle. "My, my. Rip has been a mighty busy boy."

Overstreet hiked a leg and sat on the corner of his desk. "A busy boy and a damned naughty one. You telling me this is the first you're hearing any of this?"

"Me and my horse herd fall a ways outside the whirl of current events," Lone said dryly.

"Okay. But your ranch ain't that many miles north of where...and what about those two owlhoots you just brought in?" Overstreet scowled. "Them being members of Hardessy's gang for as long as anybody can remember can't possibly mean they just happened to be passing through the neighborhood without being part of the hit on the train."

"Maybe they showed up late for the party." Lone shrugged. Then he added the first part of the fabrication he and Charley had put together to cover his bringing the bodies into town. "Or, more likely, the gang split up once they'd freed Rip—to confuse their trail for any posse that might form to give chase—and I got lucky enough to have Cramer and Redsleeve set a course smack through my spread."

"They say something to indicate that?"

"Not hardly. They didn't show up for a social visit, Keith. I caught the bastards tryin' to make off with a couple of my horses," Lone explained, layering on some more fabrication. "Reckon they meant to run with some spares to make better time wherever they was headed. I objected, then we had a sort of argument involvin' some

.44 caliber cuss words. I ended up doin' a better job of arguin' than they did. I didn't fully recognize 'em until it was all over."

Overstreet wagged his head as if in amazement. "You make it through the damnedest scrapes. You shoot it out with a couple of the toughest nuts around, they bite the dust, and you're lucky enough to come away with only a fresh bullet hole in your hat."

"Hey. To me, that ain't all the way lucky," Lone grumbled. "I'm real fond of this hat, just got it proper broke in. Now one of those jackasses went and punched a hole in it."

"Well the good news about the bad news is that you won't be short money to buy a new one."

"How so?"

"Because of the individual bounties those two jackasses managed over time to get slapped on their stupid heads. That's how you recognized 'em, wasn't it?" Overstreet pointed lazily to a couple thick layers of Wanted posters spiked to a cork board hanging on the wall. "Somewhere up there are papers on Redsleeve and Cramer. Dead or Alive, as I recall, and a couple tidy sums offered as I also recall. Some time or other those dodgers and the mugs plastered on 'em have been plenty wide. I know you didn't brace 'em for the bounty money, but you'd be a damn fool not to cash in. In addition to needing to buy a new hat, you can't tell me you'd pass on a chance to add to your horse stock, would you?"

In truth, Lone had been quite aware of the bounty rewards offered for the pair he'd brought in. Rather, Charley had. Claiming payment, after putting on the appropriate surprise act, was another part of the plan he and Charley came up with to get the most benefit possible out of Lone's trip to town. To start with there'd only been the goal of learning all the latest information available on the status of things in the aftermath of Hardessy's rescue. But then, tacked onto that, came the notion to broadcast how Lone got the better of Redsleeve and Cramer all on his own—knowing the news would quickly reach the rest of the gang, no matter where they'd gone to ground, and purposely omitting any mention of the role Charley had played in order to maintain his being dead facade.

The idea behind this whole tack-on, crafted in Charley's devious mind, was to dangle two potential "lures" that might get a response out of Hardessy. If the gang boss was obsessed with making certain of Charley's demise to the degree Cramer had indicated, then maybe he'd smell something suspicious about Lone's tale; wondering what had caused the men he sent to apparently veer off course and somehow end up victims of a small-time horse rancher. If this bugged Hardessy sufficiently, maybe he'd be careless enough to risk trying some additional follow-up and thereby expose himself. A second possibility, even though individual members of outlaw gangs weren't known to be particularly loyal or protective of one another, was the chance that a desire to dish out some plain old-fashioned revenge on the man who took down two of their outfit *might* come into play and also provide an opening.

Either way, if acted upon, it essentially set up Lone as a stalking horse. This was a point Charley went to great lengths to drive home before he'd let Lone agree to it. The matter was settled by Lone stating flatly, "If I'm in this with you, then I'm in all the way. I've never before directly crossed paths with Hardessy's bunch. But I've heard plenty about the hell they've raised. Like you said —they're overdue for bein' scraped off the face of the earth. If I can help get that done, then I'm more than willin' to pitch in."

CHAPTER SEVEN

RIP HARDESSY CAME AWAKE AND SLOWLY, CAUTIOUSLY opened his eyes. The way a man learns to do after spending time behind bars. Through guarded slits, his gaze swept wide one way and then back the other. For just a moment he appeared somewhat bewildered. Then his face relaxed, his eyes opened full, and he pushed up to rest on one elbow atop a bedroll spread near the back of a wide, shallow cave.

Six feet away, about half the distance to the narrow, ragged-edged mouth of the cave, another man was squatting beside a campfire, lifting the flame on the tip of a burning twig to the freshly rolled cigarette clamped between his lips. Hardessy had involuntarily emitted a faint grunt when he raised himself, causing the squatting man to look around just as he puffed the cigarette to life.

Grinning through a cloud of smoke, Whitey Culp dropped the twig back in the fire and straightened up. "Hey there," he said. "Have yourself a good rest?"

Hardessy looked past him and frowned at the sight

of long shadows slicing through the fading sunlight outside. He grunted. "Looks like I must have. Jesus. Is afternoon comin' down already?"

"Yeah, it is."

Hardessy's forehead puckered. He gestured toward Whitey's cigarette. "You got makin's?"

Whitey held out the quirley he'd just got going. "Here, take this. I'll build another."

Hardessy wordlessly accepted the offer. With only one hand, he had become amazingly adroit at many tasks. Rolling a cigarette was one of them, though circumstances at times dictated it being among the more challenging. Regardless, it was a fierce point of pride with the man to never accept assistance—the only exception being from Whitey, by virtue of some unspoken bond formed during their many years riding together.

After drawing in a deep pull of smoke and exhaling, Hardessy said, "Where's everybody else?"

"Kid's on lookout. Posey's due to relieve him soon, but before then he went down to the spring—says the cold, fresh water helps sooth his burns." Whitey paused long enough to light the fresh smoke he'd rolled. "River...well, he's sitting out by the grave again."

"Takin' it awful hard, ain't he?" Hardessy said.

"Yeah. Clevis may have technically been only his nephew but, after River's brother died, he raised the boy like a son. You could see that, see how it cut both ways between 'em."

Hardessy's mouth tugged down at the corners. "One of the reasons I don't like relatives riding in the same outfit. Something goes sideways and one goes down, it hits the one who's left extra hard. In this case, Clevis having been such an all-around likable cuss makes it hard for everybody." A couple years short of fifty, an even six feet in height, age had thickened Hardessy's body some but hadn't lessened its rawhide-stretched-over-barbed wire ruggedness a lick. His face was molded in solid, even features that made him still a handsome man in spite of the leathery skin and deeply ingrained lines marked by a hard life. This also accounted for an expression that seldom varied from somber. Only in his eyes did a range of emotion show; sometimes conveying gentler feelings—such as sadness, like they were doing now when discussing Clevis—but then equally capable of turning, in an instant, to fiery pools ablaze with vicious anger.

Whitey Culp, so called since boyhood due to his milk-colored hair, had in the course of the dozen years he'd ridden with Rip seen those extreme swings often enough to always be on guard against them. Whitey was two years younger than Hardessy and an equal number of inches shorter. He was deceptively frail-looking, possessing his own streak of viciousness though with a slightly slower-burning fuse. When the fuse burned down, however, the lightning in his gun hand made up the difference.

Blowing a smoke ring out the corner of his mouth, Whitey spoke matter-of-factly. "Something more to know about how hard River is takin' what happened to Clevis...something I been tryin' to keep a lid on, but got a fear is bound to boil over..."

"Spit it out. What?"

"Whenever he ain't out at the grave, River has been sitting around grumbling and aimin' the stink eye harder and harder at Posey. Posey is tryin' to ignore him, but the eyeballin' is getting sharper and the grumbling is getting' louder...you see, River is holdin' Posey partly responsible for Clevis's death."

"What? What kind of blue hell nonsense is that?" Hardessy demanded to know. "Clevis got pumped full of lead by that young federal marshal. Posey was busy dealin' with his injuries from near gettin' blown apart by his own blast."

"That's just it. The power of that blast. The way it blew way the hell stronger than it was supposed to and near tore all of us apart. River blames that—and Posey, him bein' the one who rigged it—as the fault for Clevis ending up so rattled and scared he walked into the marshal's bullets not being clear-headed enough to shoot back."

"Aw, for Chrissakes! If anybody's got a beef with Posey's goddamn triple-strong explosion, it oughta be me on account of how that wooden beam came flyin' and slammed across my middle. I ache from my ass both ways, and I can't see where—ahhh, damn!" In his agitated state, Hardessy had abruptly tried jackknifing to a sitting position, but this produced a jolt of pain so severe it knocked him back flat.

Whitey took a halting step toward him. "Rip! You okay?"

Wrapping both arms around his battered middle, Hardessy responded through gritted teeth, "Does it *look* like I'm okay? I feel like I been busted near in two by the granddaddy of all mule kicks. Jesus!"

Kneeling beside the prone man, Whitey took the half-smoked cigarette that had fallen from his mouth and tossed it into the fire. Then he said, "Lift up the front of your shirt. Let's have a look at where you took that hammering."

Moments later, after Hardessy had tugged his shirt-front out of his pants and undone the buttons, Whitey's expression became one of deep concern. "Holy balls. Your whole stomach area is bruised as purple as an overripe grape!"

"Sounds familiar," Hardessy rasped. "That was about the color of the blood I pissed before I lay down for that nap."

"Why the hell didn't you say something? The sound of that and the look of this damn well might require attention from a doctor."

"Yeah. Like we got one of those somewhere handy by," Hardessy said wryly. Then: "I'll be okay. I just tried to sit up too fast is all, forgot I need to take things slower for a while."

A flicker of movement filled the cave entrance as a lanky young man came through. Once inside, Darrold "the kid" Memford, youngest member of the gang, paused to regard Whitey and Hardessy. "I thought I heard somebody holler. Is everything okay?" he asked.

"That wallop I took in the explosion is crampin' me up some," Hardessy explained. "I aggravated it by moving too sudden."

Darrold moved closer and stared down at Hardessy's still exposed stomach. "Oh, wow. That don't look good at all."

Hardessy glared at him. "Ya think?"

"You want I should go fetch River? He knows some healin' stuff. Maybe he could do a poultice or at least wrap it in a way that would ease you some."

"I don't see how no poultice is gonna do any good," Hardessy grumbled.

"You never know," Whitey countered. "Kid's right about River knowing a thing or two that might help, though. Wouldn't hurt to let him have a look."

Hardessy scowled. "Hell yeah, why not? While you're at it, climb up on some high point and holler out in case any stray folks are wandering by who might want to come take a gander at the purple-bellied freak. We can charge admission!"

"Oh, put a boot in it, you stubborn ass," Whitey told him. Then he gestured to Darrold. "Go ahead and fetch River. Let's hear what he has to say."

As soon as the kid was gone, Whitey turned back to Hardessy and said, "If nothing else, River tending to you will help get his mind off Clevis. At the same time, it'll give you a chance to try and ratchet down those sour feelings he's harborin' toward Posey."

"Yeah, one way or other I got to not let that get out of hand," Hardessy allowed. "There are enough threats piled up against us on the outside without goin' at each other's throats internally."

"Wouldn't think it'd be hard for everybody to see it that way."

"And speaking of outside threats and concerns, the fact Redsleeve and Cramer haven't made it back yet ain't doing nothing to make me feel any better either," the gang boss stated. "We parted ways with 'em yesterday morning. We made it here *this* morning, even after bein' slowed by packin' Clevis's dead body and the injuries to me and Posey. Wouldn't you think those two oughta be catching up before much damn longer?"

"Before too much, I suppose. But they had to backtrack to the train wreck site to begin with, remember. And they would've got caught by that same storm as hit us," Whitey pointed out. "I don't think there's cause to get overly worried, not just yet."

Hardessy frowned. "With that damn nigger Marshal Bourbon in the picture, there's always cause for worry. Man, much as I was looking forward to you boys bustin' me free off that train, I was looking forward almost as much to the chance for puttin' an end to that Black sonofabitch and shaking him off my tail once and for good. Then when that holy hell dynamite blast blew everything all crazy and the last anybody saw was Bourbon flyin' through the air...damn! Hard as I want to believe he *must* have been broke to pieces, I can't rest proper 'til I know for certain. You understand?"

"Yeah, Rip, you made all that plenty clear," Whitey said, "when you sent Redsleeve and Cramer back the way you done. Now relax and give 'em time to do their findin' out, like you want. In the meantime, take it easy and don't get yourself all worked up again."

"Yeah. Yeah, you're right," agreed Hardessy. He closed his eyes and lay quiet for a minute. Then, still with them closed, he said, "Wish I knew, also, how Mona is makin' out. Figurin' there was bound to be a delay in getting those tracks cleared and fixed after that explosion, ain't likely she's made it to Ogallala yet. Be a comfort to know when she's settled in okay."

"Everybody—even though the others don't know the full of it yet—have got reason to want Mona doing okay," said Whitey.

"You mean on account of the money, of course. That's understandable, I get it. Me, I got added reasons."

"I know. But, for a while, we'll all just have to have

faith where Mona's concerned. Be too risky to try and check on her for certain right now. Thing about it, though, she's done a pretty good job so far of showing she can be counted on."

Hardessy smiled and gave a faint nod. "Yeah, I sensed that about her right off. Have to travel a long way to find any who give you that feeling, and it's damn seldom a woman. But Mona's different."

"I hope you're right about her."

"She came through so far. She got word to you, didn't she?" Suddenly a wince of pain gripped Hardessy's face. Once it passed, he said, "Where's that bottle of whiskey I was nippin' on earlier?"

"You drained it before you dozed off." Whitey frowned. "I can grab you another but, if that bruising means some inside damage, is guzzling whiskey a good idea?"

Hardessy formed a sly grin. "Come on, old pard. Is whiskey ever a *bad* idea?"

"It's led to plenty of bad results."

"Speak for yourself. Whiskey may have led me astray fifty or a hundred times. But it never let me down, not when I needed it the most...now how about grabbin' that fresh bottle?"

CHAPTER EIGHT

THEY WERE BACK THERE, SURE AS HELL. TWO OF 'EM.

The night was too clear and they were too sloppy at tailing somebody—especially somebody as savvy as Lone McGantry—for there to be any doubt.

Lone was only about half an hour out of North Platte when he first became aware of them. His initial thought, considering the hour, was that the likeliest explanation for other riders exiting town this late must be cow hands who'd overdone an evening of saloon-hopping and were now kicking up dust to get back to their ranch in hope of grabbing a couple hours sleep ahead of call to daybreak chores. It didn't take long, however, to note how the behavior of this pair didn't fit with that notion. Cowboys coming off a night on the town were usually whooping it up some, boasting about who out drank who or a favorable run at one of the gaming tables, maybe relating a dalliance with some willing dolly. Or, at the very least, doing the opposite— lamenting some experience that made them wish they'd stayed away and lost neither the money nor the sleep.

But these hombres were doing none of that. They were being way too quiet. Or trying to be. They also seemed to be maintaining a controlled distance behind him. This struck Lone as curious. Then it made him suspicious. Putting things to a bit of a test, Lone gigged Ironsides to a slightly faster pace for a while. The men behind him adjusted to hold the same gap between them and him. Easing back and going even slower got the same result.

Okay, so the shadow riders clearly had some kind of interest in him. But what? And why?

The portion of Lone's visit to North Platte aimed at covertly learning as much as he could about the aftermath of the train explosion that freed Rip Hardessy had gone well, even better than expected, and he was anxious to get back and report what he'd found out to Charley. The secondary part, to draw attention to himself for gunning the two Hardessy men and thus hopefully prod some careless retaliation out of the gang leader or his men, would take some time to see if it bore any fruit. Or so Lone and Charley had figured. But could it be that the clumsy oafs clopping along behind him now were already reacting to the ploy, making them somehow a part of Hardessy's crew? It didn't seem possible, not this soon. The way the whole territory was stirred up over the daring and reckless strike on the train, members of the gang had surely fled with all haste and gone to ground somewhere where they'd hunker until things died down. That was standard procedure, the only sensible thing...and yet that hadn't been the case for Redsleeve and Cramer. Hardessy had sent them back, against all convention, to make sure about Charley Bourbon. So was there a chance he was so obsessed—Cramer's word—to be certain Charley was done for that he sent *a second pair* as some kind of guarantee?

Whatever they were up to, Lone damn well didn't like the two fogging behind him. And he had no intention of letting things play out until they got around to making a move when it suited them.

Travel between North Platte and the small settlement of Sarben, off to the northwest, was regular enough to have worn a distinct trail through and over the undulating terrain of the Sandhills. Even at night this made an easily discernible course to follow. Lone's spread lay more directly north, however, meaning there came a point where he veered off the better-worn trail and set straight up across open country. Normally he would have stuck with the main trail a couple miles farther before making his turn, but tonight he didn't wait that long. He'd consider it a final test to see if those behind him also left the main trail. If they did, then whatever the dumb bastards were up to he'd make sure went different than they intended.

While the heart of the Nebraska Sandhills is essentially a sea of grassy, treeless, rolling hills, there is among those hills—some of which rise up sharply to nearly five hundred feet—also numerous gullies, washouts and blow-outs, jagged rock outcrops, and even a smattering of shallow ponds sometimes containing patches of quicksand. In short, even on a clear night it is a landscape one needs to strike out across with a measure of caution and keen awareness.

Lone knew the Sandhills, especially these lower reaches along the hinge of the panhandle, as good or better than any man alive. So when those tailing him did indeed turn off the main trail in his wake, he smiled a wolf's smile and thought ahead to exactly where he would lead them.

The spot he had in mind wasn't far. Less than a mile. The lead-up to it was an expanse of gently rising and falling low hills. Awash in the light of myriad bright stars and a partial moon, the surrounding grassland took on a bluish silver tint and the still air was heavy with the scent of the spring grass and wildflowers recently bathed and nurtured by the previous night's rain. A damn shame he couldn't be drinking all this in and savoring it peacefully, Lone thought, instead of having the enjoyment of a quiet evening ride ruined by interference from a couple of jackasses. Only thing for it, he consoled himself, was to turn the tables and ruin their evening to a greater degree.

Ahead, a pair of high hills hove into sight. One sloped off to the east, the other to the west. As Lone got closer, he came to the spill-out end of a broad, shallow wash that snaked between the hills, formed over a long period of time by run-off from the humps of higher ground. It likely had gotten worn some more during last night's storm, but the day's sun and the sandy soil had absorbed the latest flow quickly, leaving the floor barely damp now under Ironsides' hooves.

Lone steered his big gray into the snaky, empty watercourse. The tall hills loomed on either side. The base of each stretched out in long, gradual curves for more than a hundred yards. As it passed between them, the wash grew deeper for a ways until, nearing its northern end, it became narrower and shallower again. It also went into a sharp twist, almost fish-hooking around the back side of the east hill. There it abruptly ended, flaring out briefly and then pinching shut. The land beyond the pinch point extended on grassy and relatively flat once more, but before that the slope on the back side of the east hill was split open by a rocky ridge, partially collapsed. This left a ragged pillar of rock, about eight feet tall, standing apart from the smaller pieces of rubble and thrusting up just to one side of where the wash ended.

Lone gigged Ironsides up out of the wash, over the low bank of the pinch point and onto the flat grass. There, he quickly reined up and dismounted, pulling his Yellowboy from its saddle scabbard. Tugging the gray to one side and ground-reining him in a pool of shadows thrown by a jagged point of the broken ridge, Lone returned to the pillar standing beside the pinch point and pressed into position there. He waited.

The thud of horses' hooves coming down the wash grew closer and pounded a bit more rapidly, signaling some apprehension on the part of the approaching riders since the juke in the wash had taken Lone momentarily out of sight. When they rounded the fish hook curl and saw the flared section of wash and then the pinch point directly ahead, the two shadowers balked and jerked hard on their reins.

That's when Lone edged out from behind the pillar and stood in full sight, the Yellowboy aimed level from his hip. "Right about there is a good spot for you boys to hold real still," he barked loud and clear. "And if you don't want to catch a bullet, keep those hands high and empty!"

Except for a couple muttered curses to quell the confused, nervous pawing from their suddenly halted horses, the two wide-eyed men now under Lone's gun did exactly as ordered. His vision long since adjusted to the night's starry illumination, Lone was able to make out the features of the pair with reasonable clarity. Both were strangers to him and both were cut from similar cloth. Shabby, unwashed and unshaven, hair spilling long and greasy from under the wide, half-wilted brims of battered felt hats. The stockier of the two was wearing a pair of bib overalls with one broken strap so that a corner of the bib hung down in front like a flop-eared pup. The other was a considerably leaner specimen with an elongated neck displaying a large knob of an Adam's apple bulging through the growth of whiskers. Neither appeared to be packing a sidearm, but each had a Henry repeating rifle thrusting up out of his saddle boot.

After several beats of eyeball to eyeball silence, the lanky one said, "Who be you to halt our way and poke a rifle gun in the faces of me and my brother, mister? If we be trespassin' on private property or some such, we didn't see no signs agin' it." He had a twangy southern accent. Tennessee or maybe Kentucky, Lone guessed.

"No signs posted against foggin' a fella's trail neither," Lone grated in response. "But in my book there oughta be. 'Specially when it's done so sloppy as to be downright insultin'."

The one in the bib overalls said, "You're gonna hafta chaw that a little finer, bub. We don't know what you're talkin' about."

"You're a liar," Lone snapped, flat and sharp.

Both men went rigid in their saddles, bristling visibly.

Lone gave a warning thrust with the muzzle of the Yellowboy. "Too bad if you don't like hearin' it, but you damn well know it's the truth. Now, before one of you tries pukin' out some mealy-mouthed excuse, I want each of you—one at a time—to reach across with your off hand, pull out your saddle gun real slow, and drop it to the ground. You in the bib britches, you go first."

Bib Britches glared fiercely and hesitated for as long as he dared, but then with grudging slowness proceeded to do as told.

While he was, the lanky one said to Lone, "You're makin' a big mistake, mister. We be the Cutcheon brothers—I'm Mort, he's Remus—from down Memphis way. We came north lookin' for honest work but ain't found nuthun' hereabouts 'cept cold-shouldered Yankee cattle pushers and high stuck noses lookin' down on poor southern trash. We saw you back in one of the saloons and heard how you got yourself a horse ranch you're workin' to get a-goin'. Happens me and Remus don't know much about cattle critters, but we by-gum know horses. So we thunk maybe you'd give us a chance to—"

Lone interrupted him, gesturing with the Yellowboy. "Your brother is done shuckin' his hardware. Now it's your turn."

"Okay, okay," Mort said irritably. "None of this would be called for if you'd just listen to what I'm—"

"To the mealy-mouthed excuse you're tryin' to puke out," Lone finished for him. "Didn't you hear me say I was expectin' that and can't you see I'm too smart to buy a word of it?"

"Bein' mule stubborn ain't the same as bein' smart," Remus grumbled.

"Not that it's a very high bar to jump but, since I'm the one with the drop on the both of you, I'll settle for

claimin' that at least makes me smart-*er*. Now, instead of
wastin' more time—how about one of you fine southern
gents go ahead and tell me the real reason you been
followin' me?"

"Go to hell," Remus spat.

"We was headed back to Memphis and I reckon we
made a wrong turn," sneered Mort.

Lone regarded them, his teeth set on edge. Then he
exhaled out through his nose a ragged breath he hadn't
realized he was holding. "You know, Mort, thinkin' back,
I realize I was wrong about not buyin' a word you
spouted a minute ago...the part about you and Remus
bein' looked down on as nothing but southern trash.
You got that part right as rain, leastways as far as how
folks hereabouts likely see you. What that means, the
more I reflect on it, is instead of draggin' this out any
longer I could just go ahead and blow the liver and
lights outta you two and nobody in these parts'd hardly
notice or give a damn even if they did."

Mort didn't like the sound of that. His sneer had
disappeared. "You'd do that? Without fair cause?"

"He's bluffin'," rasped Remus, but not with quite as
much conviction in his voice as he was trying for.

Lone's mouth curved once more in a wolf's smile.
"For a minute I thought you might be after the bounty
money you heard I claimed back in town. But even you
lunkheads would've understood that didn't get forked
over to me right on the spot. So now I'm the one who
understands...the horses. I can see by your mounts you
appear to know good horseflesh, makin' that another
truth you told, Mort. Only you went right to lyin' some
more with that phony shit about wantin' a chance at
horse wranglin' work on my ranch...what you really had

in mind, after followin' me to find out where my spread is located, was to do some wranglin' alright." Lone's eyes blazed in the silver-blue starlight. "Once you'd caved in my skull with a rock or back-shot me, you sorry sons-abitches was gonna wrangle away my whole herd and push 'em up into South Dakota for a quick sell-off. Tell me *that* ain't the straight of it, you lowdown pieces of crud!"

"Now hold on a minute, you," protested Mort. "You be throwin' out a lot of ackasations you ain't got a lick of proof for."

"I got proof enough to suit me."

"Okay, I admitted me and my brother are on hard times and feelin' kinda desperate, didn't I? So maybe—just maybe—we took a notion to foller and see if this one-loop operation of yourn had anything to offer. We was thinkin'—again, just thinkin'—we might fob a few head to gain us a grub stake. But just a few, not so much as to wipe you out. And we sure-fire wasn't plannin' to do you, the way you said, as part of it. We ain't killers."

"No, you're practically a couple choirboys," Lone said sarcastically. "And as far as stealin' horses, one ain't no different than a dozen or fifty. It rates hangin' all the same."

"To hell with that! We ain't done nothing to rate no rope dance," declared Remus. "And I won't hear no more of it!"

"Long as you're on the wrong end of this Winchester, you'll hear whatever I got to say," Lone told him. "And I say I got every right to swing you varmints from the closest tree I can find. Even was I inclined to go to all the bother of marchin' you at gunpoint back to town, I doubt the marshal there would see it any different."

"I warned you about hangin' talk!" Remus bellowed, making a sudden grab at his chest with one hand.

"No!" hollered Mort, realizing what was happening before Lone had any chance to figure it.

With their rifles tossed to the ground and neither man visibly packing a short gun, Lone had made the unforgivable mistake of feeling a bit too smug and having slightly relaxed his readiness. It damn near cost him bad.

What Remus turned out to be grabbing for was a short-barreled hideaway revolver tucked in a specially sewn pocket inside the folded over bib of his overalls. It was clearly something he'd relied on in the past and something he'd practiced bringing quickly into play. The fisted revolver came out from behind the flap of cloth in a blur of speed. But no matter how fast Remus was or how much Lone was caught by surprise, it wasn't enough to beat the already cocked and aimed Yellowboy. The repeater bucked and roared in Lone's grip while Remus's gun hand was still in motion, swinging to try to get lined on target. The slug from the Yellowboy punched high into Remus's chest, knocking him out of the saddle and sending him into a backward somersault off the rump of his horse.

"Nooo!" Mort hollered again, this time dragging it out in a mournful wail. And then, even as his brother was toppling away, he flung himself from his own saddle.

Lone had automatically levered a fresh round into the Yellowboy. Seeing Mort spring from the back of his mount, his first thought was that he was dropping to try and aid his fallen brother. But no, when Mort hit the ground he made no move toward Remus at all, but rather began scrambling to retrieve one of the discarded Henrys. Lone cursed and snap-fired another shot, this bullet kicking up dirt an inch from Mort's groping hands.

Mort jerked back for just a moment but then lunged forward again, reaching once more for the rifle. Lone jacked home another round, but his two previous shots had panicked the horses and now they began shifting and hopping, inadvertently blocking another try at Mort. Lone leaped down from the bank of the pinch point and charged in between the skittering critters. He reached Mort just as the lanky Tennessean was swinging up the Henry rifle he'd finally managed to grab hold of. Lone swept his foot in a side kick, knocking away the barrel of Mort's gun. Then, stamping the kicking foot back down firm and leaning in as he twisted sharply at the waist to create full momentum, the former scout smashed the butt of his rifle savagely against the side of Mort's face.

CHAPTER NINE

"So you just let him go?"

Lone bristled at the question from Charley Bourbon. "*Just* let him go?" he echoed. "You make it sound like I sent him on his way with a bouquet of flowers and a picnic basket full of goodies. I don't figure most folks would see leavin' Remus with a busted jaw, a dead brother to be buried, and stripped of all weapons as exactly pampered treatment. What was I supposed to do? No matter how big a piece of trash he was, I couldn't just shoot him in cold blood. And the option of takin' him back to North Platte for a jail cot and a doctor and an undertaker to do the plantin' of his brother—that, to me, seemed like more damn kindness than he deserved."

Charley waved a hand placatingly. "Okay, okay. Didn't mean to ruffle your feathers so. Jesus. The main thing is you got through another scrape with your hide still intact."

"Yeah. And speakin' of hides," replied a still scowling Lone, "gettin' back here to check on that chawed up, half burned one of yours was another thing I had to take into consideration. You'd been left untended for quite a spell as it was. Didn't appeal to me to stretch it out even longer for the sake of dealin' any more than necessary with those pesky hillbillies." Outside the kitchen window of Lone's soddy, where the two men sat at the table talking, the first pale smudges of dawn were poking above the eastern horizon. "Plus," Lone continued, "I was also anxious to get back with the information I learned from Keith Overstreet on account of I figure it's gonna make some differences how we go from here."

"I appreciate you frettin' about me. So, to get that out of way," drawled Charley, "I'll tell you I'm feelin pretty damn decent. After your doctorin' and then near a full day and night of doin' nothing but restin' and healin', I reckon I oughta. There's been no dizziness, no fever, no ill effects I can tell 'cept for a touch of lingerin' weariness."

Lone nodded. "That's good to hear."

"And now, thanks to the new duds you brung me and especially *this*"—Charley waved the smoking pipe Lone had picked up for him in North Platte, then used it to also indicate the store-bought hat and clothes piled on the tabletop between them—"I figure what sliver of healin' I got left to do will go even faster and better." He paused to contentedly puff a cloud of smoke, then added, "No man with tobacco cravin's can be expected to fetch around proper if he's fightin' withdrawal miseries."

"Sounds like, instead of just bein' concerned for your back injuries, I should've been equally worried about your sufferin' due to bein' separated from a pipe and tobacco," remarked Lone.

"Maybe so," Charley allowed. "But, based on what you found out from your marshal friend, a whole new and urgent worry for us is the condition of my young partner, Hank Wordell. If he's still alive yet shot to hell and only hangin' on by a thread under some Ogallala doctor's care, I need to get to him pronto and see if there's a chance he can pass on anything that might help nail the bastards who sprung Hardessy and did the damage to both of us."

"To do that, it sounds like you're also sayin' you're ready to give up the dead man act."

"Not much point any more, is there?" Charley's face bunched with a fierce scowl. "Seems plain it's time for me to throw away my damnedable suspicions and crafty plans where Hank is concerned and get back to what and who I really am—a stubborn-ass law dog needin' to put my nose to the ground and get busy sniffin' out some lowdown skunks the same old-fashioned way I always have."

"You'll get no argument on that from me. In fact, I like the sound of it," said Lone. "But let's not forget one thing before you go chargin' off. All kidding aside about the healin' effects of tobacco and what not, you still went through a helluva rough ordeal and ain't no way you're at a hundred percent yet. The ride to Ogallala, just for starters, is near thirty miles. You really feel up to takin' out on that?"

"Damn right. You just worry about keepin' up with me."

Lone grinned wryly. "Guess there wasn't much doubt

how you'd answer. So okay, that's what we'll do. But, if you don't mind, I been near twenty-four hours without sleep. A couple hours of shuteye will do me, but I better grab that much or maybe I *won't* be able to keep up with you. While I'm doin' so, how about you use the time to get yourself ready and put some trail supplies together for us? Be sure to include some of those new bandages and salves I brought back, just in case. On the way out, we'll also need to swing by a neighbor of mine so I can ask him to keep an eye on my spread while I'm gone. We should still be able to make Ogallala by sunset."

Charley replied, "Like you said, I can't argue any of that. You go ahead and stretch out your bones for a spell. I'll have myself and the other stuff took care of before I wake you."

WHITEY CULP STOOD outside the cave mouth, a few feet off to one side, smoking a cigarette. He was leaned back against a bleached, wind-polished slab of sloping rock whose surface, which had still been cold from last night's chill when he first settled against it, was now quickly warming under the wash of early morning sunlight.

Whitey held statue still, his only movement being to periodically lift the cigarette to his mouth, take a hard drag, then let the smoke dribble slowly out through his nostrils. All the while, his face remained expressionless and his gaze appeared focused somewhere distant and indistinct.

What lay within actual range of sight from Whitey's vantage point was a vast sprawl of broken land made up of high, blunted sandstone cliffs with their faces scarred by irregular vertical seams and fissures—as if gouged by a giant hand reaching down with long, gnarled fingers. At the base of these ragged furrows, many choked by yucca and bramble brush and here and there a clinging clump of evergreen growth, ran a tangled maze of narrow, snaking arroyos bottomed by a mix of gravel and stubborn grasses. The hideout cave currently being occupied by the Hardessy gang was about a third of the way up one of the more gradually sloping cliff faces, cut in between a pair of weedy fissures with a short strip of flat ledge in front. Nearby, down on the flat but hidden deep in the notch of a much larger fissure, was a rare patch of meadow providing graze for the horses and also a small, spring-fed pool for water. It was a location long used by outlaws on the run and needing a place to lay low for a while, the secret of its location closely guarded yet nevertheless passed on from time to time to those deemed trustworthy enough to rate knowing. Rip Hardessy had been deemed such on a past occasion and had now led his current crew here.

Whitey had just taken his final drag off the quirley and was crushing the butt under a boot heel when another man emerged from the cave. This was River McIvey, the oldest member of the gang. He was as many years past fifty as Rip was short of it. Despite a hard life fighting poverty as a child, then fighting for the losing side in the war before fighting Indians for the winning side afterward then eventually taking on a life of fighting the law, he was still mentally and physically sharp. Of average height and build, he had a grizzled beard and a wild mane of white-streaked hair, but could always be counted on when there was need to ride hard and shoot straight. He'd previously worked with some other outfits before joining with Hardessy, always with high marks from any he'd ever ridden alongside.

Looking around, Whitey asked, "You get him to take some more of your tea?"

"Some. He dozed off after he took it. It's only biscuit soda and some brown sugar, an old remedy for soothing ulcers. There's more ingredients that should go with it, but that's all I got." River shrugged. "Way he chases it down with whiskey, I don't know how much it matters."

Whitey frowned. "Yeah. I wish he'd lay off on that some. In case he's got stuff busted up inside, he—"

"Oh, he does," River cut him off. "No doubt in my mind."

Whitey's expression soured all the more. "You figure it's pretty bad?"

"Afraid so. When Darrold showed up to take over for me, he told how Rip had moaned and thrashed through much of the night." The other four men, minus Hardessy, were standing six-hour lookout shifts. River had just completed a turn, having been relieved by Darrold Memford, and, when he got back to the cave, Whitey had asked him to minister some to the gang leader before sacking out to catch himself some shuteye. "I could tell," River commented further, "it was pretty unnerving for the kid to have to hear."

"Wasn't pleasant for nobody—least of all Rip," Whitey replied tersely. Then, taking some of the edge off his tone, he added, "But I know what you're saying. Listening to a tough nut like Rip carry on like that... well, it can only mean he's got to be hurting fierce not to be able to hold it in."

"You said he told you he's been pissing blood?"

"Uh-huh."

"When I was in there just now, he coughed up some too. And by the look of the stained hanky he wiped his mouth with, it wasn't the first."

"Damn. So he ain't getting no better, not at all."

"Worse, I'd say."

"In other words, he's in need of a doctor."

"In my opinion, yeah. For sure." River's forehead puckered above bristly white brows. "Even then, I don't know if just any sawbones would do."

"What's that supposed to mean?" Whitey growled.

"I mean, depending how bad he's busted up inside, it might take a skilled surgeon to go in and have any hope of making a difference."

"You mean carve him open? Jesus Christ, old man, you're making it sound worse by the minute!"

River spread his hands. "I'm just laying it out the way I see it. And, comes down to it, I don't think I'm telling you much you ain't already been thinking on your own."

The scowl that had been clutching Whitey's face let go slowly. He heaved a ragged sigh. "What it really comes down to," he bit out through clenched teeth, "is that it don't make a damn one way or the other... sawbones or skilled surgeon or even a lousy horse doctor...our chances of puttin' Rip in the hands of any of 'em is the same. Zero."

"That's a rotten summation. I can't offer much better, though. Except," River said, "maybe not to be so quick to give up on Rip's natural damn toughness. If anybody could pull through something like this, it'd be him."

"Yeah, there's always that," Whitey allowed, though

with limited conviction. "And it's how you and me are gonna sell it to the others, regardless. Yeah, Rip's having a rough go of it right now—but he's hangin' on and it's just a matter of time before he pulls through." He paused to eye River intently. "Got it?"

The old man shrugged. "Fine by me. That'll be our story...but don't you think Rip himself is gonna figure out the truth?"

"If he does, he does. But we ain't gonna say or do anything to help him think in that direction," Whitey insisted. "Besides, Redsleeve and Cramer ought to be showing up sometime today. If they bring a report confirming that nigger marshal is dead and nothing's left of him but a busted up, burned up chunk of charcoal, think what a lift that'd give Rip. Hell, it might even be enough to go ahead and actually set him to healing!"

CHAPTER TEN

HIRAM NEEDLES WAS THE LAW IN OGALLALA. THE NEW law. Six months prior he had been specially appointed by the town council to replace Marshal Cliff Halsey after Halsey was shot and killed breaking up what should have been a routine saloon brawl. As he fell victim to a fatal bullet from a hideaway derringer, Halsey had gotten off a trigger pull of his own that snuffed out the wick of his killer. So Needles started with a clean slate. By the terms of his appointment, he also started with greater authority than what Halsey'd had—Needles wore the star of a county sheriff, giving him jurisdiction over the town *and* the surrounding sizable chunk of real estate that comprised Keith County.

Both Lone and Charley had heard about these changes but neither had been to Ogallala since they took place. Lone seldom had cause to pass through the once notorious cattle town, despite his recurring visits to relatively nearby North Platte. In recent years, however, there'd been a couple of occasions where he had some dealings there, each ending up involving Halsey. As a result, he'd come away with a favorable impression of the man, both personally and as a lawman. Enough so that it was sad news to hear of his sudden demise.

As far as his replacement, Lone had never heard the name Hiram Needles before, knew nothing about the man. Charley, on the other hand, had a smattering of information that he shared on their ride from Lone's ranch. "Been a fair while ago," he related, "but I brushed elbows with Needles once or twice. Real stiff-necked, no-nonsense, graveyard serious type. Leastways that's how he struck me. Made a smidgen of a name for hisself cleanin' up a couple rowdy towns in the Four Corners area as I recall. Fancied hisself the second comin' of Wyatt Earp, the way I read him. Only trouble was, he came along a dozen or fifteen years too late—all the *real* rowdy towns had already been tamed."

Lone chuffed. "Sounds like he's still runnin' a mite late. If he's lookin' to build a name for himself here-abouts, Ogallala's wildest days—the ones that made eastern newspapers write about it as 'the Gomorrah of the Plains'—have pretty much come and gone."

"Maybe, maybe not," said Charley. "The ghost of Cliff Halsey'd probably argue that some. And with Needles all of a sudden havin' an exploded train, a daring prisoner escape, a shot-up US Marshal on his hands, and the whole Rip Hardessy gang runnin' loose right in his back yard...hell, he's likely got brand new visions of glory sparklin' in his eyes like a kid on Christmas morning."

"Never thought of that," Lone allowed. Then: "If that's the case, though, it could be he'll see you showin' up—risin' from the dead and all, aimin' to settle your own score with Hardessy—as something that'll take the sparkle out of his eyes on account of bein' a threat to slice off a piece of his glory."

"Too damn bad if he does! I've had my sights on Hardessy a helluva lot longer than Hiram Needles has," came the barked response. "The first order of business when we hit town is to find my partner. That he's also still alive and has a chance of pullin' through is my biggest hope. Then, I freely admit, my next hope is that Hank maybe saw or heard something before Hardessy and his rescuers rode off, leavin' both of us for dead, that might be a lead to where they were headed, what they next had in mind." Charley's expression hardened with resolve. "But make no mistake, I'll be goin' after Hardessy again, regardless. I won't let up until I put that bloodthirsty bastard toes down in the dirt!"

Lone remarked dryly, "He better hope you catch up with him soon, while you're still feelin' kinda weak and rundown...otherwise, he's gonna be in big trouble."

They arrived in Ogallala later than Lone had predicted. It was well past sunset, leaving the town wrapped thoroughly in the murkiness of evening. A useful array of street lamps were lighted, however, and Lone knew the layout well enough so that they had no trouble navigating to the desired address. It was a two-story wood frame building, freshly white-washed and very trim looking, located on a corner lot just off the main drag of Spruce Street. A neatly printed sign on a post in the narrow strip of front lawn read: *Maxwell Frake, M.D.*

Lone and Charley dismounted and tied their horses to the streetside hitch rail. Lone couldn't help but notice that Charley moved with notable signs of stiffness and fatigue. Neither was surprising, of course, considering everything he'd recently been through. In recognition of this, Lone had modified the pace of their just-completed long ride as much as he could, which was why they were getting in later than he'd initially estimated. By all rights, in his condition Charley should have held off such exertion for at least another day. But a not uncommon trait among men like him—and Lone as well, when it came right down to it—was to too often let stubbornness and pride override good sense.

There were lights glowing warmly in the windows of the house and behind an opaque oval of glass that decorated the front door. As Lone and Charley started up the plank walk leading toward the ornate door, a figure abruptly stirred out of a pool of shadows off to one end of the front porch. This movement was sudden enough and unexpected enough to cause Lone's right hand to drop automatically to the Colt riding on his hip. Out of the corner of his eye, Lone noted the lack of any similar reaction by Charley...a sign of greater calm on his part —or a further indication of his weariness?

A moment later, any call for concerned reaction was erased by the shadowy figure stepping into better lighting and revealing itself to be a man wearing a lawman's badge. He was a tall, sturdily built individual holding a Winchester rifle angled up across his chest. "You here to see the doc?" he wanted to know.

"That's the general idea," Charley responded somewhat irritably. He and Lone had stopped walking. Charley stamped his feet wide and drew himself up to his full, formidable height. Hard-eyeing the man with the badge, he asked, "Is it customary hereabouts to have an armed guard standin' watch over the comin's and goin's of a doctor's patients?"

"It is these days," came the answer, stated flatly. "But if a legitimate patient is what you are, then you got no worry."

Charley made a production of spreading his arms and planting his fists on his hips just above the brace of .45s pouched in his black, tooled leather, double-holster gun belt. This action caused the crisp new vest Lone had bought him to open wider and reveal *his* badge pinned to the shirt underneath. "Who and what I am," he declared, "is Charles Bourbon, United States Marshal. That good enough for ya?"

"*Bourbon*? But...but you're supposed to be dead! Does Sheriff Needles know you're in town?"

"Not hardly. We just now got in," Charley told him. "I skipped stoppin' to see the sheriff because I'm anxious to check on the other US Marshal, my partner Hank Wordell, who I understand is bein' cared for inside. I take it lookin' out for his safety is why you're posted here?"

"That's right."

"I'm obliged to you and your sheriff for that consideration, Deputy...?"

"Lissom, sir. Jerome Lissom," the deputy answered so smartly Lone thought for a minute he was going to salute.

Charley smiled tolerantly. "If I can make a suggestion, Deputy Lissom—since me and Mr. McGantry here are on hand and capable of helpin' to keep an eye on things while we are—maybe you should go advise Sheriff Needles of our arrival. Anxious as I am to check on my friend and partner, I reckon your sheriff will be equally anxious to start firin' some questions my way."

A corner of Lissom's mouth quirked up. "Oh, I think you can be pretty sure about that."

Before any more was said, the house door opened and a middle-aged man in an open-collared white shirt with the sleeves rolled a quarter of the way up his forearms stood there frowning slightly. "I heard a rather loud exchange of voices. Is there a problem?" he asked.

"Not really, Doc," Lissom was quick to answer. "But some, er, surprise visitors have shown up to see your patient. This here"—gesturing to Charley—"is US Marshal Charley Bourbon."

The doctor's eyebrows lifted. "Bourbon? But we've been hearing—"

"I know. I'm supposed to be dead," Charley finished for him. "But clearly I ain't. It's a long story and one I expect I'll be tellin' more than once before this night is over. Before all that, though, I want to know about my partner, young Hank. How is he, Doc? Any chance I can see him, talk to him some?"

CHAPTER ELEVEN

ONLY CHARLEY WAS ALLOWED TO GO SEE HANK WORDELL in the adjoining room where Dr. Frake reported he was heavily medicated and confined to bed rest. While the doctor accompanied Charley back for what he said would have to be a short visit, Lone was instructed to remain in the reception/ waiting area at the front of the house. Since the furnishings included three different well-padded easy chairs to choose from, it was hardly a hardship for Lone to bide his time by plopping into one of them. He was plenty weary himself from lack of sleep and the day's long, hot ride.

As it turned out, however, he didn't have very long to get settled and enjoy the comfort. Acting on Charley's suggestion, Deputy Lissom had gone to fetch the sheriff. And so, it seemed, Lone had barely sunk back in his chair of choice before the front door swung open and Lissom came through on the heels of a tall, angular man with a sheriff's star pinned prominently on the fancy brocade vest he wore under the swept back lapels of a long-waisted charcoal gray suit coat. The stark, clean-shaven features of Hiram Needles' face were set in a stern, almost scowling expression that promptly reminded Lone of how Charley had described the man as being a "graveyard serious type." The rest of the sheriff's attire consisted of a black flat-crowned, wide-brimmed Stetson, black string tie, and pin-striped gray trousers tucked into high, gleamingly polished black boots. The ivory-handled Remington revolver worn for the cross draw on his left hip rode in a chocolate brown holster, also polished to a sheen.

Penetrating pale blue eyes swept over Lone where he remained slouched in his chair. "You clearly are not Charley Bourbon," was the conclusion announced as a result of this appraisal.

"Nope. I ain't," Lone agreed.

"His name's McGantry. He rode in with Bourbon," Lissom told the sheriff.

Needles regarded Lone thoughtfully. "McGantry... would you be the former Indian scout they call 'Lone' McGantry?"

"I would," allowed Lone. Then, grinning wryly, he added, "Not sure if I oughta be flattered or worried that you've heard of me, Sheriff."

"In perusing my predecessor's files," Needles replied matter-of-factly, "I paid particular attention to his reports on some of the more spirited events that have taken place in and around Ogallala in recent years. Your name is memorable enough for me to recall it being mentioned as being involved in more than one such matter."

"I trust it was mentioned in a favorable light."

"According to Marshal Halsey's perception, yes, that always seemed to be the case." Needles continued to regard Lone closely. "But it happens I've also heard your name connected—often rather vaguely—to other incidents. Among them, one up in the Dakotas not too far back, in some association to the downfall of the Pike Grogan gang. And, pondering it further, I believe I heard about you working in conjunction with Charley Bourbon a previous time when he ran down Fenton Eccles' bunch. From the sound of them, all laudable accomplishments, I must admit. And then, of course—prior to you showing up here this evening reportedly once again in the company of Marshal Bourbon—there came a telegram received just this morning from Marshal Overstreet in North Platte relating how you had encountered and dispatched two members of the Rip Hardessy gang whose atrocities are very much at the forefront of chaos throughout the territory."

"Okay. Reckon that explains me—or at least my name—not bein' a stranger to you."

"To be sure. Further, you being an individual with no official affiliation to the law yet having an undeniable propensity for ending up in all these violent confrontations...you can surely understand how that might cause one to wonder."

"All those twenty-dollar words you're tossin' around have got me doin' plenty of wonderin'," Lone drawled. "But one in particular, this propensididdy you say I got —think it's something I oughta have Doc Frake take a look at while I'm here?"

Deputy Lissom had to look away to hide the smile that tugged at his mouth. Needles didn't look away and certainly showed no sign of trying to hold back anything close to a smile. His mouth pulled into a straight line pressed so tight a finishing nail couldn't have been driven between his lips with a hammer. Not until he opened them to speak, saying, "Considering the grave circumstances we're in the midst of here, McGantry, your lame attempt at humor is inappropriate and, I assure you, highly *un*-appreciated!"

Lone snapped up straighter in his chair. "Climb down off your high horse, mister. Bluster and big words don't impress me a lick. If they amounted to anything, then the way you wrap yourself in 'em should've amounted to Rip Hardessy and his train blastin' crew all rounded back up by now...how you comin' with that?"

Needles purpled with outrage at this response. His mouth opened and closed but no words came out. Before he was able to find any, the door to the adjoining room through which Charley and Dr. Frake had gone earlier opened and the two men came back out.

Spotting Needles standing there, Frake said, "Oh. Good evening, Sheriff."

"I'm not so sure about that," Needles replied harshly, causing the doctor to look confused and a bit taken aback.

Ignoring those two, Lone rose from his chair and said to Charley, "How's Hank?"

The big marshal's expression was dour, on top of the exhaustion and build up of pain showing steadily more evident on him. "He's hangin' on," he answered. "He took three bullets and lost a lot of blood, so he's a long way from doin' rosy. But he's young and strong and he's stuck with it this far. I'm bettin' he can make it the rest of the way."

Appearing to have regained his composure and put aside his ire toward Lone, at least for the moment, Sheriff Needles took a step forward and addressed

Charley. "Inasmuch as you delayed advising me of your arrival in town and no one has yet seen fit to provide introductions, allow me to do so." He extended his hand. "I am Sheriff Hiram Needles, Marshal Bourbon. I wish it was under better circumstances but, nonetheless, welcome to Ogallala and, er, welcome back to the living."

Charley took his hand and rumbled out a low chuckle. "Yeah, I expect you're mighty curious about that last part. And bustin' with a whole raft of questions about it and more."

"Hardly anything I can deny," Needles said somewhat stiffly.

This exchange drew a quick frown out of Frake. "If that means what it sounds like," he said, "then I may be the one to do some denying—or at least suggest a postponement."

"What are you saying?" demanded Needles.

"I'm saying if you intend an intense question and answer session with Marshal Bourbon, which I understand may be warranted, then as a doctor I suggest you consider holding off for a bit."

"Reason being?"

"Because this man"—Frake placed a hand on Charley's shoulder—"is suffering injuries of his own from the same attack that left young Wordell so bad off. I haven't had the chance to fully examine Marshal Bourbon yet, but I understand he has numerous burns and lacerations to his back and it's clear to my trained eye he is generally exhausted and worn down. Just because he isn't as dead as we've been hearing, doesn't mean him and his stubbornness need any help pushing him closer to making that true."

"Hey, Doc, I appreciate the concern. Only I ain't—" Charley tried to say.

But Frake cut him off with: "Let me examine you and *I'll* say what you are or 'ain't.' You're right here and you've already interrupted my supper. I'm willing to give up a hot meal, what have you got to lose?"

"The doc's right and you know it, Charley," Lone spoke up. "I did the best I could and you've started healin' pretty good. But we hurried takin' this ride today and you know that too. For cryin' out loud, let the doc do what's best for you. You'll get all the way healed that much sooner."

"If Marshal Bourbon needs treatment, then by all means he should receive it," said Sheriff Needles. "But if he feels he can hold off being examined right away, then why must everyone else be in such a rush? The doctor can enjoy his supper, Marshal Bourbon and I can have our overdue discussion, and *then* he can be examined and treated. Information exchanged between the marshal and I may prove crucial to a new lead on catching up with the fugitive Hardessy once again. Need I remind all here that every second that villain is left running loose could mean—"

This time it was Lone who did the cutting off. "If you're so interested in every second countin' when it comes to runnin' down Hardessy," he grated, "then what are you doin' hunkered here in town? His gang hit that train four nights ago and you admitted earlier how you was notified about at least two of his men—the ones I ran into—showin' up only thirty miles from here. By the look of your dust-free clothes and the shine on your boots, you sure as hell ain't been leadin' no chase posses any time lately."

The purple color once again flooded Needles' face. Only this time he didn't have any trouble spitting words out of it. "You insolent wretch!" he seethed. "If you are in any way implying—"

Once again he was cut short. "Everybody smooth your hackles and back off a damn step," rumbled Charley.

"I should hope so!" seconded Frake. "This is a doctor's office, for crying out loud. There's a man fighting for his life in the next room, and my family is upstairs. Show some respect."

"Respect cuts in every direction, yet should at all times recognize rank," insisted Needles. He jabbed a finger at Lone. "This man has been nothing but rude and disdainful ever since I walked in here. I find that intolerable. What's more, Bourbon, it is difficult for me to fathom why you, a reputable officer of the law, so freely associate with such a no-account drifter who has a reputation for nothing but stirring up trouble wherever he goes."

The weariness left Charley's eyes, replaced by a scorching glare. "Mister," he told Needles, "I don't give one morsel of cold shit how hard it might be for you to *fathom* who I choose to associate with. Far from being a no-account, in my book Lone McGantry's a rare somebody I have—and would again—trust with my life. When I say to you that me and him have faced down demons together, it ain't just hot air comin' out from under my nose. And as far as *rank*, if you want to push it I will also say to you that this badge of mine just so happens to carry more weight than that piece of tin pinned to your fancy damn vest. Is all of that clear and 'tolerable' to you?"

The sheriff tried to match Charley's glare, but ended up having to look away. "Clear, yes," he said grudgingly.

Charley exhaled a slow, ragged sigh out through his nostrils. "Okay. Now I think I got a reasonable, whaty-call, compromise for this whole business of me and the sheriff havin' our discussion and also givin' the doc his crack at me." He cut Frake a direct look. "I figure I can carry on with talkin' while you commence your pokin' and proddin'...you reckon you can do what you need to do while me and Needles are palaverin'?"

"Well, I must say it would be a bit unorthodox," replied Frake, clearly caught off guard. Then, abruptly tossing a what-the-hell shrug, he added, "However, if it will help move things along, I'm willing to give it a try. It might be too crowded in my regular examining room, so we can proceed right here. If you'll take a seat and begin removing your shirt, Marshal, I'll go fetch my medical bag..."

CHAPTER TWELVE

AND SO IT WENT, CHARLEY'S "WHATYCALL, COMPROMISE"
proving to be both efficient and generally productive by
the time they were finished.

Regarding Charley's injuries, the first thing that
came from Dr. Frake's examination was a pronounce-
ment by him that the patching up done so far by Lone
was "quite commendable." However, there was still
some follow-up necessary. The doc tightened up bits of
prior stitching, then drained two of the burn blisters
before applying medicinal salve and fresh bandaging.
That left considerable attention required by the deep
shoulder gash, which had begun to show signs of infection. This meant re-opening and thoroughly re-cleaning
the wound, applying copious amounts of disinfectant,
sewing it back up. Throughout, Charley was once again
his stoic self, steadily carrying on the palaver with
Sheriff Needles, displaying only a rare wince in reaction
to some of the harsher but necessary treatment he was
receiving. In lieu of pain-dulling laudanum offered by

Frakes, he opted instead for a few hits from the bottle of redeye he asked Lone to bring in out of his saddlebags.

As far as the talk with Needles, the first thing needing to be covered was an explanation for Charley's sudden appearance after an extended absence that left everyone believing him to be dead with his charred remains just not yet discovered under a pile of freight car wreckage. Charley glossed over this rather superficially with a mix of half-truth, half-fabrication, basically erasing the part about his suspicions of his partner. The way he told it was that he'd been knocked unconscious by the freight car blast and then, upon finally coming to but still dazed and confused, had wandered aimlessly up into the Sandhills through most of the following morning. When he at last started to get a grip on himself, he was far from the site of the train attack but realized he was somewhere close to the horse ranch of his old friend McGantry. Weak and wounded, he sought him out in desperation and barely succeeded finding him before blood loss and the ravages of a storm finished off the damage already inflicted by Hardessy's crew. Lone's care and a good night's sleep had worked wonders. Then, when Redsleeve and Cramer showed up at Lone's spread the following day, only to be caught by surprise and cut down, Charley took responsibility for having Lone deliver their bodies to North Platte without any initial mention of Charley still being alive —not until he found out how things stood in the aftermath of the train blast and the status of Hardessy's escape from custody. When Lone returned with news that Hank was still alive but in grave condition in Ogallala, all other considerations were cast aside and Charley insisted on getting to him with all haste.

Needles listened to all of this attentively, somberly. He interrupted with only minimal questions and, though a dubious glimmer might have shown in his eyes a time or two, he presented no challenge to any of Charley's story. After all, the man clearly had undergone a punishing ordeal and what call did he have to fabricate anything about it?

For his part, Needles mostly only had a few embellishments and updates on what Lone had already learned from Keith Overstreet. Other than the pair who had shown up at Lone's spread, Hardessy and his gang —estimated by the surviving brakeman from the caboose to have numbered seven or eight at the time of the attack—had scattered unseen and untraceable. The brakeman was pretty sure one of them had been fatally wounded by Hank before they rode off. He also believed another had been injured, though less severely, as a result of the explosion. Railroad officials had subsequently confirmed that the freight car under which the gang's dynamite charge went off had been carrying several kegs of blasting powder—thus explaining the added ferocity of the explosion when these were additionally triggered.

With track and car wreckage at its rear, blocking the means to return to the larger town of North Platte, the remainder of the train had high-balled on to Ogallala to report what had happened. A flurry of telegrams were immediately sent out, advising the necessary halting/rerouting of all affected train traffic and notifying law enforcement officials all up and down the line. A repair crew armed with whatever could be grabbed in the way of make-do equipment and tools was assembled and loaded onto the train, which then reversed back to the site of the damage. A hastily gathered posse from Ogallala rode ahead and were met at the site by a second posse from North Platte, responding to the telegrams that had been sent out.

A number of factors—the length of time that had already passed since the gang struck, the lack of any truly skilled trackers among their would-be pursuers, the vastness and empty ruggedness of the surrounding terrain, the way the gang members had scattered and employed veteran measures to blur their sign—combined to make taking out after them an effort with slim chances for any meaningful success. Nevertheless, the gathering of determined men broke into a handful of smaller groups that scoured a wide swath in hopes of turning up something. What sign they *were* able to spot seemed to indicate the fugitives were angling roughly toward the northwest, the panhandle region. This only increased the difficulty of trying to follow them since the land out that way was more broken and ranches and towns even more sparse. The track-erasing storm that rolled in at the close of a long, grueling, fruitless day also signaled—by mutual agreement of leaders Needles and Overstreet—the calling-off of this initial chase effort. The volunteers who'd pitched in would return home sodden and weary and go back to their regular lives and jobs knowing they'd given it their best; and the lawmen would return to reports in duplicate and triplicate and input from the railroad people and others all lamenting they weren't doing enough, while at the same time working up new plans for some kind of wider sweep, a net, a way to keep relentless vigilance in hopes for the break of some promising sign—just one—that could put them back on the right track.

"For the past day or so," Needles summed up, "we have been temporarily reduced to holding out for a lead based on a sighting from somewhere—or from Marshal Wordell becoming lucid enough to perhaps provide something useful he may have seen or overheard before they left him for dead."

Charley grimly responded, "To tell the truth, second only to hopin' he was still alive and showin' signs of stayin' that way, I was hopin' for the same."

"Then you know first hand...unless your presence produced better results...he only manages brief spurts of incoherent mumbling."

Charley gave a sad wag of his head. "Afraid that's all I got, too."

"But don't give up hope," interjected Dr. Frake. "The patient's condition is stable, and he's young and strong. I'm guardedly confident he'll keep showing steady signs of improvement. What I can't foretell, of course, is whether or not he'll have anything useful to tell you, even after he comes fully around."

"Be good if he can. But, like I just said, that's a secondary consideration," Charley stated.

"Naturally," agreed Needles, whose arrogance and pomposity seemed to have lifted by some small measure. "In the meantime, one of the alternatives we were also hoping for—a sighting—gives us something requiring more immediate consideration."

"You're talkin' about Redsleeve and Cramer showin' up on my spread," said Lone.

"Exactly. Them showing up there, which I'm given to understand is basically due north of where the train strike took place, contradicts with the signs our posses picked indicating the gang members scattered toward the northwest. Plus, the appearance of that lone pair came only about twenty miles *away from* and more than twenty-four hours *after* the train strike. None of that seems to make sense. In that amount of time, no matter what direction they scattered, they should have been much farther away." Needles frowned. "Too bad you were in such a hurry to kill them, McGantry. If even one of them had been left alive, think of the valuable information he could have provided."

Lone blinked calmly. No, he told himself, Needles was an arrogant jackass clean to the bone with no notion to ever try shaking it off, not even a little bit. "In my book," the former scout replied, putting a purposeful edge on his tone, "only a fool worries about keepin' alive some sonofabitch throwin' lead at him. You do that, it's a good way to end up dead yourself. I'd rather be the one left talkin', thanks, even if the conversation is sorta one-sided."

"As far as those varmints showin' up where they did, instead of the way some of the others appeared to've gone," added Charley, "ain't that how scatterin' is supposed to work? And them laggin' behind the rest could be as simple as 'em gettin' confused in strange country the night of the train hit then needin' to lay low an extra day before headin' out again." He scowled. "Yeah, it woulda been nice to've captured instead of killin' 'em—in order to shake loose some information. And if wishes was fishes, we'd all have something to fry, as my ol' granny used to say...still, the good news about the bad news is that their number is whittled down by two. Settlin' for that much ain't all bad."

"I suppose that's one way of looking at it," Needles allowed sullenly.

Lone gave it a beat before saying, "How about we back up once more to Hank's mumblin's. Mind if I ask what it was in particular he mumbled? I mean, was it names, words, animal grunts—what? Reason I ask, if Hank was tryin' to pass on something he might've overheard about where the gang meant to split off for, but was only able to get it out in bits and pieces on account of the shape he's in, what he managed to mumble might sound like gibberish to certain folks but not necessarily others."

Needles scowled. "No offense, McGantry, but you're not sounding too far from gibberish yourself. What point are you trying to make?"

"Just this: I know this territory, even out across the panhandle, better than the rest of you combined. Not uncommon for folks in certain areas to have odd or peculiar names for places close about 'em—names that wouldn't necessarily make sense to folks from elsewhere. So my point is that possibly a word or two out of Hank's mumblin's that haven't made sense to anybody so far, maybe *would* have meanin' to a different set of ears—like mine."

"By God, that just might be so!" declared Charley.

Needles' frown didn't waver. "Sounds awfully thin to me."

"I don't see what there is to lose," said Dr. Frake, reaching into his shirt pocket and withdrawing a small notebook with a pencil clipped to it. "Happens I've been jotting down all or most of what the patient has had to say on different occasions."

Lone and Charley stepped in closer and the doctor began to read from his notes. "Okay, right from the beginning, he not surprisingly called out 'explosion!'

and 'fire!' He did that two or three times...then he called out for Charley more than once."

Hearing this, Charley's already mournful expression deepened even more.

"Several times," Frake continued, "he repeated what sounded like 'tabey' or 'taybo'...and 'claw the land.'"

Charley's face scrunched in thought. "He mentioned a sweetheart down in Kansas somewhere. Wichita, I think. Doggone, what was her name...Tammy? Something like that, but...no. Tabitha, that's what it was."

"So what sounded like 'tabey,' could've been 'Tabby'—like what you might call somebody short for Tabitha," suggested Lone. "And 'claw the land'...was that maybe 'law of the land,' something that might be driftin' in and out of the thoughts of a young fella in pain but still particularly proud of bein' a peace officer?"

"That was Hank. He was almighty proud of wearin' a badge," confirmed Charley.

"Other words he repeated," Frake went on, "were 'cave' and 'deep down'...and, though I didn't write down any of the exact words, he roundly cussed Hardessy and his whole crew in some of his lengthier ramblings."

"That's it?" said Lone, trying to keep the disappointment out of his voice. "Nothing other than talk of a deep cave as far as something that might be a landmark or a destination?"

The doc shook his head. "Afraid not. Like I said, he repeated a number of things. And, other than the prolonged cussing of the outlaws, most of what he said was in choppy segments..." Frake's voice trailed off as he began making a closer scan through his notes. Then: "Okay. Here's something more he repeated several times, but it was always choppy and slurred...'Spellum' or 'spillen,' and that was around the time he mentioned the 'deep down' cave...I don't have anything more."

Lone went quiet for a minute and now it was his face that became scrunched deep in thought. Until, rather abruptly, he said, "Spellman! Could that have been what Hank was sayin'?"

"Well, I-I suppose. Like I said, his speech at that point was rather slurred. But, yes, he could have been trying to say 'Spellman.' If so, what does it mean?" Frake wanted to know.

"If I had a map, I could show everybody," Lone said. "Way up in the northwest corner of the panhandle is a little town called Spellman. Come to think of it, it may not show as even a spec on some maps. It's just a little pissant of a place. Sowbelly Canyon ain't far from there, though, so there's sure enough broken land thereabouts and the likelihood of some caves. Any way you cut it, it'd make pretty good hideout territory for owlhoots on the run. And it fits with what appeared to the posses as the northwest aim of the fleein' varmints."

"How far is this Spellman?" Needles asked.

"Two, three days of steady ridin'," Lone told him. "And before you ask, no, they got no law there nor telegraph to notify 'em even if there was. Leastways that's how it was the last time I was through, and I can't think of any reason it's likely changed. Hell, more likely it dried up altogether."

"Then why would anybody mention it as a destination in the first place?"

"Don't mean it had to be the *specific* destination," Charley responded. "When they're talkin' about some distant place, folks sometimes speak in general terms and say the name of a nearby town or landmark of some kind, though it ain't necessarily the exact spot they mean to end up. Like a body announcin' 'I'm headed for Colorado' when they're only just goin' as far as a small town or some ranch across the state line. Could be Hank was tryin' to pass on that he heard one of Hardessy's bunch say they needed to get headed for Spellman, with the others understandin' what he really meant was the hideout cave close by."

"In that case, if they were only making a general reference, how did Hank know to mention a cave at all?" Needles pressed.

Charley glowered. "How the hell do I know? Maybe it was some separate comment Hank overheard. Look, we all know we're graspin' at straws here, tryin' to catch hold of even a nubbin of a lead. But ain't nobody ready to bet the farm on anything we've said, not so far."

"That's good to hear," Needles said sternly. "I'm as anxious as anybody to grab hold of a lead—a good, solid one. I just don't want to get swept up in something too wildly speculative."

"There's some more of those twenty-dollar words again," Lone said with a clenched jaw. "I know it chafes to play a hunch and come up empty, Sheriff. But it chafes a helluva lot worse to *not* play a hunch and find out later you came up empty when you wouldn't've had to but for lack of showin' the guts to make a stab at it."

Needles' eyes blazed. "What is that even supposed to mean, damn you? If you are once again questioning my courage or dedication to duty, I—"

"Sheriff! Get a grip—both of you," Charley demanded sharply.

"All I'm sayin'," Lone blurted, "is that if a certain party took time to do some thinkin', he might see where it wouldn't come at no big cost or risk to send a wire to the town of Harris. It's located just a few miles west of Spellman, on the Wyoming border, and is big enough to have a marshal and some deputies and a telegraph office. Word could be sent to let 'em know about our bit of admitted speculation. They most likely have already heard about the train strike and the escape of Hardessy. They oughta appreciate a warnin' the polecats *might* be headed their way, even if it's only a guess. Could be those Harris law dogs will take a notion to go give the folks in Spellman a head's-up and have a general look around while they're in the area. Never know what they might see and, like I said, makin' a stab at it wouldn't come at no big cost or risk."

"I gotta say, that don't sound half bad to me," said Charley. He looked at Needles. "Yeah, I know—it's thin and it's based on speculatin' over just a handful of words. But what else have we got? Zero, that's what. If nothing else, we'd be lettin' the folks up that way know to be on the lookout for their own good...if you're reluctant to send the wire, Sheriff, I will myself."

"Not tonight, you won't," Dr. Frake was quick to say. "That is, as your physician, I'm advising you shouldn't. You've done enough for one day. Too much. You're exhausted, even if you're too stubborn to admit it, and you need to build up your blood and get fully rehydrated. No matter who sends that telegram, no action is going to be taken on it tonight. So I urge you to also involve yourself in nothing more tonight. Eat a hearty meal and then get yourself into bed for a full night of sound sleep. You can pick up all this other business again in the morning."

Lone added, "Sounds like some mighty good advice for you to take, Charley. Think I'll even follow it myself."

"Come morning, I'll go ahead and send that telegram," Needles said moodily. Then, cutting a cold-eyed gaze in Lone's direction, he asked, "Do you happen to know the name of the Harris marshal, McGantry?"

"Last I knew it was Morningstar. Ben Morningstar. He's part Indian, a good man."

"No matter who notifies Morningstar," Charley said, "I'll be joinin' you at the telegraph office in the morning, Sheriff. I'd better get a wire off to headquarters and a few other places to spread word I ain't dead after all—disappointin' as that might be to some."

As Frake finished tucking the notebook back into his pocket, he looked up and suddenly said, "It occurs to me, Charley...Marshal Bourbon...that everything I just recommended for you can be had right here. I have a spare recovery bed in the room just past Hank's. It is very comfortable and quiet. You can take supper with my wife and I, she's a wonderful cook and I'm sure there's plenty. Then you can get immediately to bed. I'll make sure you get some important fluids and a relaxant to ensure solid sleep. You'll be conveniently on hand for me to check your wounds and dressings first thing in the morning, and you'll be close by in case Hank comes around further and does some more talking. Seeing you would be bound to help perk him up."

Charley looked reluctant when Frake first started. But the part about being close by in case Hank stirred anew made a difference. Still, because it wasn't his nature to impose, he said, "Geez, Doc, I dunno. I feel like I'd be crowdin' you and your wife and, not only that, but hoggin' up a hospital bed meant for somebody who might really—"

"If somebody shows up who needs that bed worse than you," Frake cut him off, "I'll boot you out in an instant. Okay? Now accept my offer, doggone it. It's in your best interest and it'll make things easier for me too."

"Take him up on it, Charley. Don't be a lunkhead," put in Lone. "I'll take care of our horses. Then I'll grab a meal and a hotel room for myself. I'll be fine. Meet you back here in the morning."

"Reckon I'm outvoted," Charley gave in with a sigh. Then, grinning, he added, "But, I gotta say, I'm glad of it. I'm powerful obliged for your offer, doc, and happy to accept."

Frake looked at Lone. "Sorry I don't have accommodations to offer you, Mr. McGantry."

"No problem. I understand, doc."

"I always have accommodations at my place," Needles said dryly, showing for the first time a hint of anything resembling a smile—the same kind you'd find on a hungry coyote.

Lone matched the semi-menacing display of teeth. "Thanks, but I'll pass on that particular invite. Was I to accept, don't think it'd gain me much in the way of a restful night's sleep. The way you and me been hittin' it off, I figure I'd spend too much time once checked in wonderin' how hard it might be gettin' checked back out."

CHAPTER THIRTEEN

MOUNTED AGAIN ON IRONSIDES AND LEADING CHARLEY'S gelding (which the old marshal had taken to calling Blessing because, he said, that's what finding him at a crucial time had felt like), Lone rode away from Dr. Frake's place and swung down Spruce Street. It was full dark now, but with Spruce running through the heart of the town's business district it was lined with several street lamps. Plus, Lone's route took him past a string of brightly lighted saloons with illumination spilling out their windows and making pools of gaudy color on the dusty, rutted street.

The saloons were a leftover reminder of Ogallala's notorious heyday, and also a reminder that heyday wasn't necessarily tamed down all the way. What was more, it was a Friday night, meaning an uptick in the number of cowboys from the surrounding ranches were bound to be showing up on the lookout for a good time. On the second-floor balcony of one of the saloons, representing a particular version of a good time always in demand, two gals displaying bare shoulders and painted lips sat smoking cigarettes. When they looked down, measuring Lone with weary, half expectant gazes, he smiled up at them, pinched his hat and kept riding.

His destination was Dutch Kroeger's livery down near the end of the street. As he approached, he did some calculating and came to the reckoning it had been nearly three years since he'd seen the old Dutchman. Though he'd passed through Ogallala more than once in that span, they'd all been brief stops with no call to stable Ironsides. Still, if Dutch heard he'd been around but hadn't at least bothered to swing by and say a quick hello, he would likely—and rightfully—be in a mood to do some grumbling about it.

It didn't take long to find out that was exactly the case.

"Well, well, well. Looky here...if it ain't the ree-nowned Injun scout Lone McGantry. Who, in spite of all claims for bein' top notch at trackin' and trailin', somehow can only seem able to find his way to the doorstep of an old friend every fourth or fifth time he's in the neighborhood."

Lone drew rein before a livery barn that had one of the sliding double doors at its front rolled part way open. He could see half of the center aisle and a row of horse stalls stretching back on the inside. There was a lantern hanging on a beam about a dozen yards in, beyond that the cavernous interior of the building quickly turned to dense shadow. To one side of the open sliding door there was a combination tack room and office that glowed with the light of another lantern. Dutch Kroeger was emerging from this room as he issued his greeting.

Lone leaned a forearm down on the horn of his

saddle and aimed the most disarming grin he could muster at the burly liveryman. "Does that mean you ain't happy to see me, you cantankerous ol' cuss?"

Dutch stopped and folded his fence post-thick arms across his barrel chest. His beefy face, bracketed by a pair of bristly muttonchop sideburns that had a few more flecks of gray in them than Lone remembered, bunched into a scowl that failed to project any depth of real anger. "On the contrary," he grumbled. "I been lookin' forward to seein' you for the express purpose of bein' able to tell you what a slippery, rude son of a sidewinder I think you to be!"

"That's all?" Lone's grin stayed in place. "I expected you to have a bigger head of steam than that built up for me."

"That's the guilt in you, knowin' it's what you deserved."

"Maybe so," Lone allowed. "Look, my apologies for the times I passed through town—though I think you're stretchin' the number, by the way—but didn't poke my head in to say a quick hi. All I can say is that on those occasions I had some trouble barkin' at my heels and needed to stay on the move. Tarryin' for any friendly chats along the way just wasn't in the cards."

Dutch eyed him for a beat, scowl unwavering. Then his face relaxed and his mouth stretched into its own grin. "Hell, you think I didn't figure as much? Knew you had to have some kind of good reason. But I still couldn't pass up a chance to chouse you some as soon as I got the opportunity." He strolled closer as he was talking, until he stopped and reached up to gently rub Ironsides's velvety snout. "Besides, I didn't miss seein' you and that weather-beat mug of yours near as much as this fine, big gray stud who everybody knows is too good for you...ain't that right, Ironsides boy?"

Lone swung down from his saddle. "That's good to hear. If you got room to put him up for a couple days or so—him and this other critter belongin' to a friend of mine—then you and Ironsides will have plenty of time to get caught up on gossip and such."

"Yeah, I got plenty of room," Dutch said, taking Ironsides' reins and then reaching to also take those of Blessing as Lone handed them over. "Couple days, you say?"

"Thereabouts. Depends on how certain things shake out come tomorrow."

"Sounds like there might be a story worth hearin' behind that remark. You got time to sit and take a touch with me, do some chin waggin' while we're at it?"

"I can do better than that," said Lone. "I ain't had supper yet. Unless you've already had yours, after these horses are took care of I'll buy. Then we can wrap some grub, a drink or three or four, and some chin waggin' all together."

"You got yourself a deal. And we won't even have to wait on takin' care of the horses." Dutch turned his head and called over his shoulder into the barn. "Oscar! Get on out here, will you?"

A minute later a gangly, shuffle-footed young man in baggy, faded clothes and a pair of down-at-the-heels work shoes emerged from the open double door. Under a thatch of unruly rust-colored hair he had the intelligent but wary eyes of somebody who's endured a steady diet of hard luck and hard treatment for much of their life. "Yessir, Mr. Kroeger?" he asked.

"You can leave the rest of that stall cleanin' go 'til

mornin',", Dutch told him. "Instead, I want you to take these two horses and put 'em up. Give 'em top treatment —rubdowns, fresh water and hay, grain, and clean stalls. Got it?"

Oscar nodded obligingly.

Dutch jabbed a thumb. "This here is my friend Lone McGantry, you've heard me speak of him. And this big gray is Ironsides. He's a special animal."

"Anybody can see that," replied Oscar, his eyes going wide. "Boy, he's a beauty! You can bet I'll take real fine care of him—and the other horse, too."

"I know you will." Dutch's expression softened. "Now listen. By the time you get done seein' to those horses, you'll need to get headed home. Me and Lone will be goin' up the street, he's invited me to have supper with him at the café. But before he showed up, I heated me a pan of venison stew there in my office. I don't want it to go to waste. You're welcome to it, so long as it don't ruin your appetite for your ma's supper when you get home. I don't want you hurtin' her feelin's and gettin' us both in trouble. Hear?"

"I understand, Mr. Kroeger," Oscar said solemnly. "Lucky I worked up a good appetite cleanin' those stalls. I won't let your stew go to waste, and I'll be sure to put a proper dent in Ma's supper too."

"Good enough." Dutch held out the reins of the two horses. "Get to carin' for these animals then. And I'll see you back here in the morning."

"You bet. Evenin', Mr. Kroeger...nice to've met you, Mr. McGantry."

"Same here," Lone called after him, after he'd snagged his rifle, saddlebags, and possibles pack off of Ironsides. Then, as he and Dutch watched the lad lead the horses on into the barn, he added, "Seems like a nice kid."

"He is...too damn nice for the rotten breaks his life has handed him," Dutch said in a bitter tone. When Lone eyed him questioningly, he lowered his voice and elaborated more. "That mother he's headed home to—a widow, she claims—is a pathetic slattern, a drunk and an opium addict, who the boy remains slavishly devoted to and protective of. She has him convinced she suffers from 'melancholia,' whatever the hell that is, and can't help herself. I hired Oscar six months ago. He has a great touch with horses, works like a dog, and I pay him good, all I can afford. But practically every cent he makes goes to his mother's addictions." The burly liveryman snorted disdainfully. "Goin' home to his ma's cookin'? What a laugh. That hag wouldn't know how to cook even if she *didn't* spend all their money on what she calls her 'medications.' What few scraps of food the boy holds out money for, he has to fix for himself. That's why, two or three times a week, I find an excuse to cook too much of something in the way of good, belly-fillin' grub. Then get him to take the extra off my hands in a way that don't seem like charity."

"You better watch out," Lone warned dryly, "elsewise you're gonna ruin hell outta your reputation for bein' nothing but an ornery, hard-headed liveryman and horse dealer. It might even slip that you're half human."

"Aw, it just burns me up, that's all," grumbled Dutch. "Seein' a decent kid like Oscar gettin' such a shitty end of the stick yet still pluggin' ahead and workin' hard to do right. Goin' so far as takin' care of the person who's draggin' him down when she oughta be the one lookin' out for him. You know how many young pups would take even just a small piece of bein' dealt such a lousy hand and use it as nothing but an excuse to feel sorry for themselves—an excuse to turn bitter and lowdown themselves? Pick up a gun, most likely, and start—"

The rest of what Dutch was going to say got cut off by a sudden commotion coming from inside the barn. First there was the sound of Oscar's voice wailing, "Hey, what are you doing? No!" Next came a second voice, clearly that of a man, harsher and louder but spewing words in an unintelligible garble. Then Oscar again, shouting angrily: "Put that down! Don't you dare—" This ended with the thud of a heavy blow landing and a responsive grunt of pain.

By that time, both Lone and Dutch had spun around and were running toward the barn. Lone's longer legs carried him to the lead. He'd instantly cast aside his saddlebags and possibles pack but still had a firm grip on his Yellowboy, swinging it at his side as he ran. Dutch carried no weapons except for a pair of meaty, calloused hands now balled into rock hard, melon-sized fists pumping in time with his fiercely churning legs.

Just before he reached the open sliding door, Lone heard a distressed, angry shriek coming from Ironsides. This propelled him even more. He plunged through the door and started down the center aisle that ran between rows of horse stalls, eyes scanning wildly ahead. Then he saw the source of the commotion.

It was occurring halfway down the length of the barn, illuminated by the lantern Oscar had carried with him when he led the horses back and then hung on a support beam at the end of the divider separating the two stalls where he'd intended to put the animals. Blessing was already in one of the stalls, mostly out of sight except for part of his chunky, unmistakable rump showing. Ironsides was still out in the aisle, pawing discontentedly in front of the other stall. He was being held in place, his reins clutched in one hand not by Oscar but rather by a lean, shabbily clad individual whose face was blurred by shadow under the wide, floppy brim of the hat he wore. In his opposite hand this hombre was wielding a three-tined hay fork and sprawled at his feet lay Oscar, bathed clearly enough in the glow of the hanging lantern so that there was no missing the bloody gash on his forehead.

Lone ground cautiously to a halt. Dutch came up behind him and also stopped, breathing hard.

The man with the pitchfork hollered, "Tha's raht. Hol' yer asses raht ther! Try comin' closer, I be spikin' this pup to th' floor lahk a ca'fish onna gaff hook!" His voice and words seemed oddly strained, distorted. But their meaning was clear enough, especially when he extended his arm and held the hay fork with its tines pointed menacingly down at the prone Oscar.

"Jesus Christ, I know who that is," Dutch exclaimed in a breathy half-whisper. "I bought a horse and saddle off him earlier today! He asked to sleep in my loft tonight, but I said no."

Even though spoken low, this comment carried well enough in the tense quiet that filled the barn for the pitchfork wielder to have no trouble hearing it. "Tha's raht!" he crowed again, loud and harsh. "White trash not good 'nuff t' sleep in yer shit-stink barn. But I came back an'way an' lookit th' prize"—here giving a jerk on Ironsides' reins as his voice grew even more strident—"it brung me!"

The man's face thrust out from under the shadow of

his hat brim at that point, revealing a homely, bewhiskered countenance made even homelier by massive purple swelling all along its left side jawline. Lone winced at this revelation, not from the unpleasantness of the sight but rather from recognizing who the battered man was.

"Cutcheon!" he bit out through clenched teeth.

Mort Cutcheon bared his own teeth in a vicious grin. "Damn raht it's me, M'Gantry, you murdrin suvvabitch," he croaked, his mouth working tortuously due to his broken jaw, courtesy of Lone's rifle butt. "Ya thot you an' me was done, dincha? So did I. But looky here...that rotten bitch Fate has finally dealt lowdown ol' *me* a high card to play."

"If your beef is with me," Lone told him, "then let's keep it that way. Go ahead and play that high card you think you got, but lay it down against me—leave the kid out of it!"

"Hell with you! I be th' one says how this goes," Mort snapped back. "Fer starters, shuck yer g'belt. Then th' rifle. Lay it down, kick it over t' me."

Lone remained standing motionless. His ice cold stare met Mort's pain-fueled glare. After a handful of tense seconds, Lone's head twisted slowly, once each way. "No," he said flatly. "I hand my guns over to nobody, especially not the likes of you."

"I ain't bluffin'!" Mort fairly shrieked. His extended arm trembled and the points of the fork's three curved tines dipped lower. "This kid be eatin' steel in another second, you don' do like I say!"

Lone shook his head once more. "I don't want to see that boy hurt, but I never laid eyes on him until a few minutes ago. He don't mean enough to me to trade my life for. But if you put the steel to him, I won't make the same mistake as last time—you'll be dead half a second after you do."

"Lone!" Dutch hissed in his ear.

Lone ignored him and spoke again to Mort. "I'll one more time make the mistake of lettin' you live, though, if you drop the fork and back away. Then if you still want a place to sleep tonight, the sheriff will be happy to take care of that."

Mort's eyes were wild with pain and rage and indecision. Despite his flat gaze and outward display of steadiness, Lone's nerves were jumping under his skin like frenzied things trying to break free. He was taking a hell of a gamble and the chip he was betting was Oscar's life. On his run into the barn, Lone had racked and cocked the Yellowboy that he was now holding down along his right leg. It would have been an easy thing and a reasonably certain shot for him to swing the muzzle up and plant a slug in Mort...except for the hay fork hovering over Oscar's openly exposed stomach. There was too much risk Mort might still thrust it down in reflex, or even just drop it and let it sink of its own weight into flesh and intestines.

Believing the tormented, vengeful Mort was very likely to go kill crazy on everybody if guns were handed over to him, Lone was ready to instead shoot and take the risk if he had to. But he was clinging to a sliver of hope there was still a chance that the indecision he saw in Mort's eyes might yet pay off.

Suddenly, however, Mort's indecision drove him a different way. He spun away from the fallen Oscar and stepped closer to Ironsides, grabbing him by the bridle with his free hand and edging partly in behind the big gray's head. At the same time, he whirled the hay fork around, took a shorter grip on the handle, and brought the tine points to within an inch of Ironsides's throat. "Now, you suvvabitch," he jeered at Lone. "You no care 'nuff 'bout th' boy, eh? But I seen how you value this stud. How 'bout now, then? You got no shot at my head for fear hit horse. And, if you try for my legs, one o' these tines find jugular 'fore I go down!"

He'd made a crafty, unexpected move that gave his new threat plenty of teeth. Maybe not all of them quite as sharp as he was counting on, however. True, from the shoulders up he was largely obscured by Ironsides' head and by the shadows hanging thick out on the edge of the lamp glow. But there was still a slice of Mort's ugly, half-swollen face showing. It would have been a risky shot to take, yet not out of the question. It was a matter of whether or not Lone felt desperate enough to try it. Ahead of that, though, one other option streaked through Lone's mind. A move so unorthodox it would be viewed as crazy even if it worked.

Knowing he couldn't afford to fall into the trap of indecision such as he'd seen in Mort's eyes, the former scout made up his mind, crazy or not.

Tightening his grip on the Yellowboy, bracing himself to swing up the muzzle and slam the rear stock to his shoulder, he hollered, "Ironsides, stand tall!" Instantly reacting—in the manner he'd been trained as one of a handful of modest tricks Lone had taught the big gray mainly as a way to fill idle camp side hours over the many years when it was just the two of them together out in remote places—Ironsides jerked his head high, pulling sharply away from Mort and the pitchfork tines, at the same time raring up on his hind legs. The startled Tennessean was yanked off balance and the pitchfork nearly fumbled from his grip. A second later it dropped altogether from lifeless fingers as Lone's Yellowboy roared and planted a bullet square in the center of Mort's forehead.

CHAPTER FOURTEEN

SHERIFF HIRAM NEEDLES WAS NOT A HAPPY MAN. HE stood in the middle of Dutch Kroeger's livery barn, fists planted on hips, glaring disapprovingly at Lone. "This must be some kind of record even for you, McGantry," he stated. "You've been in town...what? Three, four hours? Yet in that brief amount of time you've already managed to shoot and kill somebody."

"You got the timing down pretty good," Lone replied calmly. "But don't you think it's also worth mentionin' the little detail about it bein' a matter of self-defense? As well as defense of others?"

"Indeed. And let's not forget to include the defense of a horse, too, if I understand fully."

Lone bristled at the lawman's snotty tone. "You damn right. A horse worth about ten Mort Cutcheons. And, if you want to squeeze the rag a little drier, do you remember that exchange you and me had back in Dr. Frake's office about leavin' alive dangerous varmints in order to maybe get something useful out of 'em?"

Needles scowled. "So what's your point? How does that have anything to do with this business at hand?"

Lone swept a hand to indicate the sprawled carcass of Mort that somebody had thrown a horse blanket over. "Because, two nights ago, I tangled with the varmint layin' there at your feet, the one responsible for this business at hand, and made the mistake of lettin' him live when I had the chance and every right to pinch his wick out permanent-like. See where it almost got me —and others as well?"

The sheriff's scowl didn't falter. "That's quite a tale. But all it really amounts to is yet another example of your dubious habit of attracting and dispensing violence, fatally or otherwise, wherever you go."

"What the devil ail's you, Sheriff?" demanded Dutch Kroeger, who'd been standing by listening and had heard all he could take without speaking up. "The wrongdoer here is nobody but the dead man, Cutcheon. Without an ounce of provocation, he assaulted my hired hand Oscar and then threatened to kill him unless Lone forked over his guns. If you'd seen the wild craziness in his eyes, you'd've seen he damn well had killin' on his mind and gettin' his hands on those guns would have turned it loose—likely on all three of us. You ought to be havin' some appreciation for Lone *stopping* that, not findin' fault with him the way you're actin'."

"The fault I find with Mr. McGantry," responded Needles, keeping his voice calm and even, "goes back further than this single incident. Yet it *is* this incident that has brought gunplay to my town and left a dead body in its streets. I find that problematic, regardless of anything else."

"In that case," drawled Lone, "at least part of your problem is about to be took care of. Unless I miss my guess, it looks like there's a couple fellas here to handle cartin' off the body."

What he was referring to was a pair of men making their way through the crowd of gawkers who had gathered out front and partly inside of Dutch's livery barn. And it was quite an interesting sight the pair made. Marching in the lead was a short, plump hombre wearing a silk top hat and a swallow-tail suit coat with a carnation tucked in the lapel. This, Lone knew from previous dealings in Ogallala, was Herman Offheimer, the local undertaker. Following him, pushing a large, flat-bottomed wooden wheelbarrow, was his assistant Bertram, a muscular Black man also wearing a swallow-tail coat but minus any kind of hat, silk or otherwise, on his clean-shaven head.

"We are here for the dearly departed," announced Offheimer, emerging out of the nearest of the murmuring onlookers.

"Wasn't much 'dear' about that wretch," Lone grunted.

Ignoring him, Needles gestured to the blanket-covered body and said to the undertaker, "I trust it's obvious who your customer is."

"Indeed," acknowledged Offheimer. Then, gesturing in turn to his assistant, he bade him, "Go ahead and prepare the subject for transport, Bertram." He spoke with a faint German accent.

This directive was, of course, a rather elaborate way of saying to load the body on the wheelbarrow. Since Mort was of sufficient size to make handling his literally dead weight something of a chore, even for the power-fully-built Bertram, Lone stepped forward and lent the undertaker's man a hand. It was the least he could do, he figured, since he was the one responsible for putting Mort in such a hard-to-handle condition.

While the body was being loaded, Needles said to Offheimer, "You didn't happen to see anything of Dr. Frakes on your way here, did you? We sent for him also, to tend an injury received by another individual."

"I saw nothing of the doctor," the undertaker answered rather stiffly. "He administers to the living, I take care of what he cannot."

"That's a fine howdy-doo," harrumphed Dutch, overhearing this exchange. "The dead get quicker service than the living."

Sitting on the ground nearby, leaning back against the end post off a stall and holding a bloody bandanna to the cut on his head, young Oscar said, "It's okay, Mr. Kroeger. The doc must be busy with something else. My cut ain't that bad, it ain't even bleeding no more."

Before Dutch could reply, there came a new ripple of motion and murmuring from out of the crowd clogging the front of the barn. Deputy Lissom emerged from this, wearing his habitually stern expression.

Looking around, regarding his deputy for just a moment but then looking past him, the sheriff said in an impatient tone, "Where's Frake? Didn't he get the word he's needed here?"

"No," Lissom answered. "He couldn't, on account of he got called out of town on an emergency."

"What emergency?"

"Leon McSwain got himself gored by one of his

bulls. Tore him up bad enough so's his family was afraid to try and move him," explained Lissom. "They sent the daughter, Laurie, in to fetch the doc. She showed up right after you and McGantry left, ridin' in all in a lather, begging the doc to come right away. So he did. Grabbed his bag and followed Laurie on horseback, without even bothering to hitch up his buggy."

"That's hard luck to hear," replied Needles, sounding sincere. "I've met McSwain. Seems like the kind of decent, hard-working family man that every community needs more of." He paused to cast a side-long glance over at Offheimer, then added, "I trust you'll understand my sentiment in saying I hope McSwain doesn't turn into another case where the doctor is unable to deprive you of a new customer."

"A noble sentiment, Sheriff. I, too, hope for Mr. McSwain's speedy recovery. Despite what you and others may think, I never cheer for fatalities in order to bolster my business." Then it was Offheimer's turn to pause and smile thinly before adding, "I don't have to... Fate and Father Time keep me satisfactorily busy."

"And don't forget me, Offheimer, you old ghoul," spoke up Lone. "As the sheriff is so eager to point out to anybody who'll listen, I've sent a fair share of business your way on this and other occasions when I've been in town."

"That's why it is always good to hear you're in town. You need to come around more often," Offheimer told him.

"That's a matter of opinion," Needles growled. "Okay, Offheimer, you've got loaded up what you came for. You can be on your way. Not that I need to remind you, but send your bill to the county clerk and it will be taken care of."

At this, a frowning Dutch said, "Only because I pay enough in city and county taxes to not want seein' any of it wasted, I'd advise somebody checkin' the dead man's pockets. I paid him good money for a horse and saddle earlier today. Unless he cut a helluva swath through the saloons in between, there oughta be enough left to cover plantin' expenses."

"Which, if that is the case, I would have brought to proper attention anyway," Offheimer was quick to declare, with an accompanying glare in Dutch's direction.

"Maybe so," allowed Needles. "But, as I should have thought of and in accordance with proper procedure, a legal representative needs to inventory the personal effects of a homicide victim. Harold"—here addressing a second deputy who'd been pacing back and forth in front of the pack of onlookers, keeping them from pressing closer—"you go along with these two and log said items when you get to the mortuary."

After Deputy Harold had bobbed his head in acknowledgment and then turned to forge the way for Offheimer and the wheelbarrow-pushing Bertram to depart through the crowd, Needles swung his attention once more to Lissom and said, "You'd best get on back to your post at Dr. Frake's house until relieved. If there's any change in the condition of Marshal Wordell, naturally, let me know right away."

"Will do, Sheriff," said Lissom, starting to turn away.

But Lone stopped him, saying, "Just a minute, Deputy. I been wonderin' why Marshal Bourbon ain't shown up if he heard about a fracas in town involvin' me. Is he okay?"

"He's fine," Lissom answered. "When the doc saw he had to ride out on that McSwain emergency, he got Charley to go lay down in the extra recovery room and take some medicine to help him rest and relax. It worked pronto. Charley was snoring and sleeping real deep by the time we got word about the shooting. Mrs. Frake, who is kind of a nurse, said she thought it best not to bother Charley unless it was truly necessary."

Lone nodded. "Sounds like good advice. I'm glad you took it."

"Now can we proceed with my deputy getting back on duty?" said Needles, clearly annoyed by Lone's interruption. Next, turning to the crowd, he addressed them as he began spreading his arms in wide, pushing away motions. "And, while we're at it, the rest of you people need to disperse and clear away now. There's nothing more to see here. Get along with you, go on back about your own business."

With a minor amount of muttering grumbling, the onlookers broke apart and began drifting off as advised. Soon the barn and the street out front were empty of all but the last two or three stragglers. This left only Needles, Dutch, Lone, and Oscar on the inside, with the latter still sitting at the end of a stall with the bandanna held to his lacerated skull.

The sheriff, wearing an expression of genuine concern along with a trace of frustration, looked down on the young man. "With the doctor gone, I'm not sure what to do for you, lad," he said. "Your head still hurting bad?"

"It's let up quite a bit," Oscar answered. "My bleeding has stopped too. I'll be okay."

"That's brave of you to say. But I'm not so sure that should be the end of it. If Dr. Frake's wife functions as a nurse, perhaps we should have her take a look," suggested Needles.

"No, I don't want to bother her. I'll be okay," Oscar said again.

"How about your mother? I imagine she must have patched up more than a few of your past cuts and scrapes. Right?"

It was hard to read the look on Oscar's face at this suggestion. But Dutch's reaction, as observed by Lone, was clearly disapproving. Prompting the former scout to say, "Tell you what. I got a look at that head gash right after it happened, and I think it's something I could take care of okay. I'm pretty sure it'll need a couple stitches to close proper, though. You willin' to trust me, Oscar? The sheriff here can testify how, earlier this evenin', he heard no less than Doc Frake himself say I did a 'commendable' job sewin' and treatin' all the explosion wounds on my partner Charley."

When Oscar looked questioningly at Needles, the lawman set his jaw tight before raking out a grudging reply. "I must admit that was the doctor's assessment. It seems our Mr. McGantry possesses not only skills for tearing flesh and bone asunder but, when the mood strikes him, also for mending same to a serviceable degree."

"What he just confirmed, amid all those twenty-dollar words, is that I ain't half bad at what I'm proposin'. So what do you say?" Lone asked Oscar.

Before Oscar could answer, Dutch said, "Since none

of us have eaten supper yet, I'll throw in a kicker. We get the stitchin' and patchin' out of the way, I'll pick up the tab for steaks and all the trimmin's over at Mabel's. Be a good way to start buildin' your system back up for the blood you lost, Oscar. How's that sound?"

Oscar couldn't hold back a wide grin. "A steak dinner for a couple stitches? I say that sounds like a pretty fair trade to me!"

CHAPTER FIFTEEN

ONCE THE HORSE HE WAS MOUNTED ON HAD FINALLY BEEN brought to a halt, Maxwell Frake felt hands digging roughly at the nape of his neck, fingers tugging to undo the knot of the bandanna tied around his head and over his eyes. The blindfold had been in place throughout the nightlong ride from the McSwain farm, where his captors seized him after arranging the ruse that brought him there. Laurie McSwain's part in said ruse had been forced by those same villains, holding her parents at gunpoint and threatening to blow both their heads off if she didn't cooperate fully by fetching the doctor with the made-up emergency fabrication scripted for her.

In the past hour or so, Frake had sensed through the folds of cloth covering his eyes a lessening of total blackness, a pale grayness seeping in that told him—along with the passage of time—morning must now be upon them. When the untying of the knot was completed and the blindfold was removed, the doctor kept his eyes closed for a few moments longer and then opened them slowly. The stabbing brightness of sunlight made him blink and caused his eyes to water a bit, but felt good nonetheless.

As soon as his vision was fully clear, Frake swept his eyes in search of Laurie McSwain. Like him, she also had been bound and blindfolded and forced to come on this all night ride. The thanks she got for the desperate cooperation she'd given. Now she was a hostage to squeeze another round of cooperation, this time out of her parents, forcing them—under threat of never seeing her alive again—to continue the charade of Leon McSwain's injury along with claiming to have no idea what happened to the doctor after he'd paid his mercy visit and left. All of this aimed to delay any pursuit of the two men—Whitey and Posey, they called each other —who were orchestrating all of this. Though they never said it outright, Frake came to the conclusion the pair must be members of the Hardessy gang he'd been hearing so much about of late. Why their flight from the events behind all the talk hadn't taken them farther away, the doctor had no way of knowing. But his conviction of who they were, what they were part of, remained.

Frake was relieved to see that Laurie appeared a bit disheveled but otherwise showed no outward signs of harm. He'd already formed an admirable opinion of her, back at the McSwain farm, when he saw her display of pluck and nerve in the face of the rough talk and threats from the two outlaws. Her assurances to her mother to stay strong, stay calm, and admonishments to her father to refrain from trying anything reckless had helped keep a distraught, very tense situation from getting out of hand. Even Frake himself had felt some-what steadied by her comportment.

"Alright. Easy part's over, now we got some walking and climbing to do," said the man called Whitey, a wiry, average-sized individual with spikes of the pale hair that undoubtedly gave him his name poking out from under the brim of his hat. As he spoke, he reached up with a short-bladed knife to cut away the strands of rope binding Frake's wrists to his saddle horn.

"Good God, man," protested Frake. "Is there no rest for us? Not a moment to stretch our legs, have at least a drink of water?"

"You'll get your drink of water, and then soon enough a chance to stretch your legs," Whitey responded harshly. "As far as rest, you'll get that after you do your job, medicine man. And you'd better do it right, elsewise your rest might be the long, permanent kind. Now get down off that horse."

Frake swung stiffly, awkwardly down out of his saddle. His thigh muscles ached, his feet felt half numb, the small of his back throbbed like someone was tapping on it with a hammer. For a moment he feared he might be unable to stand. But he managed it, steadying himself against the side of his horse until the feeling returned to his feet and his legs held up in spite of momentarily threatening to cramp.

When a canteen was held out to the doctor, he grabbed it with both hands, tipped it high, and thirstily guzzled its tepid contents. The water flowing down through him had an amazingly revitalizing effect. They'd stopped only one time during the night, and that only briefly—just long enough for their captors to hold canteens to the mouths of Frake and Laurie so they could gulp a few swallows.

Lowering his canteen now, Frake again looked over

at Laurie. She too had been cut free and was standing on the ground beside her horse, drinking from a canteen of her own. Then, sweeping his gaze wider, Frake for the first time took a good look at their surroundings in the bright wash of morning sunshine. It was not very heartening. For as far as he could see in any direction there was nothing but high, rugged slopes of bleached sandstone cut by irregular vertical slashes. Some of these gouges were wider and deeper than others, some clogged with yucca and bramble brush, a few containing splashes of evergreen. The bottom ground where they had halted appeared to be part of a narrow, twisting arroyo—one of many snaking along the base of the slopes, Frake judged—its floor mostly sand and gravel with a few spurts of stubborn grass poking up.

"Where in God's name is this place?" Frake said, only partly under his breath.

"Take a good look," sneered Whitey. "Don't matter what you call it, all you gotta know is that it'd be plumb foolish for either you or the girl to try and make a break from here. You'd either get lost or fall and break your neck—or both. No matter, we'd catch up and find you anyway."

"Nobody gives much of a shit about your neck, Doc," spoke up Posey, a stocky, swarthy-faced man with a wide, thick-lipped mouth and brooding eyes under a ledge of thick brows. "Lucky for you, though, you got the skills for another purpose. But the pretty, made-for-nuzzlin' neck of Miss Sassy here? Seein' that or any other part of such a fine package get bruised the wrong way would be a downright shame."

"Never mind that," snapped Whitey. "Go ahead and

take the horses over by the spring with the others. Strip 'em down and hobble 'em after they're cooled and watered. Then join us up at the cave."

Somewhat sullenly, Posey gathered up the reins of the four horses and started leading them away. Whitey watched him for a minute, then turned his attention to Frake and Laurie. Gesturing to a barely discernible path that reached up along the side of one of the wider crevices, he said, "Grab your bag and head on up, Doc. It's a little steep, but not too bad if you take care where you place your feet. Girlie, you follow. I'll be right behind, keepin' a close eye. Remember what I said about trying any funny business."

The ascent only took a handful of minutes and, as Whitey had indicated, was not overly difficult. When they reached the ledge out front of the cave mouth, young Darrold Memford stood waiting with a Winchester braced on one hip. He greeted Whitey, then explained, "I saw you riding in from the lookout. Thought it'd be okay to come down for a minute. Have any trouble?"

"None to speak of," Whitey told him. "Got our medicine man and there's no posse riding up our backsides. I'd call that a case of so far so good."

"Sounds like."

Whitey tipped his head toward the cave. "How's he doin'?"

Darrold's forehead puckered. "He had another mighty rough night. River's in there with him now and seems to have him settled down some." The kid paused and his eyebrows lifted dubiously. "Don't know how settled he'll stay when he sees you, though. He was awful riled when he heard what you'd gone off to do."

"Let me worry about that," Whitey responded with a mild grin. "Ain't the first time he's been riled over something I did. He'll get over it."

"Hope so," said Darrold, looking somewhat uncertain. "Well, I'd better get back on lookout. Good luck."

As the kid slipped away, Whitey cut his gaze to Frake. "Okay, Doc. Let's get in there and find out if you're able to do anything to make it worth the risk I took and the ass chewin' I'm about to get..."

CHAPTER SIXTEEN

AFTER STITCHING AND PATCHING THE CUT ON YOUNG Oscar's head, Lone had joined him and Dutch Kroeger in enjoying a hearty steak supper. Then Lone sought out a hotel room with a comfortable bed that drew him into deep slumber about thirty seconds after he stretched out on it. Waking with the dawn next morning, as was his habit, he washed and shaved using the basin and pitcher of water provided with the room, donned britches and boots and a clean shirt dug out of his possibles pack, then headed out to face the new day.

First stopping long enough for a cup of coffee in the hotel dining room, he proceeded on to Dr. Frake's place to reunite with Charley. He found the marshal also already awake and anxious to be out and about. He was deemed well rested and fit enough to do so by Alma Frake, fulfilling her nurse's role in the absence of her husband who was not yet returned from the emergency he'd been called out on the previous evening. This was unusual though not unheard of, she stated, though it appeared of some concern to her. In the meantime, she seemed to be handling things with cool efficiency, including the examination and release of Charley and a report that Hank Wordell's condition remained stable but otherwise unchanged.

Thanking Mrs. Frake for her hospitality and care, Charley explained he had to go take care of some business, starting with the telegrams he needed to send, but promised he would return to check in with the doc once he got back. He and Lone then took their leave.

On the way to the telegraph office, Charley wasted no time questioning Lone about last night's fracas with Mort Cutcheon (which Mrs. Frake had informed him of only this morning) and complaining over not being notified more promptly. Lone gave him further details of the incident and countered his complaint by pointing out that not involving him right away was due to a combination of the medication he'd been administered and the doctor's advice to leave him rest. This seemed to settle the matter, except for a parting grumbled remark, "If you'd've beefed that lowdown skunk in the first place, then he never would've showed back up to make trouble in the second place."

To which Lone replied, "You law dogs may have a long arm, but you sure fall short on singin' the same tune. You say I'm too slow at mowin' down hombres who get in my way, Needles ain't done nothing but bellyache just the opposite—how I'm too *quick* on the trigger."

"I'll stand for you arguin' with me, but don't use that pompous horse's ass to do it," Charley warned gruffly.

Speaking of Needles, when they got to the telegraph office they found out the sheriff had already been there to send off the message to Marshal Morningstar up in the town of Harris. At least he could be counted on to keep his word. So Charley then went about making good on his stated intent of notifying headquarters and a couple close personal contacts that the reports of his death were, for the time being anyway, not accurate.

That done, the marshal proclaimed as to how—due to last night's supper with the Frakes getting cut short by the doc being summoned away on the emergency call—he was starving for a big breakfast. Without rubbing it in about the fine meal he'd had there previously, Lone led the way back to Mabel's, saying only that he'd heard it was a place that served good food.

Upon arriving, it was quickly evident that a lot of folks must have heard the same. The restaurant was packed. But Lone and Charley experienced the dubious luck of having no trouble finding a spot to sit when they got motioned over by Hiram Needles to join him and his deputy, Jerome Lissom, at their table.

"We're just finishing up," the sheriff greeted, "but before we go I'm glad for the opportunity to review some things with you, Marshal Bourbon. I must say, you appear well rested and having benefited from your stay with Dr. Frake."

"True enough," Charley allowed. "The doc—and his wife, in his absence—took good care of me. Same with my partner, though there's no change in him yet. I'll be checkin' back more later, hopefully with the doc havin' returned by then."

Needles frowned. "Frake is still away on that emergency call from last night?"

"That's right."

"How far out of town is the McSwain farm?" Needles asked his deputy.

"Less than a dozen miles," came the answer.

Needles frowned. "Seems rather odd the doctor would be tied up for so long only such a short distance away. I'd expect it to be something he could have taken care of by now at the scene or, if it was too serious, brought the patient back to town for more extensive treatment."

"The McSwain girl, Laurie, said it was a pretty bad gore and they were afraid to move her pa," Deputy Lissom reminded everybody.

"That was before Dr. Frake was there to treat and stabilize the wound. That would have made a difference," the sheriff countered.

"For what it's worth," said Charley, "Mrs. Frake don't seem overly concerned. A little maybe, but not too much. Not yet. She said it was uncommon but not unheard for her husband to once in a while be kept away overnight by such matters."

"I guess if she's not too distraught by it, then I needn't be either." Needles heaved a sigh. "It's not like I don't have plenty of other concerns to occupy myself with."

"I'm due over there to take my turn on watch," said Lissom, draining the last of his coffee and sliding back his chair. "I'll keep a close eye on things and let you know right away if there's any changes."

Needles nodded. "Yes. Good. Be sure to do that."

As the deputy was departing, a plump waitress came over with a pot of steaming coffee from which she filled cups for Lone and Charley before taking their breakfast orders. When she offered to also refill Needles' cup, he waved her off. The waitress's demeanor remained cheerful, in sharp contrast to that of the lawman. He sat gazing broodingly into his half empty cup all during her presence.

When the waitress was gone, Charley said, "You mentioned you had some things you wanted to review, Sheriff. Something in particular you lookin' to go over?"

"Some new developments. None of them much to my liking," Needles replied. He paused, his eyes sweeping the crowded restaurant. When his gaze came back to Charley and Lone, he said, "I was at the telegraph office earlier. Sent off that wire to the marshal up in Harris."

Charley nodded. "I know. We just came from there ourselves."

"I still think that whole Spellman business is a long shot. But, with nothing better to go on at the moment, it can't be ignored." The sheriff paused again, his frown deepening. "While I was taking care of that, I received some incoming messages I find considerably more bothersome."

"How so?"

"A handful of railroad executives apparently got together following the Hardessy rescue incident and—understandably irate, I suppose, over the damage to their train and track and of course the death of one of their employees—decided it would help the capture of those responsible if sizable rewards were offered to achieve that end. Namely, twenty-five hundred dollars for the recapture of Hardessy himself. Fifteen hundred for the apprehension of any man proven to have participated directly in the rescue. And a thousand dollars for information resulting in any of the preceding."

Lone emitted a low whistle.

"Jesus. You add that to the rewards already hangin'

on the head of Rip and some of the others, you end up talkin' one serious pile of money," declared Charley.

"Exactly," Needles said sourly. "And you know what that inevitably means...money-grubbing bounty hunters swarming in from every point of the compass. The professionals and, almost as bad, the first-time amateur fools who see a chance at that kind of pay-out being some kind of wonderful opportunity."

"Not to mention," Charley added, "all the well-meanin' citizens who are gonna come runnin' to report every stranger or odd-actin' character they lay eyes on. In no time at all, you and your deputies are gonna have more leads to check out—most of 'em worthless—than you can shake a stick at."

Lone took a drink of his coffee and made no comment. He understood much of what the two lawmen were lamenting about. But the mention of bounty hunters, especially in such an disparaging, all-encompassing way, stirred mixed emotions in him. The love of his life—Velda Beloit, forever and tragically snatched away from him only a few short years ago—had been a bounty hunter. The daughter of a lawman and at one time carrying a badge herself, she had broken from the strict confines of *The Law* to bring her father's killers to justice when they were crafty enough to flee beyond the expected limits of her badge. It was this experience, having to deal on her own with evil-doers who knew how to avoid the law's grasp by slip-ping in and out of boundaries and jurisdictions, that caused her to continue chasing down such with the broader freedoms of a bounty hunter. She played the game straight, however, focused on meting out justice and ridding the West of scum. She kept her methods legal and worked with local authorities whenever possible. The unfortunate truth, however—as Lone was well aware and as Velda had been too—was that many bounty hunters, maybe most, didn't operate the same way. Their kind were bloodthirsty manhunters strictly in it for the money and their methods were often as ruthless and nearly as law-bending as those they went after. It wasn't uncommon for them to operate more like *bounty killers*, and it was their ilk who made a stench in the noses of lawmen for practically all who took up the trade.

What was more, Lone happened to know that Needles' concern for that kind of manhunter starting to come around was a hell of a lot more certain than the sheriff realized. Or, apparently, Charley either. Even before the two lawmen had begun airing their laments, the former scout's always-scanning eyes had spotted a particular pair of men in the midst of Mabel's customers. He hadn't thought too much about it at first glance. But now he had reason to consider their presence further, and there was nothing good about the conclusion it brought him to.

Heaving a sigh, Lone said, "Though it might spoil everybody's breakfast, which is to say the one you just ate, Sheriff, and the ones me and Charley are fixin' to... you fellas oughta look around and take a particular gander at the two hombres sittin' at that round-topped table off toward the far corner. See 'em?"

Needles and Charley did as suggested. Needles's expression didn't change much except to take on a trace of puzzlement. But Charley's scrunched up pronto. "Aw, shit," he muttered in response.

"What? You recognize them?" Needles wanted to

know. "I can see where they look like an unsavory pair, but—"

"Aye. They're all of that and more," Charley assured him. "They're exactly what you were just frettin' about —two of the scuzziest bounty hunters on the prowl anywhere."

"But so soon?" questioned the sheriff. "I got word myself only an hour or so ago about the added reward being offered by the railroad."

"Only that railroad money is just the *latest* bein' offered for Hardessy. Remember?" reminded Charley. "Him and some of his men had some pretty hefty rewards ridin' on their heads already. Couple of vultures like these two could've just happened to be prowlin' in the area when they heard about the train hit and decided to make a swing this general direction to see if there might be some pickin's for them. They hear about these added dollars, you can bet they'll be stickin' close."

"Damn the luck," grated Needles.

"You can say that again. You couldn't hardly have got a worse draw. The heavyset, buck-toothed one," Lone elaborated, "is Boris 'the Wild Boar' Bemis. He's a brute, likes to break bones and throttle fellas. For gun work, he prefers a cut-down Winchester 'mare's leg'...the tall, lanky one is Sylvester 'Slick' Tennebow. He's a silk-tongued weasel, a conniver and throat cutter. Equally fast with a six-gun and a blade and, they say, with the ladies too."

Needles eyed him. "You seem to know an awful lot about such charming gentlemen."

Lone eyed him right back. "For somebody in your line of work, you don't seem to know enough."

"Alright, the both of you. Jesus," growled Charley. "Ain't we got enough else to worry about without you two pawin' at each other?"

Both Lone and Needles looked away from his glare. Lone swung his eyes back to the pair under discussion and said, "Looks like our boys have noticed our gawkin' and talkin'. They're gettin' up to leave."

But he was wrong. Bemis and Tennebow indeed got up from their table, but rather than exit the restaurant they threaded their way over to stand before the table occupied by the three men who'd been taking so much interest in them.

Tennebow smiled the wide, ingratiating display of teeth that had helped earn him his "Slick" handle. "Morning, gents. Marshal Bourbon...McGantry...Sheriff. Thought we'd mosey over and be sociable. Renew old friendships with two of you, introduce ourselves to Sheriff Needles here."

"You got a real careless way of tossin' around that term 'friendship,'" Charley advised him.

Slick's smile didn't falter. "My mama taught me that to make a friend, you got to *be* a friend."

"Very well," said Needles in a flat tone. "You've introduced yourselves and acknowledged what you deem an old friendship, thus fulfilling any obligation you felt to be sociable. Is there anything else?"

"Well you sure as hell ain't bein' very sociable," grumbled Boris.

"Then it should be clear that's because I have no intent nor feel any obligation to be."

Now Slick's smile went away. "You know, mister, fancy words don't keep what they're wrapped around from still being damned rude. Ain't the fact you're a public servant supposed to obligate you to a certain amount of civility and fairness? What's clear is that those two sitting with you have prejudiced you against us—see? I can use big words too—without you ever giving a fair hearing to our side. How is that right?"

Needles scowled. "Okay. What *is* your side? And be quick in the telling."

"For starters," Slick responded, "my name is Sylvester Tennebow and my partner is Boris Bemis. We are, by trade, fugitive recovery agents."

"Bounty hunters."

Slick shrugged. "Not a term we prefer. Regardless, our right to pursue wanted fugitives for payment of reward money offered for their apprehension is a long-established legal right. We consider ourselves quite competent at what we do and we work with local law authorities to the best extent we can. Toward that end, please be advised, Sheriff and Marshal, we plan to be working hereabouts in pursuit of the outlaw Rip Hardessy and his gang."

"What makes you think they're anywhere in this area?" Needles asked.

"Call it a hunch, for now," said Slick. "The train hit that sprung Rip out of custody—which I know Marshal Bourbon is well familiar with—took place just east of here. And, as I'm sure you aware, Sheriff, your posse reported sign of the gang then scattering this general direction, maybe some north. That adds up to this being at least a good starting point."

"Also," spoke up Boris, "just a couple days ago, two of the gang was spotted and shot back near North Platte. Suggestin' maybe the lot of 'em didn't scatter so far after all." He narrowed his gaze and focused it on Lone. "But then, you know all about that piece of business, don't you, McGantry?"

"Happens I do, yeah," Lone allowed.

Slick cocked an eyebrow. "How is it, Sheriff, that you seem so disapproving of what my partner and I do, yet you're sitting down to breakfast with McGantry who—in case you didn't know—promptly put in a claim for the bounty pay-out on those men after he beefed 'em?"

"The difference bein'," Lone answered before Needles could say anything, "was that I killed those two polecats because they was tryin' to steal horses off me. Afterward, when I found out there was money ridin' on their heads, you damn right I laid claim for it. I'm tryin' to build up my ranch, and money to buy horses don't come easy."

Boris's mouth spread in a sly grin. "Yeah, I heard that about you, McGantry. How you was startin' up a small horse spread to run in your old age. That what brung you over this way, then? Lookin' to buy more stock?"

"I'm always on the lookout for good horseflesh," drawled Lone. Then, his gaze fixed meaningfully, he added, "Trouble is...I keep runnin' into jackasses who get in my way instead."

CHAPTER SEVENTEEN

THE RETURN OF THE WAITRESS WITH HEAPING PLATES OF food for Lone and Charley put an effective end to any further conversation with the two bounty hunters. They excused themselves and departed with annoyingly smug looks on their homely mugs. Needles, clearly agitated by the pair in general and by their display of brazenness in particular, took his leave only a handful of minutes later. It was a safe bet he'd be spreading word among his deputies, directing them to keep a close eye on Tennebow and Bemis.

Once they had the table to themselves, Lone and Charley wasted no time digging into their grub. Around a forkful of scrambled eggs, Charley said, "Nobody can claim things ain't been interesting since we hit this burg. But the problem is that none of it has gained us anything meaningful as far as closin' in on Hardessy and his bunch."

"Reckon so," Lone allowed. "Though, for some reason, I can't help but feel we're nibblin' on the edges of some things that might yet turn out to amount to something."

"I hope you're right. But the only thing I feel us nibblin' on is what we happen to be fillin' our faces with. Not that that's all bad, mind you."

They ate in silence for a couple minutes. During this, a new customer entered Mabel's. He was a tall, sturdily built young man, appearing to be in his middle to late twenties. He was dressed in standard trail garb but with a short-waisted jacket of brown suede that was a cut above standard. A flat-crowned Stetson perched at a faint tilt on his head, a Colt .45 rode high on his right hip. He walked with an easy, measured grace. He didn't exactly have the look of a gun hand, but neither did he come across as just another cowboy on the drift between stints of ranch work.

Out of habit, the eyes of both Lone and Charley tracked this newcomer's entrance without any special interest. But when Lone's attention returned to the task of spearing another slice of bacon off his plate, Charley's gaze lingered on the new arrival as he hitched up a stool and seated himself at the lunch counter.

With the bacon successfully fork-impaled and raised partway to his mouth, Lone paused to ask, "Something about that hombre ranklin' you, Charley?"

"Not sure. Something about him strikes me half-assed familiar, but dogged if I can say why or from where. That's what rankles me, the not bein' sure."

Lone went ahead and pushed the bacon into his mouth and then, as he chewed, said, "Well, if he was anybody who amounted to anything—some owlhoot needin' his ears pinned back—I expect you'd remember okay. So my advice is to quit worryin' about him and worry about finishin' your breakfast instead."

"Aye. And sound advice it is," agreed Charley, getting back to work cleaning his plate.

A minute later, however, the attention of both Lone and Charley was drawn back to the man now seated at the lunch counter. More accurately put, their attention was drawn by the loud, angry voices of two other men who were suddenly confronting the stranger. The pair had crowded up close behind the young man's stool, fanned apart so that they were positioned at angles off each of his shoulders. On his left was a squat, bow-legged character wearing a cowhide vest and a check-ered shirt. On his right, a gawky, scarecrow-looking specimen who was all bony elbows and long, stilt-like legs. Both were bleary-eyed and unshaven, having the look of hungover wranglers who'd done a night on the town and hadn't made it back to the ranch yet.

"Now, you cocky sonofabitch, you're in *our* town," the man in the checkered shirt was proclaiming loudly. "And me and my pal Henry are lookin' forward to givin' you a taste of the same kind of welcome you gave us when we came to yours!"

"Yeah. We're lookin' forward to it a whole lot!" agreed stilt-legged Henry.

The man on the stool swiveled slowly around to face his accusers. He eyed each in turn, then said in a measured tone, "Can't rightly say I recollect you fellas. But I recognize the type well enough. When you say we had some kind of past dealings in my town—you mean Gothenburg?"

"There!" said Charley in a hushed voice. "That's where I know that jasper from. Name's Bartles. He is—

or leastways was—a deputy for the Gothenburg marshal who nabbed Hardessy before he ended up breakin' free from our custody."

This went unheard by the trio involved in the disturbance, even though the general hum of voices and the scrape of silverware on plates had died down across the breadth of the restaurant as other customers were craning their necks to see what the fuss was about.

"That's right. Gothenburg," confirmed Checkered Shirt, keeping his bloodshot eyes narrowed and locked on his target. "About six months back, we was deliverin' a prize bull sold by our boss to a buyer on one of your local ranches. When we stopped in town afterward to have a little fun before headin' home, you didn't like the fun we was havin' and threw us in your lousy jail over it."

"Yeah, actin' all high and mighty and throwin' your weight around behind a tin star," jeered Henry. Then, cutting a sidelong glance over at his pal, he added, "But he don't look so high and mighty now, 'thout that star to hide in back of—does he, Loomis?"

At this point, a stout, rolling pin-wielding woman wearing a flower-patterned apron and iron gray hair pulled into a severe bun came marching out from the kitchen area behind the serving counter. This, evidently, was Mabel herself and she soon made it clear that her establishment wasn't the place for old grudges to be settled—unless it was with her rolling pin.

"Henry Bates and Loomis Reed, you two drunken louts, I'm warnin' you for the last time about bringin' your rowdy ways into my place and disturbin' my other customers!" she declared. "Now quit botherin' that man and get out of here. Get out and stay out—and this time I mean it!"

"What about this out-of-town skunk?" Loomis wailed. "You sayin' he can stay but we got to leave?"

"That's exactly what I'm sayin'. He ain't the one botherin' nobody."

"The hell he ain't!" protested Henry. "He's botherin' the shit outta me, and not for the first time. And I ain't ready to be done with him until—"

"You'd better be done, and you'd better get headed for the door before I bounce this rollin' pin off your empty skull!" Backing up her threat, Mabel made a couple well-practiced swipes with the heavy wooden cylinder.

Henry glared at her. "It's a good thing for you you're a woman, else I'd snatch that thing away and make you eat it."

"Come ahead on, I'll meet you halfway," Mabel responded without flinching.

But Charley Bourbon had heard enough. He rose up from his chair, all six-foot-three of him, chest swelled out full. He started around the corner of his table and said in a booming voice, "I don't think so! The only thing I think's gonna happen is that you two loud-mouths are gonna skedaddle out that door and be quick about it. But, before you go, your sorry asses are gonna apologize to the lady and all the other folks in here whose breakfasts you interrupted."

Henry and Loomis stood in stunned, hang-jawed silence for a long moment.

Instead, the one who responded was Jack Bartles, the young man on the stool. He slipped off his seat and, as he came to his feet, said to Charley, "I appre-

ciate you taking a hand, mister, but I really don't..."
Then he too suddenly froze with hang-jawed startle-
ment. Until he found his voice again, this time saying
in a strained tone, "You! But—but everybody figured
you for dead!"

That's all he got out before Henry, not impressed by
any remark about the risen dead and for damn sure not
willing to pass up an opening to get in a lick of the
craving for payback that still seethed within him, went
ahead and drilled a sucker punch hard into the gut of
the distracted Bartles. The latter was doubled over by
the blow, his knees starting to sag and breath exploding
out of him in a great gust.

"Yee-haw! Lemme have a piece of that!" crowed
Loomis as he stepped in closer, swinging one of his long
legs and crashing a bony knee to meet the descending
chin of Bartles. The man from Gothenburg was
slammed back against the face of the lunch counter,
toppling over the stool he'd occupied only a moment
earlier.

Lone was suddenly rushing forward. He'd risen
from his chair after Charley stood up but, since he was
on the side of their table closer to where the disturbance had now escalated, was positioned to get there
quicker. Three long strides, roughly bumping aside a
couple of seated diners, placed him within reach of
Henry, who remained poised over the fallen man with
balled fists raised and ready to strike again.

Lone's arms stretched out and his fingers curled into
handfuls of Henry's shirt collar. With a powerful yank,
he pulled the hungover troublemaker back toward him.
Henry yelped helplessly as he was whirled out and
around and then released with a hard shove—straight

into a beautifully timed right cross thrown by the advancing Charley.

Hearing over his shoulder the meaty thud of the blow, followed promptly by the clump of Henry hitting the floor, Lone continued on to Loomis. The bug-eyed scarecrow saw him coming and even had time to thrust out with a bony fist meant to slow his charge. But Lone easily slipped the attempt and bulled into Loomis, staggering him backward. Hooking the scarecrow's right arm, extended awkwardly after the missed punch, Lone clamped it tight in the crook of his own right arm and held it there. Then he whipped his left elbow around, viciously smashing it to the side of Loomis's head. He did this twice more in rapid succession. When he released his clamp on the arm, the lanky man collapsed like a puppet with its strings cut.

Thinking the trouble now settled, Lone turned back with intent to help Charley get the sucker-punched Bartles back on his feet.

But it wasn't that easy. In fact, the trouble not only wasn't settled—it was just getting started.

As Lone and Charley watched, momentarily dumbfounded, more than half a dozen men from tables scattered across the room all came to their feet, muttering curses and aiming angry scowls as they began shuffling toward the pair who *thought* they had just done a fitting and proper thing. At the last second, Lone realized the problem. Him and Charley—and Bartles too—were strangers, outsiders. And Henry and Loomis, never mind them being half-drunk shit-stirrers who only got what they had coming, were still from local ranks. That meant, in the eyes of those now responding on their behalf, it wasn't up to outsiders to put them in their place.

"No good deed goes unpunished," Lone said with a grimace.

"What's that?" grumbled Charley.

"Just something a fella I know is overly fond of sayin'."

"Could be he knows what he's talkin' about."

"Looks like we're fixin' to find out."

Then, with the suddenness of a starter gun kicking off a horse race, the men who'd been edging forward in a menacing clump all at once broke into an onrushing horde. They came with flying fists and feet and ramming heads. And Lone and Charley—with their backs against the lunch counter so none could easily get around behind them—braced themselves and answered in kind. Noses were flattened, teeth were loosened, ribs were pounded. Plates and cups began sailing through the air and a couple chairs were raised, meant to be swung as clubs, only to have those hoisting them and thus exposing their faces get a fist to the mouth for their trouble. More than once an unintentional blow landing on one local by another earned a fully intentional retaliatory strike.

Those not directly involved in the brawl fled out the front door or pressed themselves against the relative safety of the back wall. Behind the counter, Mabel added to the clamor by repeatedly banging her rolling pin down on the countertop and shouting in a strident voice, "Stop it, you fools! Stop it!"

Henry and Loomis both made the ill-advised decisions to struggle back to their feet. But even amid the blurred swarm of other faces, theirs made targets too prized not to take aim at once again, resulting in them almost immediately getting knocked back down.

As he fought, grabbing and twisting men by their arms and necks, delivering heavy blows with his melon-sized fists, a faint smile of borderline delight seemed to form on Charley's lips, like he was actually enjoying this. But for Lone it was different. He never took fighting lightly, not even a little bit. His eyes blazed, his teeth were bared in a permanent snarl and every blow he struck was meant to put a man down and keep him there.

In between them, though battered and sucking hard to regain his breath, Jack Bartles shoved back up to his feet and threw himself into the mix as well. His participation didn't last long, however, before the whole works was brought to a halt by the appearance of Sheriff Hiram Needles barging in through the front door with Deputy Harold right on his heels.

"Cease at once! Everybody!" Needles shouted, barely loud enough to be heard above the sounds of the brawl. To ensure he was taken notice of, he raised the Remington pistol already in his hand, pointed it up at the ceiling and triggered a thunderous round.

Silence and a stoppage of the fighting promptly ensued. Everything went quiet except for the puffs of labored breathing and the rattle of shattered ceiling plaster dribbling down onto the floor.

"What in Holy Hell is going on here?" Needles demanded to know.

It was Mabel who gave him the answer, pointing with her rolling pin and saying, "It was those two knot heads lyin' there, Henry Bates and Loomis Reed, who started it all. They lit into this young stranger over some past trouble they claimed to have had with him. When they commenced gangin' up on him, those other big galoots stepped in to stop 'em. Some rannies from else- where in the joint decided they didn't like seein' a couple of local fellas get roughed up in such a way, so they jumped in and then...well, you saw what that turned into."

Needles swept his scowl over the array of bruised, battered faces and came to rest on Charley's. "I find it surprising," he said, "that someone of your training and experience couldn't find a better way to quell such an incident than to hurl yourself into the middle of it."

Backhanding away a trickle of blood running from one nostril, Charley replied, "Apart from that first piece of business where I didn't like the two-to-one odds, I don't recollect *hurlin'* myself into nothing. After that, when seven or eight of your upstandin' citizens decided they oughta stick up for their own, me and Lone didn't have a helluva lot of choice but to throw ourselves back at 'em."

"And it never occurred to you," said Needles, just short of sneering, "that by simply displaying your United States Marshal badge you very likely could have ended the whole matter without all the fisticuffs and wreckage?"

The words "United States marshal" passed through the crowd of onlookers in a hushed ripple, accompanied by uncomfortable expressions forming on the faces of several of the participants in the brawl.

"What's occurin' to me right about now," Charley grated in response to Needles' inquiry, "is that I don't much care for your snotty tone, bub. Things popped mighty fast and I handled it like I handled it. Nobody needs you second-guessin' how it should or shouldn't have been done different."

Needles stiffened and blotches of color crept up his neck and cheeks. They quickly faded, however, and in a strained, quieter voice, he said, "To be sure, Marshal Bourbon. I trust you proceeded as best you saw fit."

Lone couldn't resist throwing in a jab. "How about me, Sheriff? You notice my admirable restraint in not killin' or even shootin' anybody this time around?"

Needles just glared without further comment.

"Before everybody gets to feelin' too cozy and satisfied," spoke up Mabel, "what about the damage to my place? Who's gonna pay for the broken chairs and dishes and the ruined meals some folks never got the chance to finish? Not to mention cleanin' up the mess."

Charley looked around, his mouth pooching thoughtfully. Then he asked, "What do you figure your cost will be to set things back right—the breakage, the spoiled food, the clean-up labor?"

Now it was Mabel's turn to look thoughtful while giving the state of things a good study. Then she concluded, "I reckon thirty, thirty-five dollars would be fair."

"I'd say more than fair," agreed Charley. He swept his eyes around the room again. "Okay. How many of you—show of hands, and don't try to dodge 'cause I can see your bruised mugs—was in on the brawl?" A count and a re-count came up with eleven, including Lone and Charley. "Alright, three bucks each makes thirty-three dollars. An extra fifty cents makes it near forty. We'll go with that. So each of you scrappers drop three-and-a-half dollars in the hat my friend Lone is gonna be passin' around, and we can wrap up this whole business."

While Lone was passing around his hat, Charley tugged aside Jack Bartles, the young deputy from Gothenburg. "Now then, son. What the devil is your reason for showin' up here in the first place?"

Bartles returned his gaze, a tormented expression on his face. "I had to come," he said. "I-I had to tell somebody that...that it's my fault the Hardessy gang knew to hit the train you and the others were on."

CHAPTER EIGHTEEN

WHITEY CULP WAS STANDING OUTSIDE THE CAVE MOUTH, leaning back against a sloping wall of rock and smoking a cigarette, when Maxwell Frake and Laurie McSwain emerged from the cave. The doctor and the girl paused for a moment, squinting and getting their vision adjusted to the bright mid-morning sunlight. Frake looked rumpled and exhausted, dark circles under his eyes, his normally well groomed hair standing on end, his white shirt streaked with dust. Outwardly at least, Laurie appeared to be enduring their ordeal somewhat better. Tall and willowy in scuffed boots, snug denim pants, and a homespun blouse that failed to hide the thrust of full, firm breasts, her years spent growing up on a farm and pitching in from an early age had better conditioned her to long hours and taxing conditions. There was a weariness in her eyes to be sure, but there was also a stubborn resolve gripping the pretty face framed by a mane of wheat-colored hair.

"Well?" the outlaw lieutenant asked.

Both Frake's expression and his tone remained flat

as he replied, "He's as comfortable as I can make him. I gave him laudanum for the pain and some spoonfuls of a medicinal syrup—complimented by McIvey's tea—to soothe him internally. He has two or three cracked ribs on his left side, so I also bound him securely around the middle to minimize irritation to them from any coughing."

"That all sounds real good, real thorough." Whitey snapped away his cigarette butt. "But what I meant was —how is he? How bad?"

Frake's mouth pulled into a tight, straight line. "In a word...bad."

"He's busted up on the inside, ain't he?"

"That's what it comes down to, yes. The cracked ribs are the least of it."

"So what can you do to fix him?"

"Under these conditions, not much more than what I just detailed." Frake's forehead puckered. "Even back home, in my office, I don't know that I could do much more. Beyond broken bones and lacerations or bullet wounds, I-I'm not a surgeon. To open him up, to try and repair whatever...I don't know how much even a skilled specialist would be able to do."

"That's a hell of a grim statement, mister."

"You think I don't know that? Do you have any idea how many times over the years I've had to give that kind of news to people? It never gets a damn bit easier, not even if—"

When the doctor cut his words short, Whitey's eyes immediately blazed. "Not even if it's a stinkin' lowdown outlaw—is that what you were gonna say, Doc?"

"None of that matters," Frake insisted. "I took a sacred oath a long time ago to heal to the best of my abilities whenever called upon. That may not be something you'd understand, but it's crucially important to me and I would never dishonor it. No matter how undeserving or disagreeable I might find a patient to be, I will always feel bound to provide my best care."

Gradually, the fire in Whitey's eyes cooled. Until he said, "Damned if I don't believe you."

"You should," Laurie said firmly. "He's an honest and honorable man, even if that's something you might have trouble recognizing."

"Best watch your mouth, gal," Whitey responded sharply. "You've been took easy on so far. Don't push your luck."

But Laurie wasn't done. "Easy? We've had no food or rest for over a dozen hours. And only a few sips of water. Did it ever occur to you that if you want this man—this *doctor*—to keep up his strength and stay alert in order to do the most he can for your injured friend, then it might be in your best interest to take decent care of him?"

Whitey first scowled at this outburst. But then, once again his expression shifted, became more contemplative. "Do you cook, girl?" he asked abruptly.

"Yes. And I have a name—it's Laurie."

"In a minute then...Laurie...you and the doc can go back inside where you'll find plenty of supplies and pots and whatever you need to make both of you a good meal. Plenty of water and coffee too, if you've a mind. After that, bedrolls will be laid out for the two of you to get some sleep. But first, I got one more piece of business with the doc." Whitey's gaze cut over and pinned Frake very directly. "Tell it to me straight...does Rip have any chance of pullin' through?"

For a moment, the doctor had trouble meeting his

eyes. But then he was able to, and his own gaze was steady and equally direct. "There's always a chance. In his case, my initial assessment says awfully slim. But, at the same time, nobody knows better than me what an amazing organism the human body is. And your man is tough, has the constitution of a buffalo ... With lots of rest and a careful, very bland diet along with the syrup and the tea—and a complete stop to the rotgut whiskey ... I still can't say it's likely, but neither will I say it's impossible for him to stabilize."

"How long before you could say for sure?"

"Not more than a couple of days. If he's going to take a turn for the better, it should start to show by then. If it keeps going the way it is now ... well, it won't be pretty and it will be clear enough to everybody."

Whitey's expression turned dark and his gaze seemed to drift off and stare at something far away.

River McIvey came out of the cave, squinting, and looked around to find Whitey. "He's wantin' to see you," he said. "Alone."

Whitey blinked a time or two and brought his attention back to the moment. "Looks like your feast will have to wait a few more minutes," he said to Frake and Laurie. Then, to McIvey: "Stay here, keep an eye on them...and get them something to drink."

––––––––

INSIDE THE CAVE, Whitey squatted down next to where Rip Hardessy lay stretched out on a bedroll. "River said you wanted to see me. You got your second wind now and are fixin' to ream me out some more for fetchin' that sawbones?"

Hardessy regarded him with heavy-lidded eyes. "It's what you deserve for pullin' such a reckless stunt, and you doggone well know it. But there are only so many ways you can tell a damn fool he's a damn fool."

"Oh, I don't know," Whitey said, a corner of his mouth quirking up ruefully. "First time around you covered a pretty wide variety."

"Like I said, you deserved it. You put everybody at unnecessary risk. But, when I reflect on how I sent Cramer and Redsleeve off to check on the fate of that damned Charley Bourbon—not to mention how my sneakin' back for that visit to Mona backfired like it did to begin with—I can't hardly duck a big share of 'deserves' for my own self. Thinkin' on it now, it's like that whole Gothenburg job was snakebit from the minute we got our hands on the money. Me getting my stupid ass nabbed again, then Clevis ending up dead and me being hammered to hell in the train attack, Cramer and Redsleeve never makin' it back...more and more frayed edges the whole way."

"Maybe. But it ain't all the way unraveled. Not yet."

"All the more reason to take extra care it don't. And I'm talkin' about one of the main rules we've always gone by. You know what I mean. Nobody who lags on account of gettin' hurt or wounded or whatever, rates affectin' the rest in any way that puts them at added risk. That includes me."

"You ain't slowin' us down or causin' us to lag. We're already holed up with no plans to ride out again any time soon," Whitey argued as he built a fresh cigarette. "And I planned the fetchin' of that doc real tight and it went by the numbers. I don't figure anybody from that town even yet realizes he's gone anywhere except on an emergency call out to the country. And when they finally get around to smellin' something fishy, they still ain't gonna have no clue where he went or why."

Hardessy worked up a frown, but not a very severe one. "And what else it still ain't is something I'd have agreed to up front. But, at the same time, it's kinda hard to hold a grudge over you lookin' out for me."

"Bad habit of mine," Whitey muttered. He stuck the newly rolled quirley between Hardessy's lips, struck a match and lit it.

Hardessy blew a cloud of smoke and then said, "Let's cut to it. What did the sawbones say about the shape I'm in?"

Whitey took his time before giving a guarded response. "What did he tell you?"

"Said I had serious internal injuries. Like I didn't already know as much."

"Uh-huh. Same thing I got."

Over a deep drag on the cigarette, Hardessy's eyes locked a probing stare on the closest thing he had to a true friend. Exhaling another cloud of smoke, he said, "Ain't it a little late in the game for us to start bullshitting each other on serious stuff? I'm in a bad way. I know it, you know it, and no matter how he cushions it in cute medical terms—leastways to me—the doc sure as hell does too. I'm bettin' he told it to you in plainer words. Tell me I'm wrong."

Whitey released a ragged sigh. "I can't. What it boils down to is that, yeah, you're busted up on the inside. Bad, just like you figure. Maybe worse. Only way to know for sure and if there's any fix to it is to cut you open. That's way past what Frake has the skills for, especially here in this cave. It's likely outside of what even the most skilled specialist could do, no matter the setting."

"Whew." Hardessy's brows arced up. "That sure enough lays it out plain, don't it?"

Whitey made no reply.

After taking another drag off his cigarette, Hardessy tipped his head back and seemed to study with great focus the curls of smoke rising up toward the roof of the cave when he exhaled. "Ain't it the shits?" he said, his mouth twisting wryly. "I spend my whole adult life slippin' in and out of the hands of law dogs and dodging bullets and hang nooses...figurin' all the while it was a near certainty I'd reach my end either from a slug or the hemp...and it turns out to be a goddamn chunk of flyin' wood from a freak explosion that has my number ridin' on it. Can you beat that?"

A coughing fit seized the gang boss suddenly, doubling him forward. He flicked away his cigarette and grabbed a blood-speckled hanky to hold to his mouth. When the coughing subsided and he lowered the hanky, it showed a thick smear of fresh blood.

"Ain't that pretty?" he said, holding it out. "When I was a kid and would get a scrape or a cut, my ma'd always tell me that rich, red blood was a sign of good health. Reckon my condition now makes that just one more of the lies the old bitch filled me full of."

Whitey took a shot at trying to counter the bleakness at least a little bit. "Something else Doc Frake said was that the human body sometimes has amazing ways of healin' itself. He also said you got the constitution of a buffalo. That don't mean I'm tryin' to smear on a layer of phony mush. But, damn it, there's still *a* chance if you don't just flat give up."

Hardessy grinned weakly and wagged his head. "Nice try, old pard. But sorry, I don't feel a damn bit of *healin'* goin' on inside of me. So what that leaves, way I see it, is for me to go to work on tyin' off some loose ends before I ain't able to come out of one of those coughin' fits. I'm countin' on you to help me get 'em took care of."

"You know I'll do everything I can."

"It involves some more risk that most would hardly call smart. Though part of it has to do with securin' the money everybody's got comin' from that job we pulled just before me gettin' nabbed. Takin' risk for money is what we do. But the rest has to do with...well, satisfyin' the wishes of a dyin' man."

Whitey said, "Meanin' you want me to bring Mona here, since she's the key to both of those things."

"Call me seven kinds of a chump but, yeah, I got a cravin' something fierce for that gal. Me stoppin' to see her, just quick-like, after we pulled that bank job and scattered with me holdin' the money like always—hell, that wasn't the first time I dallied to get in a poke somewhere before meetin' back up to go into a spell of deep, dry hidin'. But this time I got caught. Hick badge toters in a hick town. Who the hell would've ever figured?"

Hardessy paused, twisting his face into a grimace, then continuing. "When I heard them law dogs pounding on the door, there wasn't time to do nothing but hide the money under her bed, give her some fast instructions, then hand myself over. They had me cold. Tryin' to shoot my way clear would've only got myself ventilated, likely Mona too, and the law for sure would've glommed the money. I figured there'd be a better chance, once you heard I was in the clink and while all the higher-up legal shit was gettin' sorted out, for you to come back around and put together a plan to maybe salvage both me *and* the money...and you did."

"We've been over all of this before."

"I know. I just want to hear myself say it again in hopes I don't come across as soundin' *quite* so damn loco. And I want to make sure you know how much I appreciate you comin' through."

"Your gal Mona pulled her weight too," Whitey allowed. "More than I was counting on, to be honest. By the time she fed me the information on which train they was fixin' to haul you to the pen on, I had to move so fast to get everybody in place ahead of it there was no time to worry about the money. What was more, I figured what the hell—if we failed, there might not be none of us left to need money no more anyway."

"But there *are* some of us left...well, some of the rest of you anyway, the way it's gonna end up." Hardessy eyed Whitey intently. "You trust you'll find Mona in Ogallala, at Betty's, the way I told her?"

"Probably not as much as you do," Whitey answered honestly. "If I was a bettin' man, I'd see it about fifty-fifty odds."

"Then you'd short yourself. She'll be there, and so will the money," Hardessy stated with confidence. "She don't know I'm hurt. Me and her had plans. I know she's only a whore half my age who I've known just a short time. But I felt something real with her, Whitey. Like never before. We was gonna take my cut, along with some more I have stashed in a few places, and go away together. Start over, start clean."

"You're sure right about that short time business," Whitey said. "You only paid her a handful of visits while we was holed up in that abandoned old church on the outskirts of town, layin' our plans for hittin' the bank."

"I know. But it hit fast and it hit hard. For both of us. I've heard of such, but never believed it. And I sure as hell never figured it would happen to me...until it did."

Whitey's head bobbed in a faint nod. "Sounds nice. Man reaches a certain point, he oughta have a hope, a goal for some kind of settlin' down and not bein' all the time on the jump."

"Looks like I'm only gonna get a brief taste of settlin' down, old pard. But that's all right. Probably more than I deserve," said Hardessy. "I'm still gonna reach out and grab it as tight as I can for as long as I can. That's why I want you to bring Mona to me. I want to hold her in my arms, experience the warmth of a caring woman, one more time. And I...I want my goddamn hook back." Hardessy held up the stub of his right wrist and his expression turned somewhat sheepish. "I left it behind when the law took me, and I ain't felt right since. I don't want to be buried without it."

Whitey's brows pinched together. "Jeez, Rip..."

"There! See? Did you hear yourself?" Hardessy demanded. "How the hell can I be 'Rip' Hardessy without my ripper?"

"There's more to you than that."

"Is there? Thanks to dear old Ma, I've been without a hand for near three-quarters of my life." Hardessy's expression shifted again, looking angry for a moment and then taking on a strange, faraway look. "Could be that hook has been the best...and the worst...part of me."

CHAPTER NINETEEN

"I KNOW, I KNOW," JACK BARTLES KEPT REPEATING IN A mournful tone. "Nothing you can say or do will make me feel any lower or worse than the things I've already told myself."

"Don't count on that," growled Charley.

"I was a blowhard damn fool trying to impress a whore!" wailed Bartles. "But I swear to God, I never in a million years meant to—"

"I don't give a shit what you *never meant!*" Charley cut him off. "But I sure as hell know what you *did*, you mewling pup. You betrayed your badge and you queered a carefully laid plan to get a black-hearted villain delivered for a way overdue hangin'. And, in the process, you got an innocent railroad brakeman killed and damn near the same for me and my partner."

"I know," Bartles said again, half groaning. "It's been eating me up inside, squirming in my head like a snake that won't let me think about anything else. Believing you and the brakeman already dead, and hearing how your partner was barely hanging on...that's why I finally had to come forward. To see if there was anything I could do to help, to somehow—"

"Help?" Charley barked, cutting him short once again. "Haven't you done enough? But here's something you'd better get clear on what *I'm* apt to do. If Hank had been killed and I ever found out what you're tellin' us now, I'd've killed you. If it happens, he slips away and yet loses his fight to live, I may still—"

This time it was the old marshal whose words got cut short. By Lone.

"Charley! For Christ's sake, get hold of yourself!"

This exchange between the three men was taking place in Lone's hotel room. Wanting to put the restaurant brawl behind them and anxious to hear more about Bartles' claim to be at fault for the Hardessy gang finding out which train the prisoner was being transported on, they had sought somewhere they could talk in private. Bartles sat on the edge of the bed, wringing his hat in his hands; Lone and Charley sat facing him, each astraddle a straight-backed wooden chair.

After revealing at the outset how he had turned in his badge before leaving Gothenburg, it didn't take long for what the former deputy began relating next to enrage Charley almost beyond reason. Though it at last answered the nagging question of how the gang knew which train to go after in spite of the steps taken to mask the final choice, it placed Bartles in a very foolish and unsympathetic light.

What it boiled down to was a moment of boastfulness meant to impress a prostitute. Once the train had been selected and the two US Marshals and their prisoner were set to be secretly boarded just before departure, Miles Reed, the town marshal of Gothenburg, had reckoned that with Charley and Hank having assumed custody and now officially in charge, he could afford to give a break to some of his deputies who up until then had been pulling many long, tense hours guarding Hardessy. Being one of those affected by this, Bartles had elected to kick off his break by having a mattress dance with a soiled dove named Mona, a relative newcomer to town who had become a favorite partner of his (and many others) for such activities. Ironically, she was also the dove Rip Hardessy had made his ill-advised decision to dally with after him and his men pulled their bank robbery—resulting in his capture while in her company.

"I guess that's the part that started me down the path of stupidly blabbing the way I did," Bartles lamented. "Mona pretended to be shocked that the man we cornered in her room turned out to be a notorious outlaw and killer. And she acted so grateful for how we grabbed him and hauled him off before he had a chance to hurt her or do something dreadful—that was her word, dreadful. She made me feel like a big, brave hero. And me, lapping it up like a prize chump, wanted to impress her even more and have her think I was a bigger deal still."

"So you blabbed, spilled your guts on stuff you knew damn well you shouldn't," snarled Charley. "I hope you got a real good poke out of it, because what resulted— the wreckage and injury and death, the escape of a ruthless killer, all the new threats and danger he poses until he's caught again—sure didn't amount to nothing good for a lot of other people."

"I think it's pretty plain he knows all that, Charley," Lone said in a measured tone. "Give him a chance to finish his tellin'."

When Lone's gaze then cut expectantly back to him, Bartles continued. "Yeah, telling her how I was one of only a handful of men who knew about the freight run that was going to be used for the transfer, making it sound like I was practically in on the final decision—that made me feel mighty big in the moment, and she did a real good job of letting me know she thought so too. But even then, when I heard the words tumbling out of my mouth and knew it wasn't smart, I still didn't see why or how Mona would take the information and misuse it in any way."

"So what changed your mind? What makes you so sure now that she did?" Lone wanted to know.

Bartles had trouble meeting his gaze. "As soon as we heard the news about the hit on the train, everybody started asking how the gang could have known. It didn't take long before the guilt over saying things I never should have triggered my own questions. When I went to see Mona, hoping to make sure it *wasn't* her who had somehow passed on what I told her—she was gone. She'd left on a train out of town early that morning.

"My gut sank. I tried to fight believing it. For my own sake, I suppose, as much as anything. But I knew right then and there she must be the one responsible. I wanted to puke." The ex deputy stopped twisting his hat long enough to raise one hand and drag its fingers through his hair. "I was able to finish piecing it together, mostly by talking to the other girls who worked out of the same saloon Mona had. They hated her anyway, for showing up and quickly becoming so popular she began taking customers away from them. I knew about that from Mona herself. Jealousy, she claimed. But some of the others had their own side, accusing how she went out of her way to steal men away and then flaunted her popularity, rubbing it in their faces."

"Nobody gives a damn about that crap," said a scowling Charley. "Finish explainin' what convinced you she went ahead and passed the train information on to Hardessy's gang."

Bartles heaved a ragged sigh. "What else I found out from the other girls was that for a week or ten days before the bank robbery, right up to the night we caught up with him, Rip—though none of them knew who he was at that point—had been to see Mona several times. At least half a dozen. So she was clearly lying about being with him for the first time. Hell, she was probably lying, too, about having no idea he was an outlaw. Maybe she even knew him from somewhere before. In any case, there was enough between 'em for her to not only lie, but to want to help him.

"She got her chance to do that when another fella came sneaking around after we had Rip behind bars. Two different girls told me they saw a white-haired man —not an *old* man, yet an hombre with silver gray hair— slinking into Mona's room in the wee hours one morning."

"Whitey Culp, sounds like," Charley muttered.

"That's what I figure," said Bartles. "I further figure that, after he found out Rip was locked up, Whitey doubled back to do some sniffing around for a way to bust him out. Not necessarily out of loyalty but, without Lone, none of the rest of the gang had a way to get their hands on the bank money he'd rode away from the robbery with."

"So Whitey was checkin' to see if Mona might have some clue to that," Lone speculated.

"Seems like. Don't appear to have gained him anything money-wise, though. At least not right away. But it did set up an ongoing contact between him and Mona that would still turn out to have some benefit. You see, I eventually discovered that the gang had been holed up in an old abandoned church way on the outskirts of town. That's where they must have stayed for a while when they were planning their robbery, waiting for the right time when the take would be fattest due to the bank's money-on-hand riding at a high level to meet month's end paydays.

"Well, when Whitey came back to scope out trying to find some way to free Rip, he stayed there again. And when I loose-lipped the train information to Mona, that church is where she hightailed it to just as fast as she could in order to hand it over. One of the other girls remembered seeing her head out that way and thought it strange enough to mention to me. When I went to check the old church for myself, the signs of the gang having recently been there were everywhere. Fresh foot-prints all over, campfire ashes, empty tin cans and tobacco sacks, cigarette butts. Horse apples from several mounts laying thick in the grass out back...the final pieces that, when all fitted together and capped off by Mona suddenly grabbing a train out of town, painted only one picture and painted it too damn clear for it to be anything else."

"Did you tell all this to Marshal Reed back in Gothenburg?" Lone asked.

Bartles shook his head. "I was too ashamed. When I turned in my badge, I gave him the excuse I was going after the bounty on Hardessy."

"An excuse?" Charley echoed, frowning. "Or are we now gettin' down to the real reason for you showin' up here?"

The question and its tone was finally enough to cause the hangdog in Bartles to bark back some. "I said excuse, and that's what I meant. You damn bet I'm out to put Hardessy in irons again, but it has little to do with the money riding on his head. What's more important to me is trying to balance out at least a small piece of the wrong I did." He glared at Charley, his nostrils flaring. "Now, if you're gonna shoot me or beat me or bring some kind of charge against me, Bourbon, then let's get on with it. Otherwise, get the hell off my back and give me a chance to show that one mistake don't define everything there is to know about a man."

Charley's frown lifted faintly, but he made no reply.

Lone waited a moment before breaking the silence. "Ask me, Charley, anybody who steps forward to not only own his foul-up instead of hidin' it, then also stands ready to try and earn some redemption...well, that might be a fella you ought not be in a hurry to chase away."

Charley's frown appeared to turn somewhat thoughtful, but he still said nothing.

This time it was Bartles who kept the silence from extending very long. "I may have more to offer than just the *want* to try and square myself. If I'm right about a certain thing, then I can provide an edge neither of you have."

"Talkin' in riddles ain't gonna help your cause none," Lone advised. "If you got more to say, spit it out."

"The girl. Mona. She only bought a train ticket as far as Ogallala."

Lone cocked a brow. "And you figure she's still here?"

"I think there's a chance, yeah." Bartles suddenly turned more eager, began gesturing with his hands. "Don't you see? All along, ever since the robbery, everybody has expected the gang to scatter and ride off to some distant place where they'd go to ground for a spell. Yet, every step of the way, one or more of 'em keeps popping up not so far away. First, Rip himself right there still in Gothenburg to dally with Mona. Then Whitey is spotted coming back around. And there was the two other gang members who showed up only as far away as North Platte—where you tangled with 'em, McGantry. And now Mona, who clearly has linked herself with the outfit in some way, suddenly pulls foot but goes no farther than here to Ogallala. Don't it start to make you wonder if maybe the gang never meant to scatter particularly far off at all?"

"Could be the money Rip seems to've stashed before his dally with Mona," said Lone. "Maybe he ain't had the chance to get back to it yet, and that's what's keepin' everybody closer than they would've been otherwise."

A still brooding Charley finally got around to breaking his silence. "Kinda hard to think somebody couldn't have got back to the money by now. Been three days and nights since the hit on the train." His brows pinched tighter together. "Almost sounds more like a trick some old-timers used to pull—After a robbery, instead of scattering wide like everybody expected, just hunker close, practically under the noses of the local law, then sit tight and wait until the big manhunt for 'em mostly cooled down."

"I can see where that might work in a bigger town or a city," allowed Lone. "But it'd be a lot trickier hereabouts."

"Didn't we just get done hearin' how signs showed the gang went unnoticed for a week or so while they were holed up in that abandoned church just outside of Gothenburg?" Charley reminded him.

Lone conceded with a shrug.

Charley cut a hard gaze to Bartles. "Whatever they're up to, what's this 'edge' you claim to have on it that me and Lone are lackin'?"

"Goes back to Mona again," Bartles answered. "Something caused her to all of a sudden leave Gothenburg and come here. If she hadn't done that, she could have lied when I confronted her about passing on the train information and probably have been able to convince me she hadn't—because she's a good liar and because at that point I very much *wanted* to believe she hadn't. But her leaving forced me to do the checking that brought me to the opposite conclusion. The next is speculation, but I'm convinced she left and came here in order to meet up once again with Hardessy. Either directly, or by somebody who'll take her to him."

"You sayin' you think she's gonna join the gang?" said Charley, sounding dubious.

"I'm saying I think she means to join Hardessy in some manner. I don't know exactly what all that might entail. The two of them obviously hit it off. Maybe they're only looking to spend some time together while Rip burns through his share of the bank money." Bartles paused, looking anxious, and gestured for emphasis with both hands. "What I'm trying to get at is, if I'm right and it's not too late to catch Mona still in town, then I think tailing her has a good chance of leading to wherever Hardessy is currently laying low."

Both Charley and Lone had begun to show a heightened interest. They exchanged looks.

"That was my goal in coming here. Hoping I could catch up with Mona, spot her without her seeing me, and then follow her to Hardessy." Bartles paused again, his eyes searching the faces of the two men before him. "Hearing myself say that out loud made it sound even crazier for just one man to try than it did inside my head. But, like I told you at the outset, I'm determined to try and balance things some for the wrong I did.

"That don't mean, though, that I'm so crazy I wouldn't mind having somebody else standing on my side of scale with me. If you fellas shun me for what I did, I guess I'd understand. But that still wouldn't make what I just laid out a bad idea. And the edge I can bring that neither of you can—just in case you're thinking about trying it on your own—is that I know what Mona looks like but you don't."

Lone and Charley exchanged glances again.

"Like I said before...a fella you ought not be in a hurry to chase away," Lone repeated in a low voice.

After a beat, Charley shifted his gaze to Bartles. There was no longer menace showing in his eyes. "This man," he said, jabbing a thumb to indicate Lone, "is generally damn slow to extend his trust. And I'm slower still. But what I do trust is him and his judgment. To the hilt...plus, there's no gettin' around the fact you showed more sand than dust, comin' forward the way you did in spite of your blunder. And the plan you have to try and get at Hardessy through this gal Mona, crazy though it might've been for you alone, don't sound all bad—especially not if me and Lone was to climb on to help you balance that scale...so where do you propose we start lookin' for your double-dealin' soiled dove?"

CHAPTER TWENTY

BETTY MARKESON HAD COME A LONG WAY TOWARD achieving what every girl in her line of work dreamed about, promised themselves, but seldom came close to accomplishing. There was only a limited number of ways to escape once you took up whoring. You could run away from it early on, when you were still young and before it got its claws sunk in you too deep; you could find some sap who didn't know the difference between lust and love willing to marry you (though a union with somebody that dumb wasn't likely to turn into a slice of Heaven); you could work your way up through the ranks and become a madam over a string of other girls; or you could die.

Everybody dies, but a whore's death—the most common way out for countless girls—usually comes early, and often in the ugliest of ways. Sexually spread diseases. Abortion butchery. Drug and alcohol addiction. Murder at the hands of brutal customers...or suicide.

But Betty had beat it all. Well, almost. And it didn't

mean ascending to the role of a madam either, which in her eyes would never rate as being truly *out*.

No, she'd forged her own unique path with clever planning and patience. Another two, two-and-a-half years, she had been figuring, and she would e at her goal. True, she'd be forty by then. But a healthy, vibrant, still attractive forty with the means to live quite nicely, thank you, and quite independent of any expectations or needs save her own.

But now an out-of-the-blue opportunity had shown up to accelerate reaching her goal and Betty was damned if she was going to let it pass by. Even if it meant breaking some old trusts and obligations. She'd made it this far with unfailing persistence and by enduring more than a few betrayals *against* her. A lot could happen in two-and-a-half years, meaning there was always the risk something might push her goal farther out of reach. But if she took the opportunity placed before her right now, then that reach could be drastically shortened and her goal would be in hand almost at once.

Reflecting on all of this, and little else, had occupied Betty's thoughts for the past several days. But now, upon responding to the bell that signaled someone at the rear service entry to her shop and finding Boris Bemis and Sylvester "Slick" Tennebow standing there when she opened the door, the impact of mere thinking and planning now looming as a huge step closer to irreversible action, seemed to momentarily stun her.

"What's the matter, Betty-boo?" Smirked Slick, using a pet name from long, long ago. "You look like somebody stepped on your grave."

"Don't worry, honey," Boris was quick to assure her.

"We're here to see to the graves of Rip Hardessy and some others—and to keep your pretty self out of one for a long time to come."

Quickly regaining her composure, Betty adopted a cool, almost frosty demeanor. "For starters," she said, "let's get straight that no one calls me 'Betty-boo' anymore. Nor am I anybody's 'honey' unless I initiate it. For this piece of business we're about to undertake, it's strictly that—Business. The old days are long gone. As, just to be clear, are any past habits or privileges that used to be part of them."

"Well now," declared Slick. "That's a mighty high-fallutin' attitude comin' from somebody who—"

"Watch it," Betty warned.

"What the hell. You sent for us, remember?" said Boris.

"I remember all too well," Betty replied. "I also remember telling you not to come around in the daytime. You were supposed to be here last night."

"It was a longer ride than we figured. We didn't get in 'til this morning," Slick explained. "Since it's unsure when this thing might pop, we didn't reckon it'd be a good idea to hold off all day. Plus there was the thought of how we'd kill time and not draw over much attention to ourselves. So we decided coming here now was the best option."

"And if you're worried about us not bein' seen here, then maybe you oughta let us the hell in," grumbled Boris.

Though displaying a less than pleased expression, Betty proceeded to do just that. She ushered the pair inside, then led them part way down a short hallway before turning into a medium-sized kitchen/dining room. The fresh-off-the-trail scruffiness of the two men stood out in sharp contrast to Betty herself and the tidy, immaculately clean surroundings. The house that doubled as both Betty's place of business and her residence was a good-sized, two-story Victorian structure. What was originally intended to be the front parlor now served as the shop out of which she sold a variety of scented candles and rare perfumes that were the delight of the town's more upscale ladies. The kitchen and the living quarters for Betty's live-in assistant, an elderly Creole woman named Alifair, were toward the back; Betty's bedroom and private area were on the second floor.

A closely guarded secret within the town, was that a second business—one even more exclusive than the fragrances so enjoyed by certain ladies—operated several nights a week up in Betty's private area. Utilizing the skills she'd learned during her years as a more common working girl, Betty "entertained" on a recurring basis a very select and generous handful of gentlemen (many happening to be husbands to the very women who bought the expensive perfumes to make themselves more alluring to these same men). The delicious irony of the latter provided the greatest pleasure Betty derived from any of it ... Well, along with the money, of course.

Though on the threshold of her fourth decade and having endured some hard treatment early on, it wasn't difficult to see how any red-blooded male would still find Betty very fetching. Full-figured, with alert, sparkling eyes and a classically oval face framed by precisely arranged honey-blonde hair, she was quick to turn heads and hard to look away from. In her public persona as an unmarried businesswoman (widowed after a brief early marriage, she claimed) she wore appropriately modest attire, though her blouses and the bodices of her dresses all seemed to fit rather snugly and the necklines of many of the dresses tended to scoop just low enough to often display an intriguing hint of creamy cleavage.

She was wearing such a dress today, and the eyes of the neither bounty hunter were failing to take appreciative notice. Slick had nevertheless managed to tear his gaze away long enough to make a wider appraisal of things, which led him to say, "These are some mighty fine digs. You surely appear to be doin' right well for yourself, Betty-b...oops, I almost slipped there. Old habits, don't you know. Hard to break."

"Find a way. I already told you about that."

"So what *can* we call you?" Boris wanted to know. Then, gesturing to further indicate the dazzling kitchen as well as the rest of the "digs" Slick had mentioned, he added sarcastically, "Is it 'Countess' or 'Duchess' or some such these days?"

"It's still Betty, you galoot," came the answer, accompanied by a faint, fleeting smile. "It's my name, not a habit that needed to be put behind me."

"Okay. That's good to hear."

Slick nodded. "It's also what's on the sign out front. *Betty's Fine Fragrances & Candles.* Makes me wonder who's minding the store while you're back here with us."

"Not that it's any of your concern, but I have a very capable assistant who is up at the counter now."

"Say now. This really a good enough business to afford you hired help *and* livin' in all this finery...or is there maybe another of your old habits you didn't completely put behind you?"

"That's none of your damn business," Betty snapped. "The only pursuit of mine you need to know or worry about is the matter before us. The reason I sent for you. Namely, me delivering Rip Hardessy and his whole gang into your hands so you two can do your thing and we can then split the accumulated rewards riding on their heads."

"You make all of that sound awful easy," said Slick.

"When something is planned and executed properly, it *can* go easy," Betty countered.

To which Boris replied, "Well, for one thing, in case you didn't know, Rip's whole gang ain't so whole no more. A couple days ago, back North Platte way, two of 'em got cut down."

"I'm aware of that. Cramer and Redsleeve," Betty said. "But the rewards on them were pretty meager to begin with. And now the new rewards just added by the railroad more than make up the difference."

"Do you also know," prodded Boris, "that the fella who beefed Cramer and Redsleeve—a double-tough hombre name of McGantry, used to be an Indian scout but now runs a small horse ranch back to the northeast —has showed up here in town for some reason? In the company, no less, of Charley Bourbon, that nigger US Marshal everybody figured was dead."

"Too damn bad he turned out not to be," muttered Slick. "If I had my 'druthers, it'd be to conduct my business without that darky sniffin' anywhere close by."

"Well the fact he is should pose no interference to what we have going. And same goes for that McGantry person," Betty insisted. "Let them join the local sheriff in chasing their tails with no decent leads to follow. We don't have that problem."

Slick cocked an eyebrow. "You sure seem to be on top of things, I'll give you that."

"Staying well informed and well connected is the only way for a girl like me to keep from getting ground under." Betty regarded the two hard cases with a level stare. "Going back to your previous question, I'll admit that, no, I didn't acquire all you see about you by merely selling perfume and candles. Now let that be the end of that."

Slick chuckled. "You always were a cut above the rest of the pack, Betty. That's what made you so memorable."

"Then figure on me staying in your memories. When we finish this piece of business, you can add one more to the rest."

"Speakin' of this business—let's get back to it." Boris pulled out one of the chairs at the kitchen table and sat down. He let drop to the floor beside him the bedroll and saddlebags that he, like Slick, had carried in with him. "What's this magic wand you're gonna wave that's gonna spread Hardessy and his crew before us like a big ol' feast?"

Betty smiled slyly. "It's not a wand. It's a girl. Rip's girl. One the old fool has evidently fallen for like a ton of bricks. I've been entrusted to watch over her until he's ready. When he sends for her, which should be soon, then she'll lead the way directly to his hideout...and it's there your feast will be waiting."

———

MONA TRENT SANK BACK and down onto one of the rough wooden steps and trembled as alternating waves of shock and revulsion ran through her. She fought to catch her breath, not hyperventilate. Her head spun with a wild dizziness that, if she hadn't leaned against one of the walls of the narrow stairwell for support, might have caused her to spill forward down the remaining steps. Not yet twenty (in years, though vastly more in life experiences) she was supple of body and pretty of face, with full lips and almond eyes that gave her a faintly exotic look. A mane of chestnut hair, only just finger-combed at the moment, tumbled about said face and the simple dressing robe she was wrapped in displayed merely a single shapely leg, thrust out carelessly as she'd dropped back and down onto the step.

What Mona had just overheard from the kitchen area on the other side of the thin stairwell wall—the very one she was now leaning against and through which the conversation in the kitchen was continuing—was a horrendous revelation. Betty Markeson, the woman Mona had been told she could count on as a trusted link to re-joining Rip, had now, by her own words, exposed herself to be nothing short of a traitorous bitch!

Mona had no way of knowing the identities of the two men Betty was talking with. But who they were wasn't necessarily important. *What* they were—clearly bounty hunters, from the sound of it—was a different story.

Human hounds out for blood money. Sicced on by the duplicitous Betty.

Inside her head, Mona re-played some of what she'd overheard.

"The only pursuit of mine you need to know or worry about is the matter before us...namely, me delivering Rip Hardessy and his whole gang into your hands so you two can do your thing and we can then split the accumulated rewards riding on their heads."

"What's this magic wand you're gonna wave that's gonna spread Hardessy and his crew before us like a big ol' feast?"

"It's not a wand. It's a girl. Rip's girl...when he sends for her, which should be soon, then she'll lead the way directly to his hideout..."

There was no mistaking those words. Those dreadful words. It was a setup, a trap, being orchestrated by double-crossing Betty using the two bounty hunters as her snares and Mona as the bait.

Mona groaned inwardly, forcing herself to stay quiet, not make a sound that might be picked up through the thin wall by those on the other side. It was hard to believe that just moments ago she'd been coming down these steps so carefree, on her way to simply get a cup of coffee. Availing herself freely to the kitchen, making herself at home as she'd been encouraged to do, though for the most part staying out of sight in the very comfortable spare room her smiling, ever-so-accommodating hostess had prepared for her. "Any friend of Rip and Whitey certainly deserves all the hospitality I can muster—I owe them plenty from times past," the lying bitch had said.

There'd been no reason to doubt that sentiment because it so closely mirrored comments from Whitey Culp when he arranged for Mona to go to Ogallala and seek out Betty in the first place. She was a friend from way back, he'd explained, who had earned the trust of both himself and Rip.

Some trusted old friend, Mona thought bitterly.

She was starting to get angry now, starting to inwardly surge back from her initial shock over what she'd inadvertently discovered. She realized she needed to try and build on that anger. For her own sake and for the sake of Rip and Whitey and the others, she had to find a way to counter the swerve Betty and her manhunting goons were meaning to pull.

But what should she do? What *could* she do? Mona's mind raced.

She could try fleeing, escaping from Betty. She was pretty sure she could get clear of the house. But then what? She didn't know this town, didn't know anybody else in it. Running to the law was clearly out of the question. And as far as perhaps employing her charms and throwing herself on the mercy of some helpful-looking stranger...what was it Betty had said? *"Staying well informed and well connected is the only way for a girl like me to keep from getting ground under."* No, Mona dared not take the risk of turning to someone only to discover they were one of Betty's "connections."

Besides, Mona running away would do little to help Rip or Whitey. Whoever they sent to take her to reunite with Rip at his hideout could be apprehended by Betty's bounty hunters and forced to talk, to still lead *them* to the hideout, with or without Mona, where they could go ahead and spring their ambush. And since Mona happened to know that most of the Wanted posters on the gang members were *Dead or Alive*, she had little doubt the ambushers would put much effort into settling for captives.

Mona stifled another groan.

She needed time to think, to plan. To come up with something not too desperate or reckless.

Time was one of the things she had working in her favor. Since it wasn't likely Rip would send anyone for her until after cover of darkness, that gave her at least the rest of the day to try and hit on something. Her mouth twisted wryly at an ironic thought. Up to now she'd been anxious for the hours and minutes to race by, impatiently wanting to reach the point when someone would show up to take her to Rip. Now she prayed for all of that to slow down and give her time to have something figured out before then.

She suddenly thought of the money—the take from the bank robbery she was holding for Rip. The share of it due him was what they were planning to use for going away and starting a new life together. Far away. Montana or Idaho, maybe as far as California...but, given this drastic change in circumstances, maybe there was a different way to use the money, sacrifice it for the greater good. That much currency could certainly buy a great deal and wasn't the old saying that everybody has a price? Might it be possible for her to be able to buy-off Betty's bounty hunters and get them to turn on her instead?

Mona shook her head violently, dismissing such a notion as madness. What was she thinking? What would keep greedy, bottom-feeding scum like that pair gave every impression of being from gladly accepting her offer and then still proceeding with their planned ambush of the gang in order to gain the reward money, too? Absolutely nothing, that was what.

Mona shook her head again, silently cursing herself

for having such a hair-brained idea. She'd have to think a hell of a lot smarter than that if she hoped to have any chance of forming some kind of workable plan to turn the tables on Betty and her wolves.

The only other thing Mona had in her favor was that the trio had no idea she'd become aware of what they were up to. She had to keep it that way and combine it with the time she had to come up with something. There had to be a way.

For the time being, she decided, the best thing for her to do was get out of the stuffy stairwell and away from the drone of those hated voices on the other side of the wall. It didn't sound like there was anything more to learn from them, and the longer she stayed cramped and half-panicked with only the flimsy barrier between them, the more risk they might somehow sense her presence. Betty's manhunters might have instincts along those lines. Mona had heard of such.

She turned slowly and began creeping carefully back up the stairs. She wanted to return to her room where she could take in deep breaths, calm herself, clear her head. Then start thinking all over again. Fresh. Pondering hard—all different possibilities from all different angles.

There had to be a way.

CHAPTER TWENTY-ONE

THE SEARCH FOR MONA TRENT BY LONE, CHARLEY, AND Jack Bartles didn't get started right away. First, at Lone's insistence, they made a brief detour to Dutch Kroeger's livery to check on the lad Oscar. Lone wanted to make sure his stitch job from last night was holding up okay and there were no signs of infection that might require Oscar to still see a doctor. Thankfully, everything seemed okay. The lad appeared in good spirits. He said he'd awakened with a slight headache that morning, but it quickly went away.

When Oscar left any further conversation to get on with his chores, Lone asked Dutch if there'd been any issue with the boy's mother perhaps being upset about the injury to her son while in Dutch's employ.

The livery man gave a disgusted snort by way of an answer. "That pathetic old hag. By the time Oscar got home after he took supper with us, she was too drunked up and doped up to even notice the cut on his head. Instead of receiving any motherly care or concern, he ended up having to help *her* to bed." Dutch spat into the dust. "Too bad she don't stumble and fall from drunkenness some time and split her skull wide open. Be the best thing ever to happen to the kid."

Not wanting to get into that any farther, Lone told Dutch he'd be seeing him around and then, along with Charley and Jack, took his leave.

From there, this time at Charley's request, the three made one more detour before commencing their search. Perhaps nudged by the talk of Oscar's wound possibly needing a doctor's follow-up, the marshal wanted to hear the latest report by Dr. Frake—who surely must by now be back from his out-of-town call, he reasoned—on Hank Wordell's condition. Mrs. Frake's earlier assessment had been reassuring but, with all due respect to her capabilities, Charley hoped to hear something more detailed from the doc himself.

What was more, Charley stated, after seeing the doctor he reckoned it was only right for them to also take care of another matter—and that was to advise Sheriff Needles of the development concerning Mona before the three of them went too far strictly on their own. "After all, it *is* his town," he explained. "And, in his place, I know it'd make me mighty hot to have three outsiders come in and start pokin' around without the courtesy of lettin' me know what was goin' on. Plus, to give the pompous turd his due, it appears he runs a pretty tight ship around here. If him and his deputies were to pitch in and this Mona gal is still in town, then findin' her oughta go that much quicker."

As it so happened, the need for putting any extra effort into seeking out the sheriff became unnecessary. He was already present at Dr. Frake's house when they got there. Upon entering the reception area at the front, they found both Needles and Alma Frake there to greet them. Each was wearing a somber expression.

Fearing the worst, Charley was quick to ask, "What's wrong? Is Hank okay?"

"He's as he was. Stable. No change," Mrs. Frake replied, though somewhat distantly.

"Is the doc in there with him now?" Charley wanted to know.

It was Needles who answered. "No. Unfortunately, Dr. Frake isn't here at all. Mrs. Frake has been expressing her concern to me over that very thing."

"It's simply been too long," Mrs. Frake said, anguish in her eyes as well as in her tone. "No matter how serious the situation out at the McSwains, if Maxwell was unable to leave I can't believe he wouldn't have sent word somehow—via Laurie again, or somebody—to advise me what was happening. He knows he has the young marshal here to monitor, not to mention patient appointments already scheduled and other needs bound to pop up unexpectedly."

"Sounds to me like somebody oughta be ridin' out to the McSwains and makin' a check," said Charley.

"I concur," Needles replied. "A short time ago I sent Deputy Lissom to saddle up and make a trip out there."

"I hope I'm not overreacting and stirring up things unnecessarily," Mrs. Frake said, wringing her hands. "But it's just so unlike Maxwell, I can't help but think there must be something wrong."

She had barely expressed this before her worries were proven to be thoroughly warranted. From outside there suddenly came the clatter of rapidly approaching hoofbeats accompanied by the rumble and creak of a wagon.

Stepping quickly to look out the window, Needles announced over his shoulder, "It's my deputy, Lissom. And it appears like—I believe that's the McSwains he has with him. But they can't possibly be back from the ranch already."

Everyone poured anxiously out of the Frake house. A hurriedly dismounted Deputy Lissom came forward to meet them. "It's Liam and Estelle McSwain, Sheriff," he reported a bit breathlessly, swinging his arm to indicate a middle-aged couple sitting on the seat of a buckboard that had rolled up in a cloud of dust behind him. The pair looked harried, disheveled, and the woman had clearly been weeping. "I ran into them just as I was getting ready to ride out. They were on their way in to find you!"

"Where's my husband?" Alma Frake said in a hushed voice, placing a hand to her throat.

"It's a bad deal, a bad situation, Sheriff," blurted Liam McSwain from the buckboard seat. "Me and the wife been at wit's end. We held off as long as we could. Maybe too long. But we finally had to come forward— our daughter and the doc are in deep trouble."

"They have them both! Those evil, filthy men took them away!" wailed his wife.

Over the next handful of minutes, in an exchange of questions and often frantic bursts of answers and explanations, the full story spilled out. How two armed men had shown up at the McSwain house and, holding guns to the heads of Liam and Estelle, forced Laurie to go into town and bring back the doctor with the fabricated story of a serious injury to her father. Then, once she had returned with Frake, the gunmen left with both the doctor *and* the girl, using the latter as a hostage to buy silence and a continuing facade from the parents under threat of never seeing their daughter alive again if they didn't cooperate.

"They said that, come daybreak, they'd release her unharmed if they saw nobody was following 'em," husked a hollow-eyed Liam. "But all through the black night, the truth—the realization—grew in us. Those vermin couldn't be trusted. If they didn't kill her right off...or worse..."

"Don't say it!" Estelle's voice was sharp, almost strident. "A body can't help what runs through the mind, but don't say it out loud."

Looking at the sheriff with pleading eyes, Liam said, "We've become convinced her only chance—*our* only chance of ever seeing her again—is to try and find her. I got no skills to go after men like that, not alone. I need help. I'm begging."

"Of course we'll help. We'll do everything we can," Needles told him.

"What about my husband?" Alma Frake asked.

"Naturally he'll be included in our search and recovery efforts," she was quickly assured by the sheriff.

"From the description of one of the hardcases havin' silver gray hair but not bein' an elderly man—that's got to be our pal Whitey Culp, who's been a mighty busy fella lately," stated Charley.

Needles scowled. "What's that supposed to mean?"

"I'll explain more about that in a minute."

"So who's Whitey Culp?" asked Liam McSwain.

"He's second in command to Rip Hardessy."

"The escaped outlaw?"

"None other. So him headin' up this elaborate operation to fetch a doctor," mused Charley, "suggests to me something mighty important."

"More like the reason for goin' to so much trouble meanin' *somebody* mighty important," amended Lone.

Charley nodded. "Exactly."

"Quit talking in blasted riddles," growled Needles. "What are you two getting at?"

"Standard practice for any outlaw gang, and I know from past examples it's been followed by Hardessy's bunch," explained Charley, "is for the whole pack never to be bogged down or put at risk for the sake of one hurt or wounded member not able to keep up. Yet it seems clear that the reason Whitey, and whoever the other hombre with him was, must've did what they done was so Doc Frake could tend to one of their crew."

"And the only one who'd rate that kind of special treatment," said Needles, starting to get the picture, "would be Rip Hardessy himself."

"Scalds out to that as the likeliest thing, I'd say." Charley's eyes narrowed. "Could be one of the shots Hank got off put a slug in Rip. Or, from the squallin' I heard the outlaw boss do after that oversized track explosion—before I myself blacked all the way out from same—the blast might've busted him up pretty bad."

"No matter exactly why, the fact his men came here to get him a doctor indicates he must be relatively close." There was a growing enthusiasm, even an eagerness, in Needles' voice.

"So what does that change? What does it mean as far as the fate of my husband?" questioned Alma.

"It just might be to his benefit," answered Lone. "If Rip is hurt bad enough to make 'em decide on fetchin' a doctor in the first place, then it must be something more serious than can be fixed with some quick patchin'. If it takes awhile, then that means they gotta keep the doc healthy enough to do what needs doin'."

There was a moment of heavy, tense silence.

Until Liam broke it, saying, "But that don't do our daughter no good, does it? Never mind how they treat the doc, if their promise to let Laurie go was a big lie from the start, then—"

"No!" Alma cut him short. "If it came to that, Maxwell would never continue to cooperate with those villains. No matter what they did or threatened to do to him, he would hold fast to ensure the girl stayed safe as long as he did. My husband may not be a strong man physically, but for something like that I assure he would not bend!"

She delivered these words with such intensity and conviction that it made believers out of all who heard them.

"Bless you for that. It renews some hope in us," said Estelle McSwain.

"But now is the time to do more than hope," declared Sheriff Needles. "We need to form a posse and take immediate action on these new developments! Lissom, spread the word. I want twenty men deputized, armed, mounted and ready to ride in an hour!"

"That'd be just about the worst thing you can do," said Lone, the sharpness in his tone halting Lissom as he turned to re-mount.

"Why do you say that? And what business is it of yours anyway?" Needles demanded. "I certainly don't need *you* in any posse of mine."

"And I ain't askin' to be," Lone snapped back. "I want no part of such a foolhardy undertakin'."

"What's so foolhardy about it?"

"Didn't you hear McSwain say how Whitey warned against anybody followin'? Maybe he was lyin', maybe not. And maybe, since it's been fifteen or so hours, it don't matter much either way. But if you go gallopin' around out there with twenty riders, pokin' and hopin' for some kind of sign to pop up, you stand the chance of raisin' enough dust to be spotted even if they're only halfway lookin'. You think that's gonna do those captives any good?"

"And I suppose you have a better idea?" Needles sneered.

"I do. A single rider, a good tracker who could pick up the trail of those four from where they left the McSwain place. Knowin' how to read sign, he could move fast, make steady progress closin' in on wherever they were headed. And because it'd be just one man, he'd have a better chance of makin' it without bein' spotted himself."

"And I suppose that lone man—appropriately called —would be you?"

Lone set his jaw. "I'm one of the best scouts and trackers west of the Missouri. No brag, just fact... Charley?"

"He's tellin' it straight, Needles," Charley promptly responded. "If anything, he's bein' modest. Back when, he was known to spend days and weeks on end in the heart of hostile Indian Territory and, as you can see, came out with all his hair. What's more, I think he's right about this bein' a job best suited for one man. The right man that is, like him. If we was goin' in to smash the whole gang, then a well-armed posse might be the thing for that. But a chance to first get the doc and the girl out safe—that makes it different."

Indecision clawed at the expression on Needles' face. "And what are the rest of us supposed to be doing? Just wait here twiddling our thumbs?"

"Wait and be ready," Charley told him. "If Lone has any luck, *then* we follow up with full force."

"Somebody better make up somebody's mind," Lone said. "I could be halfway to the McSwain spread by now."

"There's something else," Charley said, pinning Needles with a direct gaze. "Bartles here"—a nod toward Jack—"has come forward with a related matter, an important one, that needs pursuin' right here in town. We can be workin' on that in the meantime. But first, let's turn Lone loose. Give him a chance to see what he can do."

"All right, damn it," Needles finally relented. "Go ahead, McGantry. Go! Don't lose any more time."

CHAPTER TWENTY-TWO

"SO IT'S DECIDED THEN," WHITEY CULP WAS SAYING. "The kid is goin' into town alone to fetch the money and the girl Mona. Bein' the youngest and having ridden with us the shortest time, Darrold's mug is the least likely to be recognized. And that's important on account of he's gonna have to ask some directions for findin' Betty's place, where the girl is waitin'."

The sun was near its noon peak overhead, beating down hard and hot out of a cloudless sky onto the rocky slope and slice of ledge just to one side of the cave entrance. Gathered there along with Whitey, grouped loosely around him, were Darrold Memford, River McIvey, and Terence Posey. Rip was inside the cave, lulled by the latest dose of laudanum he'd been given. The doctor and the McSwain girl were in there too, resting after their long night's ordeal.

At the mention of Betty Markeson, a lewd grin split Posey's face and he remarked, "Hey now. How about bringing Betty back, too, while the kid is at it?"

"Betty's got her own thing goin' nowadays, and it

don't have room for pawin' from any of us," Whitey answered sternly. "She's stickin' her neck out, for old times' sake, to lend a hand with this piece of business. But that's the extent of it."

"She never stood for no pawin' from the likes of you anyway, Posey," grumbled McIvey, with a slur indicating he'd been pretty heavily into the redeye already that morning.

"No. But she sure as hell *laid down* for plenty of it," Posey came back, cackling nastily.

"That's a stinkin' lie. She'd've sooner lain with a snake—she told me so her own self."

Posey hooted. "Now we're in agreement." Cupping his crotch, he added, "And I got the snake right here that ol' Betty-boo couldn't hardly get enough of!"

McIvey took a lurching step toward him. "You vulgar pig!"

Whitey wedged himself between them, planting a palm on each man's chest and spreading his arms, shoving the two apart. "Knock this shit off!" he barked. "What the hell's wrong with you fools? Don't you understand the seriousness of what we're facin' here?"

"I do," said McIvey, panting. "And I also understand that the main reason for it is this fumble-fingered so-called dynamite man"—thrusting a hand angrily toward Posey—"who must've been thinkin' about playin' with his pecker instead of dynamite sticks when he set the blast that killed my nephew and now is fixin' to do for Rip too!"

"That's a crock! Get off my back, you whiskey-soaked old bastard," Posey protested. "Clevis died from a bullet, had nothing to do with the explosion. And I keep telling all of you that the reason that blast went off so strong had to be because of something more inside the freight car—blasting powder or some damn thing—making a secondary explosion on top of mine. No way the charge I set would've done so much damage."

"Excuses!" spat McIvey. "You ain't even man enough to admit your blunders, you coward. Blunders that have done more damage to our gang than all the stinkin' law dogs in three states ever managed to do!"

"That's enough! I said knock it off and I meant it!" shouted Whitey, struggling to shove the pair even farther apart. A closer study of McIvey—his filmy, enraged eyes and the powerful stench of whiskey on his breath—gave Whitey increased cause for concern. This had been building ever since the death of the older man's nephew Clevis. It seemed like Rip had managed to quell it for a while; but now, evidently re-ignited by the gang leader's worsening condition and fueled by whiskey for breakfast, McIvey appeared hell bent on bringing it to a head.

And Posey, who previously had been trying to stay out of the aggrieved man's way and give him a chance to simmer down, suddenly picked now to decide he'd had enough.

"To hell with this!" the dynamite man exclaimed. "I've been holding a lot of stuff in and I'm damned sick of it. I've had it! You wanna talk blunders? If nobody else wants to say it, I will! Most of the blunders—one after another—that have brought us to this point can be laid at the feet of one man. And it ain't me!"

Sensing where he was headed, Whitey rasped, "Best be careful what next comes out of that mouth of yours."

"To hell with you too, Whitey. I ain't scared of you.

And that reaction shows you know exactly who I'm talkin' about."

"I'm warnin' you."

Posey jerked away from Whitey's hand still pressed against his chest and took a step back. His defiant glare swept over all three of the men now before him. "Sure, there was a time when Rip was a good man to ride behind. He planned out some prime jobs and made all of us fat cuts of money that we had some high times with. But then his luck started to turn sour, and ours along with it. He did that hitch in the Laramie pen and, out of loyalty, we scrimped and clawed and bribed until we was able to bust him out."

"And he led us straight back to more prime jobs, you ungrateful pup," snarled McIvey.

"Did he really?" Posey challenged. "I fail to remember 'em bein' all that prime. It was a string of nickel and dime hits that kept us hungry and tired and almost constantly on the run with payouts that barely stretched from one job to the next. That Gothenburg bank was finally a good take, but where's the payoff? You seen any of it, River, you old souse? You, kid?"

Whitey's eyes had become narrowed to dangerous slits. "Darrold's on his way to go get that money right now. Don't you hear so good? Didn't I just get done layin' out the goddamn plan?"

"Yeah, you laid out *a* plan," said Posey. "But who's to say it's gonna pan out? Does anybody really think that whore is gonna to be waiting where she's supposed to be and ready to hand over the money? There's further proof of how far Rip has backslid on all of us. Bad enough he got his sorry ass thrown in the clink *again* and we had to scramble to rescue him off that train. But, to make it worse, instead of stashing the bank money before he stopped off to do some diddlin'—like we was all led to believe he did—now we find out he left it with the whore he got caught pokin'. Is that smart thinkin' for somebody supposed to be *leading* us? But what does he care? He's layin' in there dyin' and the rest of us chumps are stuck holdin' an empty bag."

"Whitey!" McIvey wailed. "You gonna let him talk like that? You gonna let him run down Rip that way?"

Whitey answered without ever taking his eyes off Posey. "No, I've heard enough...Posey, you got two choices. You can shut up, pack up, and ride away from here alive. Or, if you figure on runnin' your mouth some more, then you better be ready to back it up with that smoke wagon on your hip."

"Sure, I'll go. Happy to get shed of this snakebit outfit," Posey replied. "But on the one in a million chance the kid *does* come back with that bank money, I'm owed a cut. I deserve that much, to at least be allowed to wait and find out."

"Hell with that!" howled McIvey. "The only deserves that cur has got comin' is for killin' Clevis and stovin' in Rip! Let me settle up with him once and for good!"

So saying, the older man clawed for his gun while at the same time trying to shove clear of Whitey. The latter fought to restrain him, however, curling his fingers to clutch a fistful of shirtfront and hold him in place. "No, dammit! You can't beat him and he ain't worth—"

That moment's struggle between the two men gave Posey all the opening he needed. No slouch at gun work, he'd have easily outdrawn McIvey if a one-on-one against him had gone ahead and played out. Whitey's lightning speed, though, was another matter. Facing him straight up, Posey would have stood no chance. Now, however, with Whitey allowing himself to be diverted, everything changed. And the Colt suddenly appearing in Posey's fist made it clear he hadn't missed taking advantage of the opportunity.

"Freeze, the both of you!" he ordered Whitey and McIvey. "And keep those hands high and empty."

Young Darrold, who had been silently standing by, watching with a bug-eyed look of growing concern, now blurted out, "Jesus God, fellas! What are you doing— stop this from getting any more out of hand!"

"Shut up," Posey told him. "If you were so worried about things gettin' out of hand, then you should've done something to rein in this old mossy-horn River these past days while he's been givin' me the stink eye and turnin' all of you against me for something that wasn't my fault. I got burned and battered out of that explosion, too, in case everybody forgot."

"Too bad you didn't fry to a crisp!" snarled McIvey.

"Better keep that old bastard's mouth shut, Whitey," warned Posey, "or he's gonna be a dead man."

"You're on your way to bein' a dead man yourself, if you ain't figured it out yet," Whitey responded flatly. "Even with a gun already in hand, you can't cut down all three of us before one of us plants some return lead in you."

"Nobody has to end up toes down over this. I'll go into town with the kid. If the money's there, I'll take my split and you'll never see me again. If it ain't, like I figure it won't be...well, same thing."

"After the turn you just took, we're supposed to trust you'll be satisfied with *only* your cut of the money?" Whitey wagged his head slowly, once to each side.

"Either way, you've said and done some things here I don't think I can let you just walk away from."

"You was willin' a minute ago."

"That was before you pulled a gun on me."

"Damn it, the old man forced my hand. What was I supposed to do?" protested Posey.

"Anything but turn traitor on your own, you sonofabitch!"

This declaration, issued in a harsh, raspy voice, came from the mouth of the cave. All eyes swung in that direction and locked on the startling sight of Rip Hardessy standing there. Or, rather, leaning there—propped shakily against the ragged edge of the opening, pale and hollow-eyed, with his shirt hanging open to reveal portions of purple bruising that showed around the edges of the thick wrap encircling his torso. His trembling right arm was raised, fist gripping a long-barreled Remington revolver aimed straight at Posey.

"Rip! No!" gasped the dynamite man.

Though the Remington's muzzle wavered faintly at the end of the weak, extended arm, the stare of the fevered eyes above it stabbed into their target with steel steadiness.

In desperation, Posey twisted at the waist and swung his gun arm, re-aligning his aim on Rip. Both men fired, nearly in unison.

Rip's slug tore through the trapezius muscle just above Posey's left collarbone, spinning Posey ninety degrees around and tangling his feet so that he staggered and dropped to his knees.

Posey's bullet skimmed along the rocky edge of the cave opening, barely an inch from Rip's face, splattering stony splinters as it ricocheted off in a fading whine.

The shrapnel gouging into his cheek and ear caused Rip to jerk away so sharply that his unsteady legs weren't up to the sudden shift of his weight. They buckled and spilled him to the ground.

Seeing this, McIvey cried "Rip!" and broke away from Whitey to rush toward the fallen gang leader.

Despite his own concern for Rip, Whitey knew he couldn't afford to take his attention off the still alive and dangerous Posey. His Colt filled his fist while the reports of the two guns were still shattering the air and he instantly leveled it on Posey. He triggered a shot of his own, but it was too hurried and the round cut half a foot above the dynamite man as he was dropping down.

This caused Posey to pitch himself tighter to the ground. In so doing—either purposely or inadvertently, Whitey couldn't be sure which—he flailed so frantically with his free hand that he unbalanced Darrold, who'd been standing too close to get out of the way, and dragged him down too. The kid sprawled momentarily on top of Posey, preventing Whitey from triggering another shot for fear of hitting Darrold.

But Posey had no such restraint—not as soon as he could get his gun hand thrust out from under his squirming, cussing shield. Whitey saw what he was attempting, though, and had time to react. He also pitched himself to the ground and this time it was Posey's bullet that sliced the air above him. What was more, in order to get off that shot, it had been necessary for Posey to expose more of himself than just his gun hand.

Whitey didn't hesitate to take advantage of that exposure. Lying flat on his stomach, Colt extended straight out ahead, he triggered two rapid rounds. Both of them slammed into the shoulder of Posey's gun arm. He screamed and jerked back, trying to roll away. He arched his back and kicked and shoved to dislodge the weight of Darrold, who was doing his own struggling to accomplish the same. When the kid finally toppled free, Posey twisted around and tried desperately to drag himself over to where his gun had skittered when the bullets drilled into him. He was reaching for it with his left hand due to his right being disabled from the damage to his shoulder.

Whitey pushed smoothly to his feet and, just as Posey's hand was closing around the gun, he took a long step forward and pinned both to the ground under his boot. Posey slowly cocked his head back and gazed up, his expression a mix of fear and torment. In a husky voice, he said, "I'm sorry it came to this, Whitey...I -I just felt cornered."

The eyes and the bore of the Colt barrel staring back down at him all nothing but cold, black, lifeless holes. "Sorry don't cut it," Whitey responded in a flat tone. Then he pressed the muzzle of his Colt to the middle of Posey's forehead and pulled the trigger.

Looking on, Darrold gave a startled jerk when the gun went off and then his mouth gaped, aghast. "My God," he said under his breath.

"God gave up on the likes of us a long time ago, kid. Get used to it." Holstering his gun, Whitey then made a casual gesture with his hand and added, "Roll this piece of shit over the side while I go check on Rip."

"We ain't even gonna bury him?"

Over his shoulder, as he headed toward the cave mouth, Whitey said, "He ain't worth breakin' a sweat. Let the coyotes and worms have him. Now do like I say and then get ready to ride. You still got that trip to Ogallala to make."

Leaning over McIvey where he was knelt beside Rip, Whitey asked, "Is he all right?"

"That's a dumb question. I wasn't all right to begin with," Rip answered for himself, mouth curving in a wry grin.

"Some rock chips chawed into the side of his face. Nothing serious," McIvey said. "He lost his balance and fell when he jerked away."

"Pins are awful wobbly," Rip admitted. "Took all the strength I had but, when I heard what that mealy-mouthed backstabber was sayin', I was determined to come out and 'front the lowdown bastard myself."

"Well, his mealy mouth is now shut permanent-like," Whitey assured him. "So let's get you up and back in to your bedroll...where the hell's that doctor anyway?"

"That's a good question," McIvey said sourly. "When the arguin' and shootin' started up, him and the girl must've saw it as a prime chance to bolt. So that's what they did—they're gone!"

CHAPTER TWENTY-THREE

AT THE MCSWAIN PLACE, LONE HAD NO TROUBLE PICKING up the trail of four horses leading off to the northwest. He recognized the markings of two that had recently ridden in from town—that would be Laurie McSwain fetching in Dr. Frake—and then those same two accompanied by two others, who must have been Whitey Culp and an unknown accomplice, riding away.

By the spread of the hoof prints, they appeared to have proceeded at a steady but moderate pace. The lead animal, likely belonging to Whitey, had a slightly crooked shoe on its left rear foot. The prints of one of the middle horses made shallower indentations that matched one of the sets that had come in from town, meaning it carried a lighter rider, the girl Laurie. The remaining two sets of prints had no particular distinction.

It was quickly evident that Whitey was making little or no attempt to mask their trail. The captors seemed confident that having hostages, combined with the warning given Liam and Estelle McSwain about what would happen to their daughter if pursuit came too suddenly, would buy them plenty of time. Plus, over the miles of rolling, grassy, treeless terrain that comprised the southern reaches of the Sandhills, there wasn't a hell of a lot trail masking tricks one could employ. And the tall, thick spring grass, given a few hours to straighten back up after the passage of only a few hooves, made quite an effective cover all on its own.

But not such a thorough one that the trained eyes of Lone McGantry couldn't still discern plenty of telltale signs. Especially when those he was tracking were, at least so far, locked on an unwavering angle to the west and north.

The miles fell away and the morning expired under a high, hot sun in a cloudless sky. The air hung still and heavy with heat. As usual, Ironsides plodded tirelessly at the pace Lone was holding him to.

They reached the north branch of the Platte River shortly past noon. It was running a bit high from recent rain and a touch of late snow melt out of the Laramie Mountains farther west. But, at the same fording point used earlier by their quarry, Lone and Ironsides crossed with ease. Once on the other side, Lone decided a short break was warranted. In the shade of a couple leafy cottonwood trees, he loosened the cinch of the big gray's saddle to let him breathe and cool before drinking from the river and then munching some of the rich green grass along the bank. Lone himself took the opportunity to lean back against one of the cottonwood trunks, legs splayed out wide, and eat some brief jerky washed down by canteen water.

Back in the saddle and back on the trail again, Lone saw that the angle of the sign he was following began to flatten out some and head more due east. If the speculation he and Charley had pieced together was anywhere close to being accurate—that Rip Hardessy himself was the injured gang member Dr. Frake was being forcefully taken to see—then that meant the fugitive outlaw (and presumably the rest of the gang) had to be holed up somewhere relatively close by. Figure not more than a day's ride. That would also fit with Mona Trent relocating to Ogallala to seemingly be in nearer proximity.

But, as he rode on, the thing that gnawed at Lone more and more was the question of *Where?* Where hereabouts was a likely spot, a hideout, in which Rip and his gang could be laying low? Nobody knew the area better than Lone and he was damned if he could think of a place that might effectively serve that purpose. The farther west you went, the land became increasingly more broken. That was out considerably more than a day's ride, though. In between, it was little else but rolling, grassy, empty hills stretching in every direction. Yeah, there were a few sections of sizable rock outcrops and some deep, washed-out arroyos. But nothing—at least nothing that came to Lone's mind—he'd call truly suitable for a group of men to hole up in for any length of time.

Remembering how the gang had evidently gone unnoticed for several days in an abandoned church on the outskirts of Gothenburg, Lone was beginning to think that this new hiding place of theirs might be more along those lines. Not some remote place created by nature, but perhaps a remote remnant of man. An abandoned homestead maybe ... Or, certainly not out of the question, an outlying small ranch or farm simply over-taken by the gang and claimed for their use as long as they saw fit. In such a case, what that might have meant for anyone already present when the gang descended on them was something Lone didn't want to ponder at any length.

The former scout was still grinding on all of this when, not very long after leaving the river, he spotted three riders approaching from the north. Inasmuch as it was all cattle range through here, confirmed by the sporadic clusters of beef on the hoof he'd been seeing all morning, Lone suspected the trio would turn out to be wranglers who rode for some local brand. Just in case, though, as he slowed Ironsides to await them, he slipped the keeper thong off the Colt holstered on his hip.

"Afternoon, gents," Lone drawled when the horsemen got close enough to draw rein.

"Back at ya," said the hombre riding at the center. He was of average height, stocky build, with an open, sun- and wind-burned face whose plain features fell just short of what anybody would call handsome. As Lone had guessed, he, like his two companions, was decked out in standard, well worn wrangler garb. On his left, slouched so comfortably in his saddle it looked like he was born to it, was a lanky, heavily whiskered number with sleepy eyes and a half-smoked cigarette dangling from his lower lip. On the other side was a wiry old timer with a tangled gray beard, lumpy unpeeled potato for a nose, and coal chip eyes darting busily between a bracket of deep crow's feet.

"My name's Hagen. I'm ramrod for the Lazy T," said the stocky man. "In case you didn't know, this is Lazy T range you're on."

"No, I didn't know," Lone told him. "Not by any particular name that is. I've spotted some cattle here and there, so clearly I knew I was on somebody's range. Didn't see no harm in just passin' through, though."

"That's true enough, long as passin' through is all you're doing," Hagen allowed. "You got no other business hereabouts then?"

Lone took a minute to consider the question. Moreover, he considered the old timer, the gray beard. Something about him seemed familiar.

While Lone was studying the old timer, he was studying back. He reached his conclusion first and spoke up when he did. "Say. Ain't you Lone McGantry?"

"Guilty as charged," Lone replied, grinning as recognition set in for him also. "BillyBob Whipple, you ol' rascal. Kinda far away from the buffalo grounds, ain't you?"

"Ain't no more buffalo grounds. Leastways not none with any buff left on 'em. Ain't been for years," BillyBob grunted. "And if you don't blame well know that, then maybe you ain't the sharp-eyed feller I took you for."

"Reckon my eyes might not be *quite* as sharp as they used to be, but I'm still McGantry," Lone assured him, still grinning. "And if you didn't have that mug of yours buried in so much fur, I'd've recognized you sooner."

"For God's sake, don't say nothing to talk him outta that face fur," said the lanky one dryly. "It'd mean the rest of us in our outfit'd have to look at that bare, shriveled prune mug over chow every day."

BillyBob grunted again. "If the rest of you cow

chasers ever saw these bee-yoo-tiful features of mine all the way uncovered, you'd cut them scrawny turkey neck throats of yours out of pure envy."

Hagen gave Lone a baleful look. "See what I have to put up with on a regular basis?"

"I think I got a pretty good idea."

The ramrod leaned forward and rested a forearm atop his saddle horn. "I take it you and BillyBob have had some past dealings?"

"Indeed we have."

BillyBob, as was his way, saw fit to elaborate more. "One mean winter down Kansas way, me'n McGantry shared takin' care of some Army boyos outta Fort Kennesaw. I hunted buff to feed their bellies and provide woolly hide blankets so's they didn't freeze their asses off, Lone scouted for 'em and kept the patrols from losin' their way in the snow. We made quite a team."

"For the sake of the rest of us who're havin' to put up with him these days," said the lanky cowpoke, "too bad you didn't lose this old windbag in a snowdrift somewhere down there."

Lone's grin stretched a little wider at this ongoing friendly banter.

"Never mind Felton," BillyBob countered, "he's just jealous because, after there wasn't no more woolies for me to bag, I roamed up this way and started teachin' some new cow pushin' tricks to rope twirlers like him who thunk they already knew everything there was to know."

"Jesus God," groaned Felton with a pleading look toward Lone. "Did he really shoot all those buffs down through Kansas and such, or did they start committin' suicide when they kept hearin' that godawful twangy voice of his dronin' on constantly across the prairie?"

Before Lone could answer, Hagen said, "Enough, you two. My ears are starting to ache from listening to you. Suspect McGantry's are too. Plus, we still got strays to round up and—now that we've established McGantry is an old friend of BillyBob's and not some lurkin' rustler—I expect he also wants to get on with his passin' through."

But putting the banter aside still didn't mean BillyBob was done talking. "Where is it you're headed, Lone boyo?" he wanted to know. "You still on the drift these days? Seems like I heard something about you finally settlin' down back North Platte way."

"I keep tryin'," Lone said, mouth quirking ruefully. "Got me a little horse ranch I'm just gettin' off the ground. But one thing or other keeps poppin' up to drag me away."

"So what's brung you to our neck of the woods ain't of your own choosin'?"

Lone took a minute to consider how he should answer. Under different circumstances, he likely would have been a bit cagey. But knowing BillyBob and particularly knowing how he always maintained a sharp awareness of his surroundings—something that could prove mighty useful right about now—Lone decided to tell it straight.

He started off by saying, "Reckon you fellas have heard the name Rip Hardessy. Right?"

Hagen's brows pinched together. "The outlaw? Latest being how he escaped custody from a couple of US Marshals a short time back when his gang blew the tracks under the train they was haulin' him on?"

"That's the hombre. Guess it's like they say—bad news travels fast."

"We mainly know," Hagen explained, "on account of some suspicion his gang took off in this general direction. That brought a posse out of Ogallala tramplin' through here a couple days ago, looking to catch up with 'em but havin' no luck."

"What interest you got, Lone, in plumb dangerous critters like Hardessy and his pack?" said BillyBob. "You doin' some bounty huntin?"

Lone shook his head. "Not quite. I *am* workin' with a US Marshal, though. Fella named Charley Bourbon, one of the lawmen who was on the train that Hardessy escaped from. You can understand how that's given him a personal stake in wantin' to run Hardessy back down. Long story short, me and him Charley did some business together in the past and I happened to be close enough by again this time around for me to pitch in with him once more. That's what brings me around now, tryin' my luck on the trail of those owlhoots."

"That's an awful cold trail by now." Hagen frowned. "Even if you're able to stick with it, that bunch is likely clear into Wyoming—hell, maybe even Montana—by this point."

"Could be," Lone allowed. "But there's been a couple recent developments that sorta hint maybe the gang never meant to run all that far before goin' to ground. That's what I'm checkin' out. The possibility they might be hunkered in somewhere closer."

Hagen's frown deepened. "Hard pressed to think of anywhere suitable for that. Not close anyway. Couple days farther west maybe. The land starts getting pretty ragged out that way."

"Yeah, I been frettin' the same. But the other thing I—"

BillyBob cut Lone short, saying, "'Cept maybe for the Spillin's."

The other three all looked at him in puzzlement.

"That chunk of broken land closer west. A half, three-quarters' day ride from here." The old buff hunter waved his arm. "Up north of Big Springs."

"Ain't that all low mesa?" questioned Felton. "Long, flat table land that stretches for miles."

"Yeah, yeah. There's that," allowed BillyBob in an annoyed tone. "But up toward the northeast end of the table, it tumbles away and drops off in a splatter of chawed, rocky slopes feedin' down into a tangle of lower slopes and gullies and deep-cut arroyos that trail out for a dozen or so miles. Somebody once said it was like spillings off the top of the table. So that's how a lot of locals came to call it and do yet today—the Spillin's."

"I've seen those gouged-up slopes from a distance," said Lone, looking thoughtful. "But I never heard that term 'Spillin's' before or realized how far they stretched."

"Oh, yeah. They rip things up for quite a ways. That's what got me to thinkin', after that posse came through, if I was an owlhoot on the run I might just burrow myself into those Spillin's for a while. Be mighty hard to find somebody down in there—even a handful of men—if they didn't want to be found. And as hard or harder to try and dig 'em out once you did."

"But you didn't mention any of this to the posse that came through?"

"Naw. Like I said, I didn't really think about it 'til after they'd come and gone." BillyBob scrunched up his face. "Besides, even if I had spoke up, I can't see that snooty new sheriff outta Ogallala puttin' much effort into clamberin' down in there. He might get his high-polished boots too dusty. If those deep gullies and arroyos was too rugged for Pawnee hunters to tackle in order to try and harvest the carcasses of some woolies they drove over the edge in a buffalo drop—this accordin' to old stories passed down—then that oughta give you a pretty good idea of how tough the goin' is down in there."

Lone was only half listening to BillyBob's further embellishment. The former scout's mind was racing, grinding. His thoughts were replaying and comparing some of the words and word fragments uttered by Hank Wordell that Dr. Frake had jotted down as best he could make out. "Spellum...spillen..." Things that had made little or no sense. Until now. Things that Hank must have overheard the gang mention—that they were headed for "the Spillings"—before he passed out from his bullet wounds. Information that, even while subsequently fighting for his life and conscious only in brief spurts, he'd attempted to pass on.

"Tell me, BillyBob," Lone said, his voice low and measured in spite of the excitement building inside him, "are there any caves down in that sprawl of slopes and gullies?"

"Can't say for certain, havin' never actually ventured down in," BillyBob said with a shrug. "But from lookin' out across the layout of the place, I'd say it's pretty likely there are some."

Lone set his jaw. "Okay, that settles it. I'm gonna ask a favor. It's important." He swung his eyes to Hagen. "Reckon that means I'll be askin' you to release BillyBob from any chores he owes you for a while. Like I said, this is important. More than what sounds like a chance to maybe pin down Hardessy and his bunch, the lives of two innocent hostages he's holdin' are also on the line. I need BillyBob to rattle his hocks back to Ogallala as fast as he can. Find US Marshal Charley Bourbon, and give him this message..."

CHAPTER TWENTY-FOUR

THE PHRASE *"OUT OF THE FRYING PAN, INTO THE FIRE"* KEPT running through Laurie McSwain's thoughts. But every time it did, she gritted her teeth and mentally brushed it away. Yes, she and Dr. Frake may well have traded one plight for another. But the one presently at hand—being lost and confused as far as recognizing any way out of this seemingly endless sprawl of ragged cliffs and tangled, twisting arroyos—was not as imminently life threatening as what they'd fled. At least not yet. It seemed inconceivable they wouldn't somehow find their way out before thirst or starvation claimed them. Had they remained in the hands of the outlaws, however, it was a certainty their lives would have ended just as soon as their usefulness did. Of this, Laurie felt firmly convinced.

That was why, when the violent arguing started up outside the cave and a weakened Rip Hardessy had risen and barely managed to drag himself to the opening in order to get involved—neglecting to pay proper attention to the captives as he did so—Laurie had seized the opportunity to grab a full canteen and urge Frake to join her in slipping away. Hearing a burst of gunfire behind them but realizing none of it was aimed their way, they breathed a combined sigh of relief and continued on with increased determination.

That was two hours ago.

Now, sweaty and exhausted and thoroughly perplexed as to which snakelike course might represent the way to an exit, they'd called a halt in the meager shade of an anvil-shaped ledge thrusting out of a cliff face a dozen feet above their heads. Even though shaded from direct sunlight, the rock slope they leaned back against was still barely cool enough to touch.

"Take it a little easy on that," Laurie advised Frake as the doc held the canteen tipped high. "We don't know how long we're going to have to make it last."

Lowering his hands, Frake said, "Good point. Sorry I got a little carried away." He held the canteen out to Laurie. "Although there's some fairly convincing evidence that, in situations where water is scarce, saturating oneself early on, even if it then means going without drinking for a spell, is just as effective as trying to get by on frequent small sips."

"That might be worth trying some time if a body had enough water to do the saturating part up front," allowed Laurie. "But lacking that in our current situation, I think it best to space out what we've got."

"I suppose. Your canteen, your rules."

Laurie gave him a look. "I didn't mean it that way and you know it. We're in this together and your share of what's in the canteen is yours to do with how you want. Guzzle it all at once, wash your feet in it for all I care. But I mean to make mine last awhile."

Frake smiled thinly. "I've admired your pluck throughout this whole ordeal. Though less so, I must admit, when on the receiving end."

"Pluck," Laurie echoed with a trace of bitterness. "If I truly had pluck we wouldn't be in this fix. If I'd shown enough pluck in the beginning, I never would have let those two owlhoots buffalo me into fetching you out to our ranch under false pretenses—I would have gone straight to the sheriff with the truth of what they were trying to pull."

"You did what you did in order to protect your parents. No one can blame you for that."

"But, in reality, what were the odds that ruthless, dishonorable curs like them could be trusted—that they didn't intend to kill my folks anyway? Leave no witnesses." Laurie frowned deeply. "Ma and Pa could have already been dead by the time I returned with you. Thank God they weren't, but it was still foolish of me to trust otherwise. At best, I made a deal with the devil by being willing to sacrifice your life for theirs. You could almost say I got what I deserved when I ended up a hostage too."

"That's nonsense. You deserved nothing of the kind," Frake insisted.

"Well, I appreciate you not holding what I did against me," said Laurie. "If we succeed in making it out of this rockpile and getting all the way clear of those owlhoots, maybe I can find a way to make it up to you."

"You're already off to a good start by the fast thinking you did when you grabbed that canteen and gave me a tug to follow you in making a break from that cave." Frake's expression turned somewhat sheepish.

"I'm not sure I would have had the gumption to try that if you hadn't initiated it."

"The diversion was there. We had to take advantage of it."

"There's that pluck I was talking about."

"Let's not start that again."

"Very well. But what we *had* better start again," said the doc, "is trying to find a way out of this, as you call it, rockpile. As far as I can tell, there's no one in immediate pursuit. But I think it's too much to hope that somebody won't be coming after us eventually."

"Unless the shooting we heard amounted to enough of the fools blowing each other's brains out so there are none of 'em left. Or at least none of 'em in any condition to come after us."

"That would definitely be too much to hope for. Not that I'm adverse to such hoping, mind you." Frake paused, frowning at his words. "Which is a pretty sorry statement, I fear, for a man who swore an oath to first and foremost always seek to heal."

Laurie arched a brow. "There's such a thing as being too doggone noble and honorable, Doc. Under the circumstances, I reckon whoever you swore that oath to would understand. If that don't work, look at it this way —wishing ill on those skunks is a way of seeking to heal me and you."

Frake grinned. "Okay, we'll go with that. But we still need to find our way out of these blasted rocks, whether anyone's hunting us or not."

Together they stepped out of the slice of shade. Squinting against the brilliant sunlight, they swept their eyes to all sides.

"Even if we hadn't been blindfolded when they

brought us in," Laurie said, "these arroyos and gullies all look the same. And the ones we've tried so far have all ended up the same—Nowhere."

"But the fact our captors brought us in on horseback means that at least one of them has to lead out," Frake reminded her. He lifted his gaze and scanned across the tops of the high, scarred slopes. "Okay. Here's an idea. For now, I think we should keep moving, keep searching. But if we fail to have any luck after another couple hours, the afternoon sun will have begun sinking low enough for the rock faces of some of these slopes to be cooled sufficiently so we won't risk blistering our hands if we attempt some climbing. From a higher vantage point we may be able to spot a passage leading out. Or, maybe there'll be a way directly from the bluff itself."

After quick consideration, Laurie said, "Sounds worth a try. *If* we don't find anything better in the meantime. But, until then, I agree we should keep on the move—staying as quiet as we can, and keeping our eyes and ears peeled in case of unwanted visitors."

"Pick a gully and lead the way, then," Frake told her. "They all look the same to me so one seems as good a prospect as the next."

———

"DID THE KID GET OFF OKAY?" asked Rip Hardessy, lying back on his bedroll after capping the bottle of laudanum he'd just taken a swig from.

"Yeah, he's on his way to Ogallala," Whitey assured him. "Me and River directed him to ride hard straight to the South Platte then follow it east into town. Little farther that way, but the ground is flatter and he's less apt to drift off course when dark starts to settle in."

"He won't make it before dark?"

Whitey shook his head. "Not likely. Not after the delay caused by that damn Posey. But there'll be a full moon tonight and it oughta be up by the time Darrold and Mona are started back. So they'll have that to guide 'em. And then daybreak should be comin' on by the time they're entering into the Spillings again."

Hardessy smiled almost wistfully. "Seein' Mona by morning light. Man, will that be worth wakin' up to."

"Let's hope so."

Hardessy's smile disappeared. "As in, 'Let's hope she's there to be brought back at all.' That what you meant?"

"Ain't what I said."

"I know what you said. I'm talkin' about what you *meant*."

Whitey met his glare with a level gaze. "Look. You got full faith she'll be there. With the money. I told you before, I'm fifty-fifty. Let's leave it at that. Do we need any more arguin' in our ranks?"

Hardessy held his glare for a beat and then let out a long, ragged sigh. "No, of course we don't. Hell, we ain't hardly got no ranks left ... Me, you, River, the kid. Four out of eight. Jesus...where is River anyway?"

"Went to chase down our runaways. I was gonna go, leave him to stay here with you. But he insisted otherwise."

Hardessy's forehead puckered. "You think he's up to it?"

"Time was, he was probably the best tracker in our outfit. I know what you're thinking, that his eyesight has faded considerable in the past couple years. And it don't help that he got into the hooch early this morning. Damned if I know why he took a notion to do that, but it played a big part in bringing things to a boil with Posey." Whitey scowled. "I suspect that's what made him so set on bein' the one to go after the doc and the girl—he felt responsible for stirring up the ruckus that created a chance for 'em to make their getaway try."

"Reckon I played my own part in that, staggerin' out the way I did and not payin' enough attention to those two. But the stuff Posey was spoutin' riled me so damn much I..." Hardessy let his words trail off and his face took on a brooding expression. "Then again, some of what he was accusin' me of—makin' some lousy decisions of late, doin' more harm than good for the gang— maybe he wasn't so far off the mark. Maybe his words stung so much because of the truth in 'em. You could even call my lack of attention to our captives another example of what he was—"

"Knock that shit off," said Whitey, cutting him short. "Posey was always a whiner and bellyacher, no matter how things were going. A nitpicker to somebody else's ideas but never with enough guts to put forward one of his own. As far as the doc and the girl, you were medicated and injured—nobody expected you to stand guard over 'em. I should have tied 'em up before I called my palaver outside the cave. But I counted on the two of 'em being too wore out and too uncertain of our surroundings to try and make a run for it...so everybody had a piece of that, not just you."

Hardessy's brooding expression lifted. "Always lookin' out for me, ain't you? Even when I go after myself."

"I won't argue you take your share of lookin' after," Whitey said wryly. Then, as he started fashioning a cigarette, he added, "But I've got used to it. Besides, I seem to recall you returnin' the favor by also haulin' my butt out of a tight spot or three over the years."

"I appreciate you saying so. But I'm afraid it's a one-way street from now on—to however long I got left."

"There's some more shit you can knock off. Nothing is for certain yet." Whitey took the cigarette he'd just finished building, put it between Hardessy's lips, snapped a match to it. "Once River rounds that doc back and Mona gets here, you might take a turn to surprise even yourself."

Hardessy grinned weakly through a cloud of exhaled smoke. "Maybe. You never know. Havin' my hook so I feel whole again will help too."

"Tell me about it," grunted Whitey as he fashioned a quirley for himself. "Then your lazy ass can at least go back to rollin' your own smokes."

CHAPTER TWENTY-FIVE

KILL BETTY.

That was the solution Mona kept returning to, no matter how many different scenarios she tried running through her head for how best to turn the tables on the treacherous bitch and her bounty hunter goons. That would effectively wreck their scheme, satisfy the revenge Mona was personally craving, and above all throw things into such complete chaos it was sure to warn off any representative sent by Rip, and thus keep them from walking into the trap meant to be traceable back to Rip's location.

As a result, Mona would of course end up behind bars—willingly branded a murderer. By design, this would protect her from any retaliation attempt by Betty's bounty hunters. Though the spending time in jail part wasn't a particularly pleasant prospect, Mona saw it as only a temporary misery to endure. When word reached Rip what had happened and that she was in fact being held in such a manner, there wasn't a shred of doubt in her mind that he would promptly show up to bust her out.

With this plan firmly decided in her mind, there remained only a few final details for Mona to take care of before setting it all in motion. First, there was the matter of the bank money; she needed to hide it some place where it could be fairly easily retrieved after she was sprung from jail. Since no one else except Rip and Whitey knew she was in possession of it, the hiding spot needed to be secure but not overly elaborate. In accordance with this reasoning, Mona chose to simply spread the packets of paper bills smoothly into the goose down stuffing of the two bed pillows in the guest room she was occupying. When the time was at hand, this would make reclaiming the booty as easy as ducking back into the room just long enough to grab the pillows.

This left the matter of a weapon to dispatch Betty with. Though it wasn't something she took lightly, Mona wasn't exactly a stranger to killing. She'd done so twice in the past. Once to a viciously abusive man; another time to a conniving rival "dove" who tried to poison her out of jealousy. On both of those occasions, Mona had had access to a gun. Unfortunately, she lacked one now. So, as an alternative, her first thought was to secret a knife from the kitchen and use that. Envisioning messy, in-close knife work would normally have been repulsive. Not that it still wasn't to a large extent but, for the even more repulsive Betty, Mona was willing to do what she had to.

With everything set and the shadows of late afternoon stretching long outside the windows of her room, Mona was doing a bit of final restless pacing, steeling herself, getting ready to head downstairs. Her intent was to pass through the kitchen, select her weapon, and then proceed out into the shop area in front where she would make her strike. Ideally, Mona hoped there would be some customers present in the shop, somebody to react in horror and go screaming out into the street in order to initiate the desired chaos. If nobody else, there was sure to be the old crone Alifair, Betty's ever-present assistant. She might be slow and shuffling in the normal course of things, but Mona was willing to bet that the sight of her mistress being attacked by a knife-wielding madwoman would put a hurry-up in her baggy old ass and send her out into the street raising sufficient alarm.

Having reviewed all of this in her mind, Mona paused before starting out the door and took one last look around the room that, for a little while, had held so much comfort and hope. It still held hope—but now only as a stepping off place for a much grimmer path to be followed before again finding any comfort. Hopefully once more in Rip's arms.

Mona's eyes fell on the large carpetbag containing her personal items that she'd be forced to leave behind. The thought struck her that the bag also contained a very personal item belonging to someone else...Rip's hook. Just before the Gothenburg lawmen broke down her door and rushed in to put Rip in cuffs, he'd put his hook and the bank money in her care with the promise she'd keep them for him until they were able to get together again. She'd taken care of the money, but she almost forgot about the hook. But now, remembering it, where could she find a place to hide...

A new thought suddenly seized her. Maybe she needn't try to hide it at all. Maybe there was a way to put it to use and then have it saved *for* her—as evidence in what would be her scheduled murder trial.

Crossing to the carpetbag and frantically digging into it, Mona withdrew the hook. She knew the stories of how Rip had got his name—using this prosthetic as a wickedly effective weapon for in-close fighting. Holding it in her hands, examining it more closely than ever before and for reasons far different than any she'd have ever had before, Mona could see the simple practicality of the item and at the same time sense a savage power forged into it by Hardessy's use. That power seemed to pulse up through her forearm as she wrapped the attachment straps tightly in her fist and then swung the hook, slashing the air with it.

A feral fire glinted in Mona's eyes. Why bother with a knife from the kitchen? Could there be a more deliciously fitting way to make Betty pay for her treachery than with this signature weapon of the very man she was so eager to betray?

Mona spun and headed for the door again. This time she did not pause ...

―――――

CHARLEY BOURBON, Jack Bartles, and Sheriff Hiram Needles were all seated in the sheriff's office. Charley and Jack were occupying straight-backed chairs hitched up before Needles' desk, the sheriff had just settled in behind same after pouring cups of fresh-brewed coffee for each of them. All three wore expressions conveying a mix of impatience and frustration. Acting on the information supplied by Jack regarding the likelihood of Mona Trent being somewhere in town and the idea that locating her might provide a lead to Rip Hardessy, they had just spent the past three-plus hours searching for some sign of her. Checks at all the hotels and boarding houses had turned up empty—no sighting of her by Jack and no responses of any new arrivals at any of the establishments who came close to matching her description. Then, reasoning that water tends to seek its own level, a secondary sweep through the ranks of known saloon and crib prostitutes she might have sought out to spend time among had also yielded nothing.

"Hookers tend to protect their own," Charley observed. "So there's always the chance we got lied to by some in that crowd. If we did, then the concern becomes they might go the next step and actually work at hidin' her. Makin' it even harder for us to ferret her out."

Needles scowled menacingly. "The lowlifes in this town know by now how unwise it is to lie to me or my deputies. If it comes to that, a harsh lesson to remind them will be in order."

"Things might change after dark," suggested Jack. "Gals of that trade tend to shun the daytime. Might be another round of looking and asking at a later hour will turn up some we missed the first time. Or maybe some who've had time to think it over and will be more willing to talk."

"Could be," Charley allowed. "But while the comin' of dark might work to our advantage, it ain't gonna be no friend to Lone." He turned his head and looked out the window at the thickening shadows starting to fill the gaps between the buildings lining the street. "I wonder how he's doin' out there..."

FIVE MILES NORTH OF OGALLALA, BillyBob Whipple was flattened low in his saddle and urging his wiry, hard-galloping mustang pony to keep giving it all she had. "Come on, Bessie girl, it ain't much farther now," he told her.

As the sun sank low off to the west, it painted the crests of the rolling, grassy hills out ahead of him with splashes of pinkish gold while pouring deep pools of shadow into the alternating hollows. As he topped some of the higher rises, he was able to catch brief glimpses of the town's lumpy silhouette in the distance—only to have it disappear again as soon as Bessie took him down the next slope.

"When we get there," he promised her, "you'll have earned yourself a night's rest in a livery stall with a bucket of cool water and fresh hay and grain to your heart's content."

———

FIFTEEN MILES WEST OF OGALLALA, a second horseman was approaching the town, following the relatively flat terrain along the south branch of the Platte. This rider pushed his horse steady, but at nowhere near the pace BillyBob was urging Bessie. Darrold Memford knew he had an assignment to complete, but he was feeling very troubled and reluctant about it.

Nothing was the same. So much had gone wrong in such a short amount of time. Four of the men he'd been riding with and living with and trying so hard to fit in with were now suddenly gone. Dead. And the worst was yet to come...anybody with eyes could see that Rip wasn't going to last much longer, that he would soon be next. Then what? He'd always trusted Rip to look out for him, see to it he got treated fairly. But with him gone, Darrold wasn't so sure about Whitey and River. For God's sake, they hadn't even bothered to bury Posey!

Would Whitey and River still want him around? Would they even stick together themselves? And if he brought back the girl and the bank money, would they figure him worthy of a fair cut? Darrold didn't care so much about the money, he just didn't want to go off the edge of a cliff and end up nothing but coyote bait like Posey.

The truth was, Darrold was scared. Scared of what lay behind, scared of what might lie ahead.

But he still had to do the job he'd been sent to do.

He was too scared not to.

CHAPTER TWENTY-SIX

LONE McGANTRY MOPPED HIS FACE THOROUGHLY WITH A canteen-soaked bandanna. Then, after holding the cloth over his head and wringing the remaining moisture out of it to dribble down onto his already sweat drenched hair, he re-tied it around his neck. That done, he tipped his hat upside down, filled it with more water from the canteen, and held it for Ironsides to drink from. He'd been walking the big gray for the past several minutes, allowing him to cool sufficiently.

While Ironsides drank, Lone swept his squinted eyes in a wide scan over the broken land on all sides. They'd worked their way well into "the Spillings" by now. Continuing to follow the trail of his quarry after parting ways with BillyBob and the other Lazy T men had remained relatively easy up to this point. But finding sign within all this wind-scoured, sun-bleached rock slashed by crazily twisting washes and gullies was painstakingly slow work, a challenge even for the finely honed tracking skills of Lone. Yet making such effort all the more worthwhile was an increasing conviction that these were exactly the kind of environs where an outlaw gang on the run would seek refuge. All Lone had to do now was locate that refuge without being spotted, extract the hostages, and then signal in the reinforcements headed by Charley that BillyBob Whipple had gone to fetch.

"Nothing to it," he muttered under his breath.

Ironsides lifted his dripping snout out of the hat and looked at Lone with an expression that seemed to say: *So what's new? Not like this is the first time you've drug us somewhere it ain't smart or healthy for us to be.*

Clapping his dripping hat back on his head, Lone scowled and responded as much to himself as to the horse, saying in another low whisper, "The hell of it is, there are a couple of innocents somewhere out in the middle of this over-baked rock sprawl who may be a lot unhealthier off than us. We need to try and get 'em out. That's the long and short of it."

So saying, he took Ironsides' reins and began walking again. The gray plodded silently behind, his feet encased in thick leather pouches, secured by rawhide thongs, to mute any warning clink of a horse-shoe against rock. In contrast to this precaution taken by the former scout, his ears were sharply cocked for any errant sound signaling the lack of same by his quarry. The infrequent fresh rock scuffs he spotted, providing the main spoor for him to follow, already indicated those he was tracking *hadn't* taken such measures.

Deeper into the Spillings they went. Everything silent and motionless around them. The only things that moved other than man and horse were the slowly lengthening shadows thrown by the higher rocks as the sun made its afternoon descent in the sky.

————

AFTER CONTINUING to run up against dead ends or following narrow, twisty routes that never yielded any kind of exit point, Laurie McSwain and Dr. Frake decided it was time to try the idea of climbing out. On their first attempt, they found the exposed rock face after a dozen or so feet still too hot to try and grip with bare hands. When they tried again a short time later, they picked an upward reaching crevice that quickly became impassable due to a choke point of thick, tangled bramble growth.

Dropping back down from this, they collapsed against the base of the slope, exhausted, dirt-streaked and drenched in sweat, momentarily gripped by a numbing sense of hopelessness that pressed down like a weight holding them in place. Finally, after each had taken a sip of the canteen's steadily diminishing contents, it was Laurie who once again rallied them.

"God damn it!" she exclaimed. "There's *got* to be a way out of this stupid rock pile. Probably more than one. If a bunch of lowlife scum like Hardessy's gang can find their way in and out, then we can too! The only certain way to fail is to quit on ourselves. So get up off your ass, Doc—we ain't about to do that!"

As she pushed to her feet, Frake grinned wryly up at her and said, "Some saltiness added to the pluck. There's a new touch."

"Better get used to it," Laurie told him, extending a

hand. "If we don't find a way out pretty soon, I'm only gonna get more pissed off."

They walked a ways farther along the base of the slope until they came to a shallow fissure gouged into the bleached, weather-molded face. A vertical slash that extended up to the blunted top and appeared narrow enough and clear enough to be negotiated all the way.

Gazing up, Laurie said, "This looks like it offers a pretty good chance. I can make out decent handholds along each side and I don't see any entanglements that should stop us."

"I agree," seconded Frake. "You go ahead and take the lead. You're more sure-footed. I wouldn't want to slip and fall and drag you down with me."

"Okay," said Laurie, slinging the canteen over her shoulder. "We'll take it slow and steady. Just watch where I put my hands and feet, then you do the same."

They began their ascent. The sun was hanging quite low in the eastern sky by now, leaving the rocks gratefully cooled. Dense shadows were cast in many of the deeper crevices and fissures all around them, but the shallowness of the furrow they were climbing within kept it only faintly murky.

Laurie's heart was hammering double-time. Despite her outward bravado—or "pluck" as Frake kept calling it—she was hardly without her share of trepidation. Not like there wasn't plenty of reason, she couldn't help thinking. In addition to merely getting out of this damnedably frustrating rock pile, there remained the very real threat that some member of the Hardessy gang might still catch up with them. But Laurie gritted her teeth and refused to let that thought take hold. *One battle at a time, damn it*, she told herself as she set a foot firmly and then reached for the next handhold.

Seconds later, however, after she'd pulled herself higher and was just getting her foot re-planted, she found herself eyeball to eyeball with a new menace that could not be off-put by any amount of willpower. Two feet from the new level of her face, partially emerged from a crack in the side of the wider crevice, was another face staring back at her—this one belonging to a fat, wedge-headed diamondback rattlesnake!

Laurie froze and just barely managed to restrain herself from screaming or even gasping too loudly. She held her body as rigid and motionless as the rocks surrounding her.

Recognizing something was wrong but having the good sense to be cautious, Frake whispered from below, "What's the matter?"

Laurie swallowed a wagon wheel-sized lump in her throat, not knowing whether she dared answering or not. The snake's black, soulless eyes stayed locked on her. Its tongue flicked out. Finally, out the side of her mouth farthest away from the reptile, barely moving her lips, she whispered huskily, "There's a rattler up here, just to the left of my head."

She heard Frake groan.

Then she heard the first chatter of the rattles and the snake's coils tightened ever so slightly. Inside her head, Laurie also heard her father's voice telling her long ago how a rattler won't strike when it's making that dreaded sound. *"It's a warning. That's when you need to play it smart and be at your most cautious."*

She was all in for the cautious part, but what was the smart play when you were clinging by your fingers and toes a couple dozen feet in the air with no place to duck or run?

Almost as if reading her mind, Frake whispered again from below. "We're only about twenty feet off the ground. I'm lower than you...what if we just drop, and I help break your fall?"

That sounded tempting, but only for a moment. "What if one of us breaks more than that—a leg or an ankle?" she argued. "Would that make us any better off?"

The snake stopped rattling and its coils tightened more noticeably this time. Laurie was on the brink of deciding that dropping away might not be such a bad idea after all when, suddenly, the snake's head totally disappeared, leaving only a long, wildly writhing body with a pulpy, jagged stump where the head had been. The crash of the gunshot sounded an instant later, along with a splatter of dust and rock shards as the bullet tore through and ricocheted back and forth within the vertical trough. This time Laurie was unable to suppress a shriek as she jerked reflexively away and lost both her hand grip and footing. She fell down onto Frake and the two of them went tumbling roughly to the ground together.

Stunned, much of the air jarred out of them, with a miniature avalanche of pebbles and dirt scraped loose by their fall now pouring down after them, the pair untangled and rolled away to try and catch their breath.

"Well, well, well...looky what dropped in for a visit."

The grime-smeared faces of both Laurie and Frake looked up sharply to find River McIvey standing over them. His mouth was stretched in a wide smirk and in his hands, he held a Henry repeating rifle, its muzzle making a slow sweep over the two of them.

Laurie passed a hand over mouth and then licked some remaining bits of sandy grit from her lips. "Looks like we just traded one snake for a bigger one," she muttered.

McIvey's smirk turned menacing. "Oh, that's real cute, you ungrateful bitch. Only a minute ago, you'd've got down on your knees and begged me to get rid of that rattler for you. Hell, you'd've probably got down and offered to do more than that if—"

"Shut your filthy mouth!" Frake snapped.

McIvey chuckled nastily. "What'sa matter, Doc? Your plans just get ruined for a little sumpin'-sumpin' you had in mind for the little filly now that you had her all to yourself out here in the wild wide open?"

"You pig!" Frake spat. He tried to shove to his feet but instantly fell back again, hissing in pain as he grabbed at his left ankle with both hands.

"Doc! What's wrong?" Laurie scrambled over to him.

Grimacing, Frake answered, "Blast it all! Feels like I twisted hell out of my ankle when I landed." Then, managing a sheepish grin as Laurie crouched down next to him, he added, "Looks like you were right—again—about that dropping down business. But hey, I did okay at breaking your fall, though. Right?"

Looking on, McIvey's face scrunched into a sour expression. "Oh, shut up before you make me puke. I don't care if that's some kind of trick you're tryin' to pull or if you broke that pin in a dozen different places, you're still gonna drag your ass up and make your way back to Rip in that cave."

Laurie glared at him. "For God's sake! Can't you see he's hurt and in pain?"

"Too bad," McIvey snarled. "I don't care how much pain he's in, he better drag his ass up and get a move on." He made a jabbing motion with the rifle barrel. "Same for you, Miss Sassymouth. If you're so worried about him, then give him a hand. Either that or I can arrange for you to do some limpin' alongside him. No matter which, you'd better both damn well remember I'll have this Henry trained on you the whole way."

"That sounds like real good advice for you to take your-self, bub...only, in your case, it's a Winchester Yellowboy trained square on that ugly melon you call a head."

This new voice, crisp and sharp and coming from some impossible to determine spot in the surrounding rocks, cut the air like a shock wave.

McIvey's mouth sagged open and his eyes darted every which way, but always snapped quickly back to Laurie and Frake. Then, licking his lips, he rasped, "Whoever the hell you are, don't think you got the whole bulge on this thing. I got my rifle jacked and cocked and still lined flat on these two troublemakers. You pull your trigger, my finger jerk does mine too and I'll take at least one down with me...that gonna gain you what you want?"

There was a beat of tense silence.

Until, for the second time in a matter of minutes, it was shattered by the roar of a rifle. McIvey's right hand, where it gripped his Henry above and around the trigger guard, spurted blood and splinters of cartilage as a slug smashed into it. Arm, hand, and gun were hammered off to the side, at the same time twisting McIvey's upper body half around. Before it was knocked

completely out of his grasp, the Henry discharged—
spewing a bullet that whined off harmlessly. McIvey
crumpled to his knees, clutching his damaged hand
with his good one and howling in pain.

Twenty yards away, from behind the weather-
rounded top of a high boulder, a tall, broad-shouldered
man in a buckskin vest appeared. He slipped up and
over the top of the boulder, dropped lightly to the
ground. Moving in long, smooth strides, loosely
swinging a Winchester Yellowboy in one hand, he
crossed to McIvey and stood over him.

Looking down at his victim, Lone said in a flat tone,
"Changed my mind about that head shot. Ugly as your
melon is on the outside, I didn't want to try and stomach
what it'd look like split open by a .44 slug."

McIvey gazed up at him, his face twisted by pain.
Chin quivering, he wailed, "You busted my hand, you
sonofabitch! You blasted off two of my fingers!"

Leaning over to take the six-shooter from where it
was holstered on his hip, Lone straightened up and said,
"Best get those stumps wrapped in a bandanna then,
stanch the bleedin'. Next thing, you might start thinkin'
about learnin' how to pick your nose with a thumb."

Turning away, Lone moved to where Laurie and
Frake sat looking on with expressions of mingled awe
and uncertainty.

As he reached the pair, Frake's eyes suddenly bright-
ened with recognition. In a voice coarsened by the dust
and grit he'd inhaled, he exclaimed, "I know you...
McGantry!"

Lone grinned. "I know you too, Doc. Though I gotta
say, you look a mite worse for wear than the last time I
saw you."

CHAPTER TWENTY-SEVEN

As she entered Betty's shop from the rear, Mona saw that things were almost ideally laid out for what she meant to accomplish. Two customers were present, a pair of plump, obviously pampered middle-aged ladies, well fed and well dressed, each clutching a neatly wrapped package that Mona assumed were recent purchases. They stood together up near the front door, paused to make small talk with Betty on their way out. Over behind the service counter was the crone Alifair, fussing with some items in a glass display case.

Mona moved toward Betty and the two ladies, smiling innocently and holding Rip's hook down at her right side, hidden by the pleats of her full skirt. Though the early stages of a rosy twilight still filled the street outside the broad front window, several scented candles were burning on shelves inside the shop. They gave off a warm glow and a sweet, dreamy aroma.

Betty turned at Mona's approach, looking a little surprised before producing a smile that dripped with phony charm and saying, "Oh. Mona. Good afternoon, dear."

Those were the final words of her life. Because a moment later, barely breaking stride, Mona swung the hook up and across in a savage, slashing motion. The sharpened point did its job perfectly and laid open a track of split, gaping flesh the width of Betty's throat. The victim staggered back, eyes bulging, making a liquidy choking sound as blood gushed from the wound and poured down over her proudly displayed cleavage.

Blood gushed out over Mona too. But neither that nor the fact she obviously had already struck a fatal blow deterred her from using the hook some more. She lunged after Betty, this time swinging her weapon overhand and driving its point repeatedly into the heart area of the chest, pounding Betty to the floor.

By this time the two plump women were screeching in horror, their voices reaching a near glass-shattering pitch. Flinging away their purses and recent purchases, they scratched and clawed to squeeze simultaneously through the doorway and then out into the street where their shrill screams filled the air between the rows of other businesses.

Mona straightened up from striking down Betty. She was blood spattered and her mouth was curved faintly in a satisfied, half-mad smile. She turned slowly, looking for Alifair, puzzled as to why the crone wasn't squawking and screaming too.

Then she saw why.

Alifair still stood behind the service counter. But she not only wasn't screaming, she wasn't showing any sign of fear at all. Her dark eyes, staring back at Mona, were as cold and emotionless as the twin bores of the double-barreled shotgun that lay on the countertop, also staring out at Mona.

The blood-spattered girl had only a second to understand what was happening, to realize that her plan—which had been going so perfectly—was about to be terribly and permanently ruined.

Alifair triggered one barrel of the shotgun. The twelve-gauge load hit Mona, tearing her nearly in two as it lifted her off the floor and propelled her back to slam against the side wall, knocking down three of the shelves that had burning candles on them.

Behind the service counter, the kick of the shotgun knocked the frail old woman back against a wall also, causing her to lose her grip on the heavy gun. As the gut-shredder clattered to the floor, its second barrel discharged. The blast blew to smithereens the glass case displaying several bottles of perfume along with more burning candles. This combination was hurled out into the middle of the floor where the candle flames ignited the flammable ingredients of the perfume in the broken bottles, and in a matter of seconds, the floor was a spreading mass of fire. Adding to this, some of the candles dislodged, by Mona on the opposite wall had rolled forward to the long curtains trailing down beside the front window and they'd also caught fire.

Struggling to get back to her feet, Alifair looked out to see the rapidly building inferno starting to engulf the whole shop and now she did scream.

———

"WHAT IN BLUE HELL IS THAT!" Hiram Needles thrust to his feet behind his desk in the sheriff's office as the sound of piercing screams knifed in from the street outside. And then, in the midst of those, came two closely spaced dull booms that sounded like shotgun blasts.

As Needles came rushing around the end of his desk, Charley and Jack Bartles also rose from their chairs and all three went tearing out the door. The first thing that grabbed their attention was the sight of two women running down the middle of the street, waving their arms wildly, and shouting breathlessly amid their screams: "Murder! Bloody murder!" "A madwoman is on the loose!" "It's the Devil in female form—a slashing mistress of Satan!"

The sheriff trotted forward to intercept the women as they began slowing to an exhausted stagger, gasping frantically even as they continued to wail and carry on. "Ladies, get hold of yourselves," he demanded, reaching out to take one of them by the shoulders in an attempt to steady her. "Mrs. Burke! Mrs. Kline! You must tell me what this is all about—what's happened?"

"Oh, the horror!" keened the woman in his grip, tossing her head from side to side.

By now, dozens of other people had emerged from buildings up and down the street, chattering excitedly and craning their necks to try and figure out what was going on. It was Jack Bartles who spotted at least part of the answer. Thrusting out an arm, pointing, he called out, "There! Look!"

Heads swiveled, following the line of his pointing finger, and saw smoke pouring out from the front of a building down near the end of the next block, on the opposite side of the street. The dreaded word "Fire!" spat from a score of tongues. And then, intermingled with that, Charley and Jack heard other voices saying "Miss Betty's place" and "the candle shop."

But the billowing smoke and the threat it signaled instantly became the overriding cause for concern and action.

"Fire brigade! Somebody ring the damn bell!" Needles shouted, handing off the panicked woman to a matronly type in an apron who stepped forward to assist. Then the sheriff broke into a run toward the spiraling smoke, with Charley and Jack close on his heels.

Reaching the street area directly in front of the burning building—which by now, in addition to tumbling, thickening smoke, had flames licking out its open doorway and a broken front window—they had to bull their way through a crowd of onlookers jammed in close, but not too close. Once through, they found that Deputy Lissom and another sweat- and soot-streaked man had bravely gone in before the fire got too out of hand and dragged out a pair of occupants whose bodies now lay on the ground.

Spotting Needles, Lissom stepped to meet him, his countenance twisted into a tormented expression. "This is bad, Sheriff. Real bad," he reported, the anguish in his voice matching the look on his face. "There was somebody else in there too—the old lady, Alifair, it must have been—but we couldn't get to her. God...she just stopped screaming a minute ago."

Needles placed a hand on his shoulder and said earnestly, "You did everything you possibly could. Are you okay?"

Lissom put a hand to his face and didn't answer.

The second somber-faced rescuer spoke up, saying,

"I thought I might've heard somebody else hollering from somewhere in there too. I don't know who it could have been. But then the fire got too loud and that's all I could hear."

The fire was indeed loud, the flames roaring and whooshing as they spread stronger. Burning wood crackled and snapped. Periodically could be heard odd, dull pops.

"What the devil is that?" Needles wanted to know.

"Bottles of perfume," Lissom answered, pulling the hand down from his face. "They're exploding when they get too hot."

Now came the sound of a clanging fire bell and the increasingly loud rumble of approaching voices calling, "Clear the way! Clear the way!"

"Move, damn it! Let the water wagon through!" Needles shouted impatiently, waving his arms to disperse the cluster of onlookers. Then, turning back, he said, "Somebody help move those bodies out of the way before—" He stopped short, for the first time taking a good look at the shapes sprawled on the ground, seeing the blood and the torn flesh. "My God!" he gasped. "This isn't the work of a fire!"

"No. I don't know what to make of it, sir," rasped Lissom. "At first, we didn't realize it either. We thought they'd passed out from the smoke until we got them out here and ... well, saw what you're looking at now."

Charley and Jack had moved up to have a closer look for themselves. Suddenly, Jack's hand closed on Charley's forearm, clamping tight. "Oh, Jesus," he groaned, his gaze riveted by one of the savaged bodies in particular. "That's Mona!"

Despite this recognition, not to mention the grisly

details in evidence regarding both bodies, the first and foremost demand for all present became fighting the fire and keeping it from spreading. The water wagon, with its pumps and hoses and assigned crew, rolled in and went to work. In addition, two bucket brigades—one reaching to the river, one coming from a public hand pump and trough—were formed. It was all hands on deck; men, women, even children of a size big enough to swing a bucket.

In the midst of this, a rider—a wiry oldster with a tangled gray beard—came galloping into town. He quit his saddle and hitched his lathered mustang down the street a ways, then strode closer and began looking over the throng of straining, hollering, frantically busy folks. It took a little while but, in the end, it wasn't hard to pick out a hulking, six-foot-three Black man.

Marching up behind this individual and raising his voice to be heard above the din of other voices and the crackle-roar of the fire, BillyBob said, "Are you US Marshal Charley Bourbon?"

"I am," Charley grunted over his shoulder as he passed along bucket after bucket of sloshing water. "But, in case you didn't notice, I'm a little busy right now—and why the hell ain't you pitchin' in too?"

"Because I'm busy doin' something else," BillyBob barked in response. "I brung a message from Lone McGantry—he needs your help and needs it pronto!"

CHAPTER TWENTY-EIGHT

When Whitey ducked back into the cave, Hardessy was propped up on an elbow, watching and waiting anxiously. "Well? Were you able to see anything?" he wanted to know.

Whitey shook his head. "Not a damn thing. Listened tight, couldn't hear nothing more either."

"Three shots," Hardessy said musingly, replaying his thoughts out loud. "First just one...then two more, quick-spaced. Don't make sense, any way you slice it."

"No, it don't," Whitey agreed. "It ain't like River went after 'em to gun 'em down. For sure not the doc. So I could see maybe one shot—you know, to get their attention, bring 'em in line. But three is too damn many."

"Those two didn't snatch a gun when they took off, did they?"

"No, there was no chance of that," Whitey stated firmly. "I might've been foolish enough to leave 'em untied, but I wasn't so dumb as to leave a gun for 'em to grab."

Scowling, Hardessy said, "Could be River had to

fight 'em off. Maybe they caught on to him gettin' close and tried to ambush him—you know, club with rocks or something. That could explain why he had to shoot so many times."

"Possible, I suppose. But it seems a stretch." Whitey considered, then twisted his mouth wryly. "On the other hand, I could see that feisty girl maybe tryin' something like that. But not the doc so much, he don't strike me as the physical type."

"Well, the only thing else that leaves is River runnin' into some other hombre out there," Hardessy said.

"Aw, come on," Whitey protested. "The chances of that are—"

"Damn slim," Hardessy finished for him. "Yeah, I know. But not impossible. We ain't the first outlaws to go to ground in these Spillings, in this cave. Could be some ol' graybeard remembered from times past and convinced a posse of law dogs to come sniffin' around. Or maybe it's a damn bounty hunter out for blood money."

"In either case, wouldn't they have come sniffin' before now?"

"Maybe. But until we know for sure otherwise, we got to consider it."

"So what are you saying?"

"Look. We always figured that, if need be, we could hold off a small army from the mouth of this cave. Right? And if came time to cut and run we always had an escape route up over the cleft." The gang leader's gaze was intense as he continued. "Well, my cuttin' and runnin' days are over. We both know that, one way or another, I'm gonna die right here. But while I may not be able to make a run for it, I damn sure can still make a fight of it. All I need is for you to help me get situated up in the cave mouth with some cover and plenty of ammunition."

"I think that's crazy talk. There ain't no damn posse anywhere out there," Whitey insisted.

"I hope you're right. If you are, and River comes paradin' back with the two runaways in tow, then you can give me the biggest horse laugh anybody ever got. But until then, just in case, humor me, damn it. Do it for a sick and dying man."

"Knock that shit off. You're a long way from dying." But even as he said it, Whitey was beginning to move some items to the mouth of the cave in order to create a low barricade for Hardessy to take up a position behind.

———

"THE SUREST WAY TO stop the bleeding and guard against infection," Dr. Frake was explaining, "is to cauterize what's left of those fingers and then bandage them in something far cleaner than that a filthy bandanna."

"Oh, Jesus," moaned McIvey. "That sure ain't no picnic you're prescribin', Doc."

"Gangrene setting in would be far less so," Frake told him.

"On the other hand," drawled Lone, "I could burn one more bullet and solve the whole matter with a lot less trouble."

McIvey's eyes bugged. "You'd shoot a man in cold blood?"

"A man...no." Lone's tone was flat and hard. "But a piece of trash like you..."

McIvey's eyes darted back and forth between Laurie and Frake. "You wouldn't let him do something awful like that, would you? We treated you two decent. Remember?"

"That's debatable. And, even then, only for as long as you had use for us," Laurie snapped in response.

"Oh, don't say that. Don't encourage him," wailed McIvey.

"Shut up," barked Lone. "If I let you live and the doc patches you up, will you cooperate?"

"C-cooperate how?" McIvey asked. He still lay where he'd fallen when Lone's bullet smashed the rifle out of his hand and blew off two fingers. He held his injured, bandanna-wrapped hand clutched tight to his chest. Frake had knelt down to examine it, then had straightened up and stepped away again. While he was doing that, Laurie had kept McIvey covered with his own six-shooter long enough for Lone to fade back and bring up Ironsides. His spare canteen had provided the girl and the medic the luxury of being able to drink their fill and even splash a reviving extra amount onto their upturned faces. McIvey was given a few sips too, but very sparingly.

"For starters," Lone said now, in response to the outlaw's query, "how many gang members are still up there in the cave I heard about?"

"Four," came the answer. But the moment of calculation Lone saw in the man's eyes ahead of the words told him that was a lie.

Laurie didn't hesitate to put a challenge into words. "Counting you, there were only five when we made our getaway," she said. "But we heard arguing and then gunshots. How can there still be four left?"

McIvey licked his lips. "Some tempers flared and triggers got pulled, yeah. But nobody got seriously hurt. Rip came out and settled everybody down."

"I still think you're lying," said Laurie.

"Damn it, gal! Why cross me that way? You ran off, you wasn't there to see and say for sure."

"Never mind. I stand with the girl—I wouldn't believe you if you said the sun was gonna come up tomorrow," stated Lone.

"In any event," spoke up Frake, "if Hardessy is one of the ones left up there, then he can't be considered much of a threat. Not the way he's stove in."

"Says you!" howled McIvey. "Even a stove-in Rip Hardessy is more than the likes of you three and ten more like ya could ever handle!"

"Then I reckon we'll find that out soon enough," said Lone. "Because it so happens I got a posse led by Rip's old pal Charley Bourbon due along in a little while."

"Yeah, right. Now who's stretchin' the truth to hell and gone?" sneered McIvey.

"Ain't no stretch to say that if you keep runnin' your mouth, you won't be around to see it play out one way or the other," Lone warned him.

McIvey thrashed defiantly into a sitting position. "Big talk! Do something then. Either go to work and fix this ruined hand of mine or go ahead and finish the job!"

Managing to get his feet under him, the enraged man thrust to his feet and took a threatening step toward Lone. The latter moved quickly to meet his rush, reaching with two open hands meant to grab him by the shirtfront and put him back in his place. But Lone damn near got fatally suckered. At the last second, McIvey's good hand swept down in a well-practiced move and pulled a slim-bladed knife from a hidden sheath in his left boot. He swung this instantly upward in a deadly, inward-reaching arc meant to slice open Lone's guts.

Only the former scout's lightning reflexes saved him. He managed to twist his torso to one side at the last possible instant. Instead of gutting him, the blade cut a deep track up across his left pectoral muscle and into his shoulder. Roaring in pain and anger, Lone swung his right fist around and clubbed it against the side of McIvey's head. McIvey staggered away from the blow and dropped to one knee. But he didn't go all the way down. Cursing, fueled by desperation, he thrust upright again and charged anew, viciously swinging the knife out ahead.

But this time he was met by more than just openly reaching hands. After delivering its punch, Lone's right hand had automatically dropped to the Colt holstered on his hip. The .44 filled his fist, cleared leather, and spoke its own distinctive roar. Almost simultaneously, McIvey's own six-shooter—still in the hand of Laurie—roared too. The double punch of bullets not only halted the knife wielder's forward rush, but it knocked him backward and slammed him in a lifeless heap hard against the face of the rocky slope.

CHAPTER TWENTY-NINE

IN THE MOUTH OF THE CAVE, WHERE HE'D JUST HELPED
Hardessy get situated behind a barricade of rocks and
stacked gear, the sound of gunfire caused Whitey's head
to snap around. "Two more shots," he rasped. "Pistols
this time, sounded like to me."

"I make it the same," agreed Hardessy. "That settles
it. I don't know exactly what's goin' on out there, but
River has sure hell run into something more than just
those two he went after."

"Hard to argue otherwise. Damn!" Whitey spat. He
cut his gaze to Hardessy. "So how do you think we
should play it? We can't just hold here and keep guessin'
until somebody comes swarmin' up over that ledge."

Hardessy smiled bitterly. "Speak for yourself, amigo.
I ain't got much choice. But you got options."

"Such as?"

"You could light a shuck the hell out of here. Leave
me to make the stand you just set me up for. Go intercept Mona and the kid, stop 'em from ridin' into a trap.
Then you can split the money and—"

"Stop right there! That ain't happenin', and you damn well know it. No way I'm cuttin' out on you like that."

"Then you're a damn fool."

"Maybe I am. But I ain't leavin' you in no such lurch—leastways not until I have some clearer idea what we're dealin' with. If it's only a scroungy bounty hunter or the like, I oughta be able to take care of him out there in the rocks. No matter who it is, however they managed to stumble in leaves the chance that I know the layout of these Spillin's better than they do."

"But what if it's more than just one or two?" Hardessy insisted. "You can't play cat and mouse with a whole stinkin' posse, especially if they've already done for River."

Whitey frowned hard. "If there's a posse out there—which I continue to doubt—then I'll drop back here and make a stand with you. With a little luck, there's a chance they might not even be able to find this spot."

"Sure. And with just a whisker more luck," Hardessy said sarcastically, "maybe a big-ass bird will swoop down and fly us outta here to safety."

Whitey grinned. "In that case, don't haul off and shoot it down before it's able to do us any good." Then, swinging up his rifle and stepping over the barricade, he looked back and said, "Same goes for me. I'm goin' out for a look-see, but I'll be back."

———

"FORTUNATELY," Dr. Frake was saying, "he cut mostly through muscle mass, so there's no excessive bleeding.

But it's still an awfully long, deep track. It's going to take stitches—a lot of them—to close this properly."

He made this assessment as he was kneeling over Lone, who was stretched out on the gravelly ground with his head and shoulders propped against the base of a weather-smoothed slope. His shirt, bloody and torn by the long knife stroke, had been removed and was being used as a pressure bandage that Frake was keeping pushed hard against his wound.

"In my saddlebags," grated Lone, "there are some needles and a ball of tough sinew thread. Bring 'em. There's also a bottle of whiskey—bring that too."

"I'll fetch them," said Laurie, in deference to the doctor's injured ankle.

While she went for the requested items, Frake continued examining the damage done to Lone, periodically lifting the shirt and then quickly pressing it back down again. The sun had dropped behind the high rocks some minutes past and the narrow twist of canyon they occupied was filling with shadows. Murmuring as much to himself as to his patient, the doctor said as he made these further examinations, "Went all the way up, nicked a piece of the clavicle, tore out a chunk of the trapezius...deep all the way, but luckily missing any big veins or arteries."

To which Lone grumbled in response, "You throw around those words 'fortunately' and 'luckily' kinda loose, Doc, to the ears of somebody who's layin' here split open like a catfish."

"Yes, I'm sure you're in a good deal of pain and feeling anything but lucky," allowed Frake. "But if our knife happy friend had sunk his blade a little lower in your anatomy—the way he clearly was trying for—trust me, the damage and your pain would be immeasurably worse."

"I'll take your word for it. No further convincin' needed."

Laurie returned, bearing the items she'd been sent for as well as some others. "I found a tin of healing salve and I also brought a pot from Mr. McGantry's mess kit," she announced. "I thought it would be a good idea to boil some water for—"

Lone cut her off, saying, "If you know how to boil water without a fire, go right ahead. But if you got in mind to build a fire, then forget it."

"But there's enough water in your spare canteen and plenty of dry bramble around here," Laurie pointed out. "It wouldn't take anything to gather some up and—"

"No," Lone cut her short again. "You want to blow a bugle while you're at it, or shout 'olly-olly-oxen-all-in-free' so's the rest of the Hardessy gang knows exactly where we are?"

Laurie looked taken aback for a moment, but then her brows quickly furrowed with anger.

Before she could reply, Frake said somewhat hurriedly, "She makes a good point about having some watered boiled for antiseptic purposes. And with the light fading like it is, I could use the added illumination of a fire to help see for the stitching I've got to do."

"Too bad on both counts," Lone responded stubbornly. "Don't you two understand that the shots we fired are bound to've been heard by whoever's left of Hardessy's bunch? And don't you think that, combined with their boy here"—a gesture indicating River's sprawled carcass—"not showin' back up, might be enough to bring some more of 'em lookin'? With us bein' in the hobbled up, sliced up condition we're in, the last thing we want is to make it easy for 'em to find us!"

"So what does that leave then?" asked Frake.

"It leaves us to finish doin' what we've already started. That whiskey is your antiseptic and you'll have to do your sewin' with what light you got. I suggest you get started before it gets any darker and before I lose any more juice to the point where I'll be too weak and woozy to do any good even after you're done." Lone's eyes found Laurie. "You did good with that cutter a minute ago. Quick and accurate. That your first choice for a gun?"

"I'm better with a rifle."

"Figured so. Take my Yellowboy, find yourself a high lookout spot not too far off. Keep any visitors at bay while the doc puts me back together. Can you do that?"

"Damn betcha."

Tucking River's revolver in the waistband of her jeans, Laurie snatched up Lone's rifle, then turned to make for the high rocks in long, assured strides. Watching her, Lone said, "Seems like quite a gal."

"Like the lady herself put it—damn betcha," agreed Frake. "Now then, mister, you'd better take a couple generous belts of that whiskey, for anesthetic purposes not antiseptic ones. Then lay back and grit your teeth for what's going to follow..."

———

As DUSK DESCENDED over the land, seven riders out of Ogallala were pounding hard for the Spillings. Leading them was BillyBob Whipple on a fresh mount. At the head of the posse that followed was a grim-faced

Charley Bourbon, seconded by Deputy Jerome Lissom. Jack Bartles rode with them too. The remaining three were hand-picked by Lissom as having the grit necessary to go up against the Hardessy gang if that's what it came to.

Bitter decision though it had been for him to make, Sheriff Needles felt obligated to stay behind to help fight the Markeson fire and to begin an investigation into why two women had been so savagely murdered in conjunction with it.

————

IN THE WAKE of the posse, a troubled Darrold Memford had ridden into Ogallala from the west only to soon find himself more troubled and uncertain than he'd been to begin with. He was naturally drawn to the raging fire that was occupying the attention and efforts of most everyone in town. Before he knew it, he was even pulled into a line of people transferring empty buckets back to the river, replacing an exhausted elderly lady who had to step out for a breather. It was from a particularly chatty teenaged girl to whom he kept handing buckets that he learned some startling details about the fire. How it was claiming the home and business of a fine lady named Betty Markeson. And how, if the fire wasn't horrible enough, Miss Markeson's savagely murdered body had been found inside before the flames consumed it. What was more, the mutilated body of an unknown young woman—who some were claiming was Miss Markeson's killer—was also found. It was all so ghastly and mysterious it was almost impossible to believe. And yet, at the same time, it was also thrilling enough for the girl and others in the line to keep endlessly repeating and opining about.

Darrold listened in silence (not that he had much choice as far as getting his ear bent) and all the while his head was spinning. It was bluntly clear that Betty, his contact person, his link to Mona, Rip's girl he'd been sent to take back, was dead. Did it not follow that the "mutilated body of an unknown young woman" who was found with Betty must be Mona? And, even if it wasn't, without Betty and in the midst of all this chaos surrounding the fire, how else was Darrold supposed to find her?

The more he rolled it over in his mind, the deeper fear and uncertainty bit into him. What should he do? What *could* he do? The thought of going back with neither the girl or the money sent a chill down his spine in spite of the sweat he'd worked up slinging buckets. He'd been worried before how Whitey and River might treat him—now he had to wonder even more about Rip. Lord knew he'd seen some savage demonstrations of the gang leader's temper. And he'd also seen the hunger in his eyes when he spoke of seeing his Mona again. Jesus God, Darrold didn't want to be the one to report that not only was Mona dead, but killed in an especially grue-some manner.

"This snakebit outfit" Posey had called their bunch. Maybe he was right. After all, Posey wasn't such a bad fella. Sure as hell didn't deserve the end he got. Maybe it *was* time to get out, the way Posey had tried to do before River pushed him too far and Whitey pitched in to put him out permanent-like. And then ordered him shoved over a cliff without even a scrap of a decent burial.

For some reason, that bothered Darrold the most.

Not dying, not being killed. Not even the fact that it was him, under orders, who'd shoved poor ol' Posey over the edge. But the thought of ending up that way himself, becoming nothing but a scattering of remains left lying forever forgotten and undiscovered at the bottom of some nameless gully...it sent another deep chill running through him.

No, by God, he wasn't going to go that way. Leastways he wasn't going to do so willingly, make it easy for 'em. He'd come here with every intent of doing the job he'd been sent to do. Now, through no fault of his, he couldn't deliver. Not anything. Not the girl, not the money. Darrold cringed at the thought of how that might be accepted.

The best thing for him, Darrold told himself, was to get out. All the way out. He was already partway there, what was to stop him from just pointing his pony back to the west and keep on riding? Nothing, that was what. He had a few dollars in his pocket, his needs were simple, and the horizon was a long way off. It would be days, maybe weeks, before Whitey and River got done dealing with Rip and had any chance to piece together what had happened regarding Betty and Mona ... and him.

They'd figure he made off with the money, of course. But hell, they'd probably figure that anyway if he went back empty-handed—suspecting he stashed it and was feeding them a line about never getting his hands on it. That's the way their minds worked, and that's all the chance they'd likely ever give him. But this way, riding off with the aim of losing himself somewhere between here and that horizon, Darrold reckoned he'd give himself at least *a* chance.

So he took it. First opportunity he got to fob off his spot in the bucket line, he gave it back to the lady he'd originally replaced. Then he faded back to where he'd left his pony, mounted up, and rode away without ever looking back.

CHAPTER THIRTY

"THERE," PROCLAIMED DR. FRAKE AS HE SAT BACK FROM the awkward position he'd been maintaining, injured ankle thrust to one side, in order to complete the stitching of Lone's wound. "It's sealed good and tight, though I fear it may leave a rather nasty scar since I finished it as much by feel as sight."

"Don't worry about it, Doc," Lone told him. "My ol' hide was already packin' plenty of ugly scars."

"So I noticed. It appears I wasn't the only one working in the dark."

Lone cocked a brow. "Hey. I did some of those myself. Try that sometime, daylight or night, and you'll quick see that doin' the stitches neat and tidy ain't an easy thing."

"I'll take your word for it. Now, if you have something I can use for bandaging, I'll apply some of that salve and a dressing."

"Stay put," Lone said. "I'll get my bedroll, you can cut up one of the blankets for a dressin'. I've got my last spare shirt wrapped up in there too. Damn. The one that lowdown skunk ruined was only seven or eight years old."

When he went to stand up, Lone abruptly discovered he was a bit spongy in the knees and had to grab a rock outcrop to steady himself.

"Take it easy," advised Frake. "You lost quite a bit of blood and you also downed some pretty hefty jolts of whiskey. Maybe you should set back down and let me—"

"No, you got your bum ankle to worry about. I just got to get uncramped from layin' sprawled out too long is all," Lone assured him. But his gait remained a bit unsteady for the short walk to where Ironsides stood waiting and he was glad for the chance to lean against the big gray once he reached him. "Damn," Lone muttered under his breath, "my bounce-back ain't kickin' in like it oughta."

"Maybe that's because you got half gutted and lost about a gallon of blood, you stubborn oaf," said a voice at his shoulder.

Lone's head snapped around to find Laurie standing beside him. "You're supposed to be on lookout," he said.

"Yeah, and you're supposed to be dead—about a dozen times over, by the look of all the scars on you. But you're not and, for the time being, I ain't on lookout. So why don't you go set back down, before you fall down, and let me bring you the gear you need."

Her assertiveness and the sponginess in his knees made a combination Lone didn't feel up to arguing with. He said, "Okay. Bring both the bedroll and the saddlebags if you will." Then he returned and dropped heavily to the ground beside Frake once more.

Laurie was there a minute later, depositing the

requested gear. "I came off lookout because I saw the patient appeared pretty unsteady," she explained. "I'll go back, but so far everything has been quiet. Before I go, is there something more I can help with here?"

"If you open up my bedroll, you'll find one of the blankets is worn particular thin. The doc could probably use some help tearin' that up for bandagin'. And, if he'll hold still for it, he'd likely benefit from a good tight wrappin' of that ankle of his," Lone suggested. "While you two are doin' that, if you hand me the saddlebags, I can dig out some beef jerky and coffee beans."

Laurie looked at him. "You intend to cook coffee?"

Lone shook his head. "Nobody said anything about cookin'. I'm gonna eat the jerky and chew some of the beans to get the caffeine out of 'em. I got to pump some energy back into this bag of bones the doc went to so much trouble keepin' stitched together."

"It's true caffeine is a strong stimulant," Frake said thoughtfully. "And of course there's protein in the jerky."

"What's wrong with some plain old-fashioned rest after what he went through?" Laurie wanted to know.

"Because I can't afford to rest. None of us can," Lone answered. "Not until Charley and that posse gets here."

Frake's eyebrows lifted. "You mean there really is a posse on the way? I thought that was just a bluff you were trying to run."

Lone's mouth quirked ruefully. "And I thought the same about your twisted ankle. Just goes to show. But yeah, I'm confident there's a posse on the way by now. I marked my trail into this rock sprawl so, with the stars startin' to pop and a moon soon to show, they shouldn't have too much trouble findin' us. All we got to do, once we get this patchin' finally done, is hunker down in a notch at the base of one of these slopes and hold out 'til they get here. I still got a hunch we're at risk of bein' hunted by some of Hardessy's crew."

"Then, by all means, let's hurry up and get, as you say, hunkered down," said Laurie. "You've gone and put an itch between my shoulder blades like somebody is drawing a bead on me."

"That's a good feelin' to have. Keep you alert," Lone told her. Then, as he rummaged in his saddlebags, he added, "You want to also chew on some of these coffee beans when I get 'em dug out? They'll keep you even more alert, and I've got plenty to share."

Laurie made a face. "I'll pass, thanks."

———

Voices.

Whitey could hear somebody talking. But the way these twisty damn gullies and arroyos tossed sound around, it was hard to get a bead on exactly where they were coming from. What was more, he had to be careful moving in pursuit of trying to pinpoint the source because those same natural features had a way of sometimes amplifying even the slightest scrape of a boot heel.

Whitey paused, leveling his breathing and listening intently some more. The talk continued sporadically. More than two voices, he thought. But how many more, damn it? The sound was a choppy drone with only a few snatches of words truly clear. But not enough strung together to make any sense. Did he hear something about coffee beans? And did somebody say "posse"...or was he straining too hard and hearing what he was afraid he *might* hear? Goddammit, there was no way a posse could have found its way in here...was there?

Somebody else had. Somebody besides River and the two runaway hostages he'd gone after. Whitey was pretty sure none of the voices he was hearing belonged to River. So if there was at least three voices, then that proved the presence of at least one newcomer. And where did that leave River—what had become of him?

The talking suddenly seemed to stop and Whitey felt a twinge of panic. The source of the voices had been difficult to pinpoint but at least he'd had something to try and lock on. With only silence it fell to just what he could see, and visibility was sketchy at best. Yes, the stars were shining brighter and brighter in a mostly cloudless sky, and the bare, bleached rock faces made a backdrop against which many things stood out clearly. But, at the same time, there were countless hollows and recesses filled with inky shadows capable of totally swallowing anything within them.

The moon would be rising soon, that would help. But it would still leave a hell of a lot of shadowy pools that could hide a threat.

Talk some more, damn you, Whitey's brain screamed. *Give me a stinkin' chance!*

A moment later, as if by some dark intervention, he got his wish. The voices started up again. Furthermore, there seemed to be more of a clarity this time as to where they were coming from.

Whitey hesitated, passing the back of one hand across his mouth. Was his mind playing tricks on him due to him being over anxious—or was the talk truly discernible as coming from just around the bend of a particular arroyo that snaked out ahead and slightly below from where he was poised? It certainly seemed so. Too much so not to act on it.

Slipping the keeper thong off the Colt holstered on his hip and tightly gripping the Henry repeater in his left fist—holding it high and out away from his body to keep the butt from inadvertently scraping across rock— he moved forward cautiously. He proceeded along the near rim of the arroyo, where the footing was firmer; solid rock not as likely to crumble away and spill a rattle of loose pebbles or stones.

He moved slowly but steadily, the voices continuing to guide him. He might have been able to make out more of the words now if he'd concentrated, but Whitey was too focused on getting into position, gaining sight of his target. He didn't give a damn what they were saying, he just wanted to see how many there were and what chance he had of eliminating them as a further threat. Given a sufficient opening, he could lever and fire the Henry fast enough to mow down a whole handful almost before they knew what hit them. And if that included the doctor—and the girl, too, for that matter— then so be it. The sorry truth was that the laudanum the doc left behind was about all the good he could do for Rip anyway.

Whitey reached the bend of the arroyo around which the voices seemed to be originating. As he eased around it, he saw that everything came to a pinch point of sorts that gave Whitey, on the rim he was traversing, about a four-foot gap to gaze out through between two ragged upright rock walls. Beyond was a flat-bottomed cross canyon, some thirty feet wide. On the other side, settling themselves into the base notch of a vertical crevice reaching up into a high slope, were three people. The doctor, the girl, and a tall, broad-shouldered stranger.

Whitey's pulse quickened. By God, he had 'em!

He braced himself and got set in a shooting stance. He was able to easily straddle the narrowed throat of the arroyo and press his left shoulder against the rock wall on that side. The Henry already had a shell jacked into the chamber, all he had to do was slowly, quietly thumb back the hammer as he brought the butt stock to his shoulder.

But he held for a moment, wanting to be sure all potential targets were in view. The notch where the trio was gathered reached back in far enough so that there were deeper shadows capable of hiding an additional person or two. There was no sign of River, so they almost certainly had done for him. Probably the big stranger. But he'd be held to account soon enough. He'd be the first one Whitey put down.

In addition to just his size, the stranger looked to have some bark on him. He wore a holstered Colt in a manner that suggested it was more than just for show; yet his movements seemed a bit jerky, unsteady. The doctor was obviously limping and had some kind of bandage wrapped around one foot. As for the girl, she was somewhat surprisingly holding a Winchester Yellowboy and doing so in a manner that didn't appear at all awkward. But no matter, they'd all go down fast enough when Whitey was ready to cut loose.

A horse, a big gray stallion, stood off to one side of the notch. He lifted his head at one point and seemed to stare straight in Whitey's direction. Luckily, Whitey was positioned downwind so the nag couldn't possibly be picking up his scent. After a couple seconds, the gray put his head back down and bit at some sparse, tough grass poking up through the dirt.

Okay, Whitey had seen enough. Time to go to work and clear this trash off their back trail. His finger curled around the Henry's trigger, ready for the final squeeze. He sighted down the barrel and centered on the broad chest of the stranger.

But half a second ahead of the trigger pull, the big, clumsy bastard staggered and lurched off to one side. The Henry roared, spitting flame and lead—a bullet that passed harmlessly between the stranger and the girl and hammered into nothing but the deep shadows of the notch.

Cursing in frustration, Whitey only made things worse when he so violently jerked the cocking lever of the Henry that he unbalanced himself and caused his left foot to slip on the hard, slick rock edge of the arroyo rim. His foot and leg shot down into the arroyo, violently wrenching his right leg where it was caught still up on the opposite rim. Whitey's frustrated curse became a howl of pain. His elbow and the side of his head cracked against unforgiving rock and he damn near lost his grip on the rifle. He struggled to pull his right leg down and barely managed to drop to the floor of the shallow, narrow arroyo without falling flat on his face.

And then the return fire from both the stranger's Colt and the girl's Yellowboy came pouring at him, bullets spanging off the rock walls, spraying stony shards and making mournful whining sounds as they sliced the air. Whitey made some mournful sounds of his own as he scrambled back around the arroyo's bend in desperate retreat. But not before one of the rounds punched into his lower back, off to the right of his spine, tearing through just under his ribs and bursting out his stomach. The impact propelled him forward, aiding his flight, but at the same time filling his entire body with fierce, fiery pain.

Jesus God, how had it all gone so wrong! his mind screamed. *He'd had them dead to rights. Square in his sights. It should have been so easy. But now he was the one bullet-torn and fleeing. How in hell could that be?*

Whitey knew his wound was bad. Real bad. Blood was pouring out his stomach and down the front of his leg. But he had to hang on, had to keep going. Make it back to the cave. Let 'em come then. Just let 'em. Him and Rip would make a stand and meet 'em with hellfire like they could never imagine. Just let 'em come and find out...

CHAPTER THIRTY-ONE

"YOU'RE CRAZY! YOU CAN'T GO AFTER HIM!" WAILED Laurie and Frake in near perfect unison.

"I can't *not* go after him," Lone argued. "He's wounded and on the run. No better time."

"But you're wounded too," Laurie insisted. "You're weak from blood loss, not even steady on your feet."

"Yeah, and being unsteady is what just saved me from takin' that slug," Lone pointed out. "What's more, a bullet whizzin' under your nose has a way of jerkin' a body mighty alert."

"But for how long?" questioned Frake. "You go clambering through those rocks, straining yourself, you might open some of those stitches and start bleeding again. An adrenaline rush will only sustain you for a limited time."

"Then I'll have to make it last," Lone said stubbornly as he finished reloading his Colt. "One of us hit him, I saw it plain. That means he'll leave a blood trail. If he makes for the cave, it'll lead straight to Rip and whoever else is left. I can't pass that up."

"If there's going to be a blood trail, wait for the posse you're so confident will be showing up. Give them the chance to follow it."

Lone shook his head. "That was Whitey Culp we just had a brush with, I saw that plain too. Caught a glimpse of his pale hair. He's near as tough and cagey as Rip Hardessy himself. Givin' the two of them even a whisker of time will only amount to givin' 'em the chance to squirt away. I ain't gonna risk that."

"Hardessy is in no shape to go anywhere, I tell you," said Frake. "And if you're so sure Whitey is wounded too, then—"

"Save it, Doc. I'm goin' after 'em and that's all there is to it," Lone told him. "You don't know men like them. They might be rotten and evil, but they're also boiled leather tough. They feel cornered and desperate enough, they'll chew a leg off to escape the trap."

Frake's eyes narrowed. "But you think you're tougher still. Is that it?"

"Let's hope so," said Lone, going glare for glare until the doctor's abruptly dropped away.

"Then let's hope I measure up too, because I'm going with McGantry."

This declaration came from Laurie, who had finished reloading the Yellowboy from a box of cartridges dug out of Lone's saddlebags and now stood ready, feet planted wide and the repeater hiked up on one shoulder.

Lone spun on her. "Like hell you are."

"Like hell I'm not. You don't have time to stand and argue about it, and I could out-argue you anyway. Face it, you stubborn ox, you can use me. You've seen I can shoot so in case you turn woozy or wobbly-legged out there, I can provide backup. Plus, if we get close to the cave, I'll recognize the landmarks and be able to give some advance warning that we're closing in."

Lone glared some more but Laurie gave as good as she got. Until, showing signs of relenting, he said, "What about the doc?"

"He should be okay here until your posse arrives. We can leave him River's gun."

"You know how to shoot, Doc?" Lone asked.

"I understand the mechanics. Cock the hammer, pull the trigger. Whether or not I'd ever hit anything might be questionable. But what's not questionable is that, if you insist on going, you'd be better off doing it together. I'll be okay here."

Lone's scowl returned to Laurie. "I suppose I'd have to shoot you in the foot or something to keep you from following me regardless."

"Booth feet."

"Alright then, damn it. Give Doc that gun. But when we get out there, what I say goes. Understood?"

"As long as you don't expect me to run and hide if it starts to turn rough."

"I think I got that much already figured out... come on."

———

THE MOON ROSE, full and bloated and milky white, as they began working their way back along the snaking arroyo Whitey had followed to his attempted ambush position then had retraced, at least to start with, in flight. On his second passage he had stuck to the sandy, gravelly floor of the gully rather than moving along its rim. This left footprints for Lone to track, as well as the wavering line of spilled blood too fresh to have yet been absorbed by the soil. The steadily increasing wash of moonlight, as the orb inched ever higher in the sky, helped greatly for being able to discern this sign.

"Rustler's moon," Laurie said softly.

"How's that?" Lone responded over his shoulder.

"It's just something my pa used to say...something he'd call a big, fat moon like this one tonight."

"Uh-huh. Reckon I've heard it called that, too, in times past...but tonight, for us, it's servin' as a manhunter's moon."

"I guess that would be accurate. But it sounds awfully ominous."

"Let's hope it is...for Whitey and Rip Hardessy."

They continued on in silence. Before long, the arroyo pinched closed and Lone could see where Whitey had been forced to shift to rockier, more broken ground that inclined gradually upward across the base of high, gnarled slopes. If not for the frequent spatters of blood leakage, showing black rather than scarlet in the silvery moonlight, Lone would have been hard pressed to stick with his trail.

There were increasingly frequent spots where it was obvious Whitey had paused to briefly rest, catch his breath. This was evident by the greater accumulation of spilled blood at these places. Every time he came to one of these, achingly wanting to stop and rest himself as he struggled with the constant burning in his chest and the awareness of his legs tiring, threatening to buckle at moments of added strain, Lone fought through and at

the same time found his thoughts crazily encouraging
Whitey to do likewise. *Stay with it, you stubborn bastard.
Make it to that cave. You get there and I will too...and then
we'll settle this once and for good.*

CHAPTER THIRTY-TWO

"Jesus Christ, old pard, you took a bad one. I could cram a fist into this exit hole om your belly." Rip Hardessy grimaced as he issued these words, fighting hurriedly and awkwardly with only one hand to get a pressure bandage applied to Whitey's wound.

"Then do it. Anything to stop the bleedin'," Whitey urged him between puffs of rapid breathing. "I fear I'm drained near empty."

"Not yet you ain't. Not accordin' to the way you're leakin' through these bandages the doc left behind," Hardessy told him. "What kind of buzz saw did you run into out there?"

"Just one man, much as I hate to admit. One big, lucky sonofabitch. I had him lined up for...for a certain kill shot. But he moved at the last second. Wh-when I missed, him and the girl—that feisty damn girl, swingin' a Winchester like she was born to it—opened back on me an...and nailed me before I could make it to cover."

"Don't talk for a minute, catch your breath," Hardessy said. "Here. Press your hand down here while I tie off these ends. I think I got the bleedin' mostly stopped."

Enough moonlight was pouring into the cave mouth to sufficiently illuminate the two men. Though the evening air had cooled considerably, Whitey's face shone with a thick film of sweat and his breath continued to come in rapid gulps. Also, in spite of Hardessy's advisement not to, he continued to talk. "I-I think they're probably followin' after me. I knew I wasn't up to a runnin' fight so...so I figured if I led 'em here we c-could make a stand together...I had to let you know."

"That's okay. You damn right we'll make a stand. We'll burn 'em down."

Hardessy finished securing the thick wad of bandaging over the exit wound in the side of Whitey's stomach. He'd stanched the bleeding the best he could but he could already see it leaking through. "How far behind you figure they are?" he asked.

"Not far, I don't expect...n-not if they're comin' at all. I think they are, but I couldn't tell for sure. I just kept tryin' to make it myself."

Hardessy held out his bottle of laudanum. "Here, take a swig of this. It'll help if you're in pain."

"My guts are on fire. And I wrenched hell outta my hip, too, takin' a fall."

As Whitey tipped up the bottle, Hardessy said, "It tastes like sin, but it'll take away the pain for a while."

Whitey handed the bottle back, making a dreadful face as he did so. "You were sure as hell right about the taste, I hope you're as accurate on the pain helpin' part."

Taking a hit off the bottle himself before putting it away, Hardessy said, "Ain't it a sorry state of affairs that our last drink together is gonna be a jolt of this shit while sittin' in a dusty cave, instead of sharin' some good bourbon in a rowdy saloon or the parlor of a classy whorehouse somewhere?"

Whitey regarded him. "Is that really where you figure we're at—down to our last drink together?"

Hardessy held his eyes, expression flat and hard. "Ain't no sense sugar-coatin' it, pard...you know same as me ain't neither one of us leavin' here alive. It's just a matter of how we check out."

Whitey's frown took on a puzzled bent. "Reckon that's the hard truth. But I ain't so sure I follow the 'how' part. We're gonna go out fightin', ain't we?"

"Yeah, we're gonna fight. We been doin' that, one way or other, since we was born." Hardessy paused, his forehead puckering, his gaze seeming to look through and past Whitey. "But I been thinkin' about something more than that. Beyond that...I was thinkin' about it for myself, while you were away. While I figured you still had a chance to pull foot and make a run for it. But now you've gone and put yourself on an even standing with my fix."

"We ain't exactly on even standing," Whitey said impatiently, "because I don't have a clue what you're talkin' about."

"I'm talkin' about fightin' for how we get treated *after* we're dead. You know damn well what they'll do—same as they have with dozens of other notorious hombres like us after they put 'em toes down. First, they'll collect the bounty money on us. Then, to squeeze even more out of our carcasses, they'll pump us full of embalmin' juice and wax and prop us up in display boxes so's they can charge a dime for gawkers to come stare at us. Fifty cents to get their picture took standin' next to us. After the novelty wears off, they'll slap a couple cheap pine overcoats on us and dump us in a hole somewhere. If we're lucky. Hell, if they can find a farmer willin' to shell out a couple extra bucks, they might sell us for hog food."

"That's a hell of a gruesome picture to paint," said Whitey, looking in even more pain than before.

"I agree. It's a hell of a way to treat anybody. Yet I've seen it done, and so have you."

"But what can we do if that's what they pull after we're dead?"

"We can not leave the sonsabitches anything to do it with, that's what." There was a kind of wild intensity gleaming in Hardessy's eyes now. "Looky here. I pulled this in closer"—he reached out and touched a canvas bag lying beside him—"while you were away. It's got the last of Posey's dynamite in it. Eight sticks. I don't know much about fuses and the like, but I got a pretty good idea what a blazin' hot bullet—or two—pumped into that eight pack would do."

Whitey's eyes widened. "Jesus. You mean you're thinkin'...."

"That's right. We close the door on ourselves. First I was thinkin' just me, but now you're in it the same. It'll prevent the bone-pickin' bastards from ever botherin' us anymore. Those eight sticks will make this cave our tomb. And, if there's somebody on your tail like you think and we time it right, maybe we can dump part of the cliff down on them in the process. What do you say?"

Before he could reply, Whitey had to wince through a sharp stab of pain. Once it passed and he caught his breath, he said, "I say that I think you're an even crazier sonofabitch than I thought before...but that don't make your idea a bad one. Not by a damn sight." He bobbed his head. "Count me in."

———————

LAURIE'S HAND REACHED OUT, clutching Lone's arm and bringing him to a halt. "There," she said, lifting her hand and pointing. "About a third of the way up that cliff face just ahead. See that narrow ledge poking out and running back for a ways? Centered on that ledge is the opening to the outlaw cave."

Lone studied the layout of where she'd pointed. He raised one hand and backhanded cold, clammy sweat from his forehead. He was exhausted, aching. The ledge was about a hundred yards away and roughly a hundred feet up from the base of the lumpy, wind-scoured cliff. The way Lone was feeling right then, it looked more like a matter of miles.

"You okay?" asked Laurie, moving alongside and gazing up at him.

"Still upright and movin' forward," he answered, perhaps a bit more gruffly than he meant to. "I was hopin' Whitey would lead us here. Looks like I got my wish."

"Him and whoever else is up there—now we have them all bottled up. That's good, isn't it? I mean, we can hold them in place until your posse gets here. Right?"

"That's one way of lookin' at it, I reckon—*if* there's only one way up or down from there. Are you sure that's the case?"

"Pretty sure. I can't say I had any chance to really study it firsthand. But they made a point of bragging more than once how—if anybody ever found them in the first place—they'd be able to hold off a small army because the trail up was so narrow in some places it only allowed passage for one person at a time. That much, having traveled it twice, I *can* attest to."

Lone frowned. "I don't doubt your word. Nor do I doubt they purposely made that brag. But what's hard for me to believe is that somebody as savvy as Rip Hardessy—or Whitey either, for that matter—would put themselves in a box with only one way out. Yeah, maybe they could guard the main trail real good against a full-on *attack*. But that could work just as good in reverse to keep 'em from gettin' out. Siege tactics, starve 'em into submission if somebody wanted 'em bad enough. See what I mean? Hard to think they wouldn't have *some* kind of escape route, even if it's a tricky, difficult one up over the high rocks. As long as there's that chance, we can't just wait here for the posse. Not after we've got this close."

"When you say it like that, yeah, I guess it only makes sense," Laurie allowed. "But remember, Rip is stove in so bad he's in no shape to travel at all, especially over any kind of rugged course. And, judging by the blood trail he's been leaving, neither can Whitey be much better off."

"Maybe so. But don't forget what I told Doc about what kind of men these are. Think what you just said about Whitey's blood trail—would you expect anybody who painted the ground that thick to still be going?"

"No, I suppose not," Laurie admitted grudgingly.

"Plus, there might be one or two more besides just Rip and Whitey up there. That's what River claimed, and you said yourself that you and the doc left five behind."

"But they were arguing and we heard shooting as we were making our getaway," Laurie said. "I can't believe somebody didn't get seriously hurt or killed out of that."

"Still, you can't be sure," Lone persisted.

"No, I can't. So what do you propose as a means to try and find out?"

Lone heaved a sigh. "Only thing I can figure is to work in closer. Get to a point where we maybe can catch sight of them...or them us. Find out what happens from there."

"I think I can make a pretty good guess."

"Yeah, me too. But it's what we came for, ain't it?"

CHAPTER THIRTY-THREE

THE "TRAIL" LEADING TO THE CAVE WAS A NARROW, jagged crevice twisting up the sloping cliff face. By the time they reached it and had ascended a quarter of the way, Lone was dripping sweat and breathing raggedly. He was pretty sure he'd pulled some stitches loose, but didn't want Laurie to know. When he paused a minute to rest, dropping one hip on a flat slab of rock, she asked, "You sure you want to keep going?"

"Wouldn't miss it for the world," Lone quipped. He unslung the canteen he'd brought along, held it out for Laurie to take a drink first and then took a long pull himself.

She smiled. "Maybe you should have brought some more coffee beans to chew on and wash down."

"Don't remind me. What I wouldn't give for a big mug of real, fresh-brewed coffee right about now."

"There's some added incentive for you then. They've got plenty of coffee up in that cave—once we clear the trash out of the way."

Lone thumbed his hat back and gazed up the trail.

"All I can see from here so far is the bottom of that damn ledge. If they bragged they could hold off an army comin' up after 'em, there must be some point where they can look down on this trail without pokin' their heads over and exposin' themselves. Any idea where that is?"

Laurie pointed. "There, I think. See how the slope kinda bulges out at that spot? Well, the trail swings out there too. I remember looking back when we were making our escape and I could actually see into the cave mouth from that angle."

Lone nodded. "Okay. That's our next stop then. Come on."

It didn't take long to reach the bulged-out area. As the crevice trail began following it, twisting out farther away from the main cliff face, Lone was able to look up and begin to see over the lip of the edge. Then he could make out a recessed gap that was the top of the cave opening. He stopped and dropped into a slight crouch, halting Laurie close behind him.

"Now what?" she whispered close to his ear.

"Now we say hello. Let 'em know we're in the neighborhood," Lone told her. He thumbed the keeper thong off his Colt, slowly unleathered it. A fresh surge of adrenaline was coursing through him now, making him feel steadier and stronger than he had for a while. "Stay low, but keep that Yellowboy ready," he whispered over his shoulder. "If one of 'em pokes his head too far over that ledge, don't hesitate to give him a haircut."

Then he cocked and raised the Colt, took quick aim, stroked the trigger and sent a slug burrowing up into the roof of the cave. The instant result was an angry, excited outburst of curses. But no heads poked into view.

Lone leaned back, grinning. "I do believe we got their attention."

"And I believe you might be a little bit crazy," Laurie replied.

Lone tipped his head back and shouted upward. "Rip Hardessy! Whitey Culp! That was the only warnin' you're gonna get! Any more lead sent your way is gonna be meant to do serious hurt. You can save goin' through that by goin' ahead and givin' yourselves up!"

The answer to that came as a hail of bullets that slapped blindly down above and off to one side of Lone and Laurie without coming anywhere close. When the shooting stopped, a harsh voice soon followed, hollering, "Them's *our* warning shots, you cocky sonofabitch! You want to go ahead and start tradin' the real thing, make your move any time you feel ready!"

"Fair enough," Lone called back. "We'll be good and ready when the rest of our posse gets here—the posse headed by US Marshal Charley Bourbon!"

No response for a long beat. Then: "That makes you out a liar on top of bein' a belly-crawlin' bushwhacker. Everybody knows that nigger law dog got killed in the train explosion that busted me out of his custody!"

"I guess somebody forgot to tell Charley that," Lone responded. "We had to convince the same thing to that pair of gunnies you sent back to check on him. What were their names again? Oh yeah, Cramer and Redsleeve. That was it. I guess they never got around to tellin' you about Charley still bein' alive, though, did they? On account of they were the bumblin' asses who ended up dead themselves."

"Who the hell are you?" demanded the harsh voice that by now was clear must belong to Hardessy himself.

Lone smiled slyly. It was also clear he'd succeeded in rattling the gang boss by mentioning things Hardessy couldn't figure out how he would know. Never a bad thing to put your opponent off balance.

When Lone didn't respond right away, Hardessy demanded even more impatiently, "Goddamnit, answer me!"

"What difference does it make?" Lone taunted. "My name'd mean nothing to you, and you ain't gonna be around long enough to care anyway."

"I'll be around long enough to make you pay for stickin' your nose in my business, you bastard!"

Lone issued an exaggeratedly disdainful laugh. "Time was, a threat from you might mean something, Hardessy. But face it, those days are gone. You're nothing but a stove-in bag of guts waitin' to die, and not man enough to face it."

Afterward, there would be no one—not Lone, not Laurie, not anyone left alive—who fully understood why those words triggered what happened next. First there was no response at all, just several seconds of silence. Then came what sounded like two nearly simultaneous gunshots instantly swallowed by the shattering roar of an explosion. Roiling clouds of dust and dirt and chunks of broken rock came spewing out of the collapsing cave. Loosened by this, great slabs of rock peeled away from the gnarled cliff face above and came crashing down as well. The ledge in front of where the cave had been was torn away, pulverized.

Lone had only a split second to react. To grab Laurie and twist both of their bodies violently away, hurling them out of the crevice and out over the side of the bulged-out section of the cliff. This took them off to the edge of the main flow of cascading earth and rock. They dropped freely for several feet before landing jarringly against the base slope and then tumbling in a series of bouncing rolls, all the while being pelted with peripheral dirt and debris spewed by the landslide. Throughout, Lone kept Laurie wrapped as tight as he could in his arms and legs, shielding her as much as possible against the punishing impacts.

The wind was pounded out of him and, when he tried to suck some breath back in, his mouth and nose were clogged with dirt. He tried to holler but nothing came out. The only sounds were the echo of the explosion and the rushing roar of the tumbling rocks and dirt. Bright pinwheels spun and danced inside Lone's head. And then, suddenly, everything went black.

———

GRADUALLY, Lone became aware of two things. Distant-sounding voices that faded in and out, and the throb of pain in his head and body that was stubbornly constant. He worked his mouth some, thinking he might try to speak. The taste of dirt was on his tongue and particles of gritty sand crunched in the hinges of his jaw.

"I think he's comin' around," said a familiar voice.

Lone opened his eyes. They burned and watered. For a moment, everything was blurry. Once he'd blinked away the blurriness, several faces, all hovering over him, came into focus. There was Charley Bourbon, BillyBob Whipple, Dr. Frake, Jack Bartles, and Deputy Lissom from Ogallala. Lone sensed there were others standing nearby, though he couldn't make them out in the darkness. It was still night and the moon, that manhunter's moon, though waning now, was up there looking down on him too.

When he finally got around to speaking, his voice came out hoarse and raspy. "Where's Laurie? Is she okay?"

"She's over by the fire," said Frake. "She's bruised and battered, maybe some cracked ribs, but otherwise fine. Miraculously, the same goes for you."

Lone pushed to a sitting position. This caused some pain in his back and shoulders to stab deeper, but he had so many throbbing aches up and down his whole body it really didn't matter. He looked over to where Laurie lay beside a small, crackling fire. She had her eyes closed and appeared to be resting peacefully. The sight was enough to send a wave of relief through his aching bones and muscles. Then something else that brought the promise of even more relief struck him— the smell of coffee cooking.

"Is somebody makin' coffee?" he demanded to know.

"Yeah, a couple of the boys made a pot," answered Lissom.

"I'd kill for a cup of fresh coffee!" Lone declared.

Charley smiled. "I think we can probably arrange that without such drastic measures."

"I'll fetch some," said BillyBob, moving to do so.

Lone gazed up at Charley. "You took your sweet time gettin' here."

Puffing calmly on his pipe, Charley said, "You'll have to excuse me for not bein' sorry I didn't get here in time to share in that explosion and havin' half a mountain pour down on me."

"It's a long way from bein' a mountain."

"It's still big enough I don't want it fallin' on me. Ain't everybody got an iron head like yours, you know. Besides, I already had my go-round with an explosion. I don't need another turn."

Lone turned his head and looked at the raw rubble of the blown away cliff with a haze of fine dust still hanging in the air over it. "Yeah," he muttered, "it all started with an explosion. I guess it's somehow fitting to end with one." Then, turning and looking back at Charley, he said, "It *is* ended. Right?"

Charley puffed some more smoke. "It's over, yeah. I got a feelin' there's gonna be some questions left hangin' that won't ever be fully answered. But, as far as I'm concerned, it's about as over as it's gonna get."

EPILOGUE

THE RIP HARDESSY GANG WAS FINISHED, WIPED OUT. That much was accepted and agreed upon by everybody. A number of questions related to that achievement, however—exactly as predicted by Charley—were left forever hanging fire.

There were eyewitnesses to Mona Trent's attack and vicious killing of Betty Markesan. But no one could explain why the girl was present to begin with or what had prompted her attack. None of the select townsmen who were familiar with Betty's "side business," which would have at least established a common link with her killer, ever came forward.

Mona's shotgun-blasted body, dragged out of the house before the fire consumed it, was rightfully attributed to Alifair. The latter's fire-ravaged remains, signaling how she'd somehow become trapped by the flames, were found in the smoldering rubble beside the blackened remnants of a shotgun. No one ever noticed, in the rubble, the remains of a prosthetic hook. But two more bodies were also eventually found in the basement of the ruins. Some surviving personal items and two horses left unclaimed at Kroeger's livery led to the identification of these victims as the bounty hunters Boris Bemis and Slick Tennebow. But, again, why they were ever present in the house to begin with was added to the list of unanswered questions.

Another mystery was what had become of the bank money from the Hardessy gang's final robbery. Most accepted that it had been buried in the explosion-slash-cave-in that claimed Rip and Whitey. But some insisted it was more likely that Rip had stashed it somewhere else before allowing himself to be cornered. This led, for years and decades thereafter, to various searches into the Spillings and throughout the surrounding Sandhills conducted by gullible fools who swore they had unearthed some "clue" to the money's true where-abouts. But all came up empty.

The question of possible surviving gang members also lingered. Laurie and Dr. Frake knew they had left behind five when they made their escape from the cave. Only three were assuredly accounted for. Both the girl and the doctor felt certain that at least one must have been killed as a result of the arguing and gunfire they'd overheard. But might there have been a survivor who wasn't caught in the final cave-in? Again, for years there-after there were vague reports of "a mysterious figure" roaming the vicinity, as if in search of something. But no one ever came forward to be identified.

In a small town in Idaho, however, a quiet young man appeared some weeks following the incidents in and around Ogallala. He called himself Darwin Ford and took a job as a store clerk. He remained in the town, eventually worked his way into a full partnership position at the store, married and had two children, lived to the age of fifty-seven. There was nothing remarkable or particularly memorable about Darwin, except he had a faint nervous tic and, every once in a while, he would spin suddenly around as if he expected someone had come up behind him. No one ever understood that, on those occasions, it was Darrold Memford who abruptly felt a cold draft and turned fearing he would find that the specters of Whitey Culp or Rip Hardessy had at last caught up with him...

—————

ON THE CONCRETE and more positive side of things, Hank Wordell finally regained consciousness and went on to recover fully from his wounds. He would end up serving twenty more years as a US Marshal.

Nor, not by a long shot, was Charley Bourbon done raising hell and rounding up lawbreakers all across the frontier.

Sheriff Hiram Needles squeezed all the glory he could out of helping to close down the notorious Hardessy gang and parlayed that claim into eventually serving two terms as lieutenant governor for the state of Nebraska.

Laurie McSwain recovered from her battering, helped along by a very attentive Jack Bartles, and the two were married before the year was out.

Lone came back for the wedding. But in the meantime, first chance he got, he said some farewells and then he and Ironsides quietly drifted on home to the Busted Spur.

A LOOK AT WEST OF WHITECHAPEL
JACK THE RIPPER IN THE WILD WEST

WITH A HUNGER FOR TRUTH, THIS THRILLING WESTERN WILL KEEP YOU ON YOUR TOES.

In the late 1880s, a series of grisly murders swept through the Whitechapel slums of London. The victims were all prostitutes, each found with their throats cut and their stomachs sliced open. Sensationalized newspaper accounts of the killings spread throughout England and beyond to a horrified yet fascinated reading public. Heightening interest all the more were the taunting letters sent by the killer to Scotland Yard—boldly signed *"Jack the Ripper."*

But then, abruptly, the killings stopped. The Ripper was never identified or captured, and the terror seemed over.

A few months later, however, on the American frontier in the raucous, rowdy mining camps that sprung up out of a silver boom in the Colorado Rockies, some eerily similar murders are beginning to occur among the flocks of "soiled doves" who gather to serve the men in remote camps. With no law to speak of in such places and sudden death being all too common, no one seems to take much notice.

Not until a sharp-eyed female journalist spots an possible connection and becomes determined to uncover the truth. Aided by a guilt-ridden, though equally dogged frontier detective, the pair follow a bloody trail through the rugged mountains and boisterous mining camps to try and prove if Jack the Ripper truly ceased his killing ways...or merely moved them out here—west of Whitechapel.

AVAILABLE NOW

ABOUT THE AUTHOR

Wayne D. Dundee is an American author of popular genre fiction. His writing has primarily been detective mysteries—such as the Joe Hannibal PI series—and Western adventures. To date, he has written several dozen novels and forty-plus short stories, ranging from horror, fantasy, erotica, and several "house name" books under bylines other than his own.

Dundee was born March 24, 1948, in Freeport, Illinois. He graduated from high school in Clinton, Wisconsin, in 1966. Later that same year, he married Pamela Daum and they had one daughter, Michelle. For the first fifty years of his life, Dundee worked his way up from factory laborer to various managerial positions. In his spare time, he was always writing. He sold his first short story in 1982.

In 1998, Dundee relocated to Ogallala, Nebraska, where he assumed the general manager position for a small Arnold facility there. The setting and rich history of the area inspired him to turn his efforts more toward the Western genre. In 2009, following the passing of his wife one year prior, he retired from Arnold and began to concentrate on his writing full time.

The founder and original editor of Hardboiled Magazine, Dundee's work in the mystery field has been nominated for an Edgar, an Anthony, and six Shamus Awards from the Private Eye Writers of America.